WELL BRED

WHATEVER IT TAKES

A. ANDERS

ABOUT THE BOOK

I've finally given up on having a child.

Until ex-con Jake Brand walks in. He's six foot five of ink and muscle and the farthest thing from a family man. He's also leaving in a few weeks.

So, when he offers to help out—in my restaurant and in my bed—I cave in and say yes.

But I've got rules, strict ones, to keep everything between us clear:

No touching

No kissing

No emotion

And the lights stay off. Always.

Except, it turns out, dirty talking Jake doesn't do rules.

He busts through them one by one and every time, he breaks a piece of the shell protecting my heart.

Now as we're counting down the days until he leaves, I can't help but wonder just how much of me will be left when he's gone.

ALSO BY ADRIANA ANDERS

The Whatever it Takes Series

Well Paid - coming soon

The Camp Haven Series

Kink Camp: Hunted

Possession

The Rough & Rugby Series

We'll Never Have Paris

The French Kiss-Off - coming soon!

The Dom-Com Coming soon! Subscribe to release day emails here.

Daddy Crush More available on the Radish Reading App!

The Survival Instincts Series

Deep Blue

Whiteout

Uncharted

More to come...

Love at Last Series

Loving the Secret Billionaire

Loving the Wounded Warrior

Loving the Mountain Man

The Blank Canvas Series

Under Her Skin

By Her Touch

In His Hands

To women supporting women. Together, we can do anything.

and

To Michelle, Super Assistant, Super Mom, Super Friend, and one hell of an amazing person.

AUTHOR'S NOTE

Like many (but not all) of my books, Well Bred showed up and parked itself in my brain one day, then wouldn't budge. It's been there for a couple years, the characters themselves fully formed. Kit, in particular, felt real to me and, in many ways, utterly relatable.

Like Kit, I spent years working in bars and restaurants, starting at the ripe old age of 15. Also like Kit, I found myself not too far from the age of 40 when I decided I wanted kids after all. I chose to have children, just as I'd previously chosen not to. This is a right that I took for granted at the time. I no longer do.

Well Bred is pure fiction and is meant to be just that, but it is also my (very sexy) ode to women's bodily autonomy, to the right to choose, to the power of deciding that whether or not we .

Please be forewarned that along with a good measure of breeding kink, our characters engage in primal play, including chasing and biting, and discuss doing a whole lot more.

Throughout the book, there are references to childhood trauma, loss of parents, cancer, domestic violence and abuse, addiction, cheating, murder, sexual assault, and miscarriage. There is on-page violence, although not between the hero and heroine, and there is frequent consumption of alcohol.

Rest assured that there is a solid HEA for Kit and Jake and you'll meet at least one secondary character whose story is already clamoring for room in my head.

Happy reading!

xo,

Adriana

1

KIT

I know the second he walks in that the man is trouble.

And if there's one thing I've learned in my almost forty years on this planet it's to give trouble a wide berth. Especially when it's six foot five, heavily tattooed, and muscle bound.

"Can I help you?" I ask from where I'm standing behind the bar. "We're not open yet."

He pulls off mirrored sunglasses and looks around, eyes probably still adjusting to the restaurant's dark interior. When he finally focuses on me, it takes effort to maintain my relaxed stance.

This guy, whoever he is, has the hard, confident, utterly aloof presence of a predator. I can't imagine for the life of me what's brought him to my fancy little gastro-diner on the outskirts of town.

"Looking for Kitty Esteban." He watches me, clearly aware that he's found her. "Your brother sent me."

Immediately, my tension ratchets up. "My brother?"

"Frank. Asked me to swing by and check in on you."

"*Check in* on me?" Great. Just wonderful. This is what I get for updating my brother on my life. Which, granted, has been more than a little complicated recently. Even from prison, Franco's got to micromanage. As if I haven't done just fine out here without him. Hell, I'm the one running a restaurant—albeit with great difficulty just now. He's the one who's been behind bars for the past decade and a half. "Tell him I'm good. Thanks." I go back to the produce order.

Ignoring me entirely, the man hooks his glasses into the neck of his T-shirt and moves smoothly between tables toward the bar. "Saw a sign outside. You need a cook?"

With a sigh, I shut the computer and look up. "Yeah. You don't happen to be a chef in need of work, do you?" I mime looking at a watch. "Available like, today?"

He stops right across from me, setting one heavily tattooed hand on the shiny wood counter and, for a few seconds, everything else recedes and all I see is him. He's massive. Bigger than my original impression suggested, with his arms and chest and flat stomach perfectly displayed in the kind of plain white T-shirt probably bought in packs of five. The kind of T-shirt that looks like trash on some people and on others—like this guy—is more appealing than a tux.

Short dark hair and a thick, sinewy neck frame the kind of face I don't usually bother examining too closely. *Do Not Engage*, this face says loud and clear. There's too much challenge in his eyes. His jaw's too stubborn.

This is the face of a pain in the ass.

And I've had enough of those to last me a lifetime.

"Sure," he says, laying both thick forearms on the

bar, putting him on a level with me. Or closer, at least. He'd have to sumo squat to get down to my height. "I can cook."

I can't keep the surprise off my face. "You serious?"

"My dad had a diner growing up. Started cooking before I could read. Then I did time in a few restaurant kitchens after I got out. As long as I'm not creating the menu from scratch, I can probably handle it." Thick shoulders lift in a shrug. "Until my next contract." I stare briefly at the big hand he offers. "Jake Brand. Friend of Frank's. From back in the day."

I slide my palm against his, entirely unsurprised at how rough and dry and cool his is as it engulfs mine. Suddenly, things slot in place. "By back in the day, you mean prison."

"Yes, ma'am."

"You just get out?"

"Got out twelve years ago."

"What have you been doing since then?"

"I'm a welder. I work on offshore platforms. All over the place."

I make a face. "And you want to cook *here*?"

A muscle ticks in his jaw. "Frank said your cook pulled a runner, stole from you." He looks at the mess of my bar. It's covered in piles of papers and delivery boxes I haven't had time to unpack since Keith took off leaving me in the lurch—and five hundred bucks poorer. "I'm here to help. At least until it's time for me to go."

"I need a cook, though. Not a welder. And I need one stat. Books are full for tonight and Frida can't handle a weekend night on her own."

"I've got a contract starting overseas in six weeks."

"A contract."

"North Sea Platform."

"Welding."

"Yep."

"And you want to spend your down time cooking upscale diner food for a woman you've never met?"

"Frank helped me get through the worst time of my life. He mentioned the shit hit the fan around here and asked me to swing by and help. So here I am."

The way Frank manages to get things done, even from within the state penitentiary, is impressive. And annoying.

"Is this like some prison blood debt or something?"

"No, ma'am." His sudden half-smile is scarily beautiful. "It's what you call friendship."

I manage to keep myself from rolling my eyes at him, lest I insult the only option I currently have. "Are you a decent cook?"

"I am."

"Care to show me?"

"If you show me your kitchen."

There's no reason on god's green earth that should sound lascivious, but it does. Or maybe it's my poor sex-starved libido, grabbing at straws.

Because I'm an adult—and probably ten years older than this guy—I ignore any and all innuendo, intentional or not, and lead him into the kitchen.

Fifteen minutes later, I bite into the best grilled cheese sandwich I've ever eaten. Ever.

The outside's got just the right amount of crunch, the cheese oozes out and—most surprisingly—he's served it with a little tomato, parsley, and shallot salad that tastes like sunshine in my mouth. It takes every bit of restraint I've got not to polish the whole thing off, moaning, as he looks on.

Instead, I set aside what's left of it with great regret, and hire him on the spot.

He nods toward the plate. "You should finish that."

"Let's get your paperwork done first."

"Rather not. I'm just here as a favor."

"And I'd rather be insured when you're in my kitchen," I tell him, although more than that, I want to not owe this man more than I already will. "Besides, stopping by to check on me at my brother's behest is one thing. Working for free is another."

"I don't mind."

"Well I do. I'll pay you the going rate."

I lead him to the office in back, where we get everything sorted, including tax forms that show his permanent address as being in a town just over the mountain.

"It's a bit of a drive."

"Don't mind. Pretty nice after spending weeks out on the water."

"Is that your address year-round?"

"Got a place there. Place out west and another on the gulf. I use 'em as base camps between jobs."

I glance down at his hand, which is devoid of ornamentation. Unless you count all the ink. "Married?"

A head shake. "Not much of a family guy."

"Fair enough," I manage to say, although his words needle a part of me I'd rather ignore. "I appreciate your honesty."

If only Clark had told me those words when we first got married, I wouldn't be in this position right now: overworked, out of money, and desperate for a family of my own.

Or a child, at least.

Because my dear soon-to-be ex-husband insisted he wanted kids and spent the next ten years putting it off and putting it off, until he'd put it off so long that he somehow tripped into a twenty-year-old and knocked her up. She's due any day now. So, I guess, he actually *is* a family man.

He just didn't want a family with me.

Which is fine. Good riddance. I can do it by myself. Like I built up this restaurant by myself, while he was off knocking up girls half his age.

Thank goodness for IVF. And modern medicine. And living in a place where I can decide what to do with my own body and just how I intend to do it.

"Welcome to the team, Jake Brand." I hand him a clean apron, which definitely won't fit and make a mental note to order some XXLs. "And thank you. Truly. Thank you."

"Don't mention it."

The second that clear blue gaze hits mine, a shot of adrenaline races straight through my bloodstream.

Wow. Okay then.

Pure trouble.

That was my first impression and nothing thus far has changed it.

What kind of fool goes and hires a man who looks like this one?

A fool who needed a little breathing room. At least now I've got six weeks to find someone permanent.

I just hope this isn't a decision I'll come to regret.

2

ONE WEEK LATER...

Kit

I turned forty today. Which is fine. Forty is young, everyone keeps telling me. Well, everyone except for that one reproductive endocrinologist who referred to my eggs as geriatric.

His exact words were that they were in great shape for geriatric eggs, so I guess it's a positive.

Was a positive. Was.

I'm done with the IVF. No babies. No family.

So, I'm celebrating forty or, I guess grieving, here at my bar at the end of a very long shift, with a birthday bourbon.

Two, actually. This is my second.

I pick up my phone again, open the group chat and smile at the Happy Birthdays from Trina and Beth, now married in New Zealand, Jules with her new guy in Paris, and my other friends who left town and scattered to the four corners of the globe, with their smiling, happy, complicated families.

Their kids.

My eyes blur as I look at the photos of babies and toddlers and tweens, grinning out from the warm safety of these wild, sweet families my friends have created. I'm so proud of them. And so painfully jealous.

Dammit, I'm being morose. I promised myself—and Frank when he called—not to get down in the dumps today.

Before I let a second thought stop me, I grab my phone and take a quick, sloppy, smirking selfie, bourbon glass in hand. With the lighting and the filter and the booze flowing through my veins, I look happy, which is good. The last thing I need is for any of them to worry.

Love you guys, I send with the picture, followed by a dozen hearts, before setting the phone back down with a final smack.

Looking up as I reach for the bottle again, my eyes land on the mirror behind the bar, where my image is aged, fractured through the cubist lens of antique mercury glass.

That's more like it. The real me. Weird and off-center and looking absolutely my age.

I take another long sip, barely feeling the burn now, and groan at how boring I've become.

Next year, I've got to do something for my birthday. No way am I allowed to drink and brood and let this dark, sloppy emotional sludge out into the world. My god is it pathetic. Especially because of the voicemail burning a hole in my phone.

Masochist that I am, I pick it up again and hit play, shocked for a half second when the music playing over the bluetooth speakers abruptly stops, to be replaced by the voice mail person, then the first few notes of Billy and Renee shout-singing Happy Birthday, little Erin doing her best to keep up.

I cut them off and move on to the next message, this one from the ex-husband. "Hey, Kitty. Uh, happy fortieth! Listen, I know you're probably out partying, but I need to talk to you about the restaurant. We need to re-evaluate the terms. Figured we could do this without getting the lawyers involved." My blood boils, but I force myself to listen to his bullshit a second time. "Kids are expensive." His laugh is so forced, I cringe. "Lily's tired and needs to—"

I stab at the delete button with a muttered, *"Prick."*

Yeah. Yeah, sure, take more of my hard-won money so the twenty-year-old you knocked up doesn't have to work through her pregnancy.

The pain I've managed to keep banked these past few months bubbles up and, instead of cutting off voice-mail entirely, I move on to the next message, like a bruise I'm compelled to press on.

Maybe because I've always been someone who picks at her wounds, I leave the audio on bluetooth.

"Hi there, Ms. Esteban. This is Teri from Dr. Haims' office." The sound's loud, piped everywhere in the restaurant. I picture diners hearing this, imagine the kitchen crew listening in. Thank god they've all left for the night. "Calling to let you know that, sadly, your most recent cycle failed. I'm so sorry about that." Yeah. Me, too, Teri. Me, too. "However we can get you on the schedule later this month. So give us a call to set up a time and we'll—"

A wounded sound leaves my body as I hit the end call button.

Something rattles in the back of the restaurant.

I go utterly still.

Nina Simone blares out from the speakers as the bluetooth switches back to music. Fumbling with my phone, I turn it off and listen with growing horror as the rattling becomes a repetitive scraping.

Oh my god. Is someone trying to get in the back door?

Scared sober, I slide off the stool, and stand here, completely paralyzed by indecision for the few seconds it takes my brain to catch up. Finally, I race around behind the bar and grab the metal baseball bat I keep there more as a deterrent than anything else.

Breathing hard, I raise it over my shoulder and set off, past the kitchen, down the hall, and the restrooms' bleachy fog, around the corner, where the light's not working, and smack straight into a wall that...shouldn't be here? I don't think I've ever made the kind of weird squeal I let out when I realize it's actually a chest, attached to a person.

"Whoa. Whoa, whoa, there, girl. Shit." The voice is low and familiar. "Gimme that."

Every nerve in my body's gone haywire, shorting out as I stare up at Jake, whose massive body fills the hallway. He takes a hold of the bat and gently pries it from my hands while I stand staring up at him, open-mouthed.

"Jake? What are you..."

"Fixing the store room shelves. Told you I'd stay late and get started."

"Now? Tonight?" I shake my head, squinting up at the cold blue eyes staring out from the man's face. "I thought you meant at some point in the future. Not right this minute."

Despite having worked with him every day for the past week, I don't feel like I know the man at all. He's perfectly polite, exceptionally competent in the kitchen, more than helpful with other things around the place. But he's also intimidating and a little...off, although I can't explain why. Maybe it's the sharp eyes, so often on me whenever I look his way, or the hard edge to his expression, his body, the way he holds himself, which I attribute to the time he spent in prison or the job spent working in some of the most dangerous places on earth.

He's been an exemplary employee. Everyone loves him—including Frida, the sous-chef who hates everyone—the restaurant's booming, and, oddly, given everything else, I feel *safe* when he's around.

But then, there's this *tension.*

Which I'm probably imagining.

Like now. He's holding a bat, staring down at me with this serious, almost angry look while I stand here and pretend that my nipples haven't gone inexplicably hard.

The back door rattles again, sending a sizzle of adrenaline-fueled fear over my skin. Maybe the nipple thing is fear.

Jake shoves the bat back into my hands. "Lock yourself in the office. Call 911," he mutters, low, before striding empty-handed down the hall to the back door.

I don't move. All I can do is stare at his wide back, the T-shirt stretched tight over places I didn't know muscles grew. His stride is long and heavy and fearless, his spine straight. He turns the lock, then works at what looks like a second one, then flings open the door and I don't have time to wish he'd kept the bat for his own protection. All I can do is watch as he jerks someone inside, one-handed and without apparent effort, then pins him to the wall, his meaty forearm pressed to the intruder's throat.

"What the fu—"

The words cut off sharply when Jake leans in.

"Who're you?"

"Keith?" I come up behind Jake and stare at the man I employed for four years, currently hovering a good six inches above the ground, his hands struggling to release the bar of human muscle that's got him in a headlock. "What are you—"

"This the guy?" Jake's blank-eyed stare meets mine over his shoulder. "The one who stole from you?"

I nod, dumbfounded.

Jake turns to look at Keith, head tilted at a curious angle. "You here to ask for your job back?" I'd almost think he was joking if his low voice wasn't so deadpan. "Position's been filled, asshole."

"Bitch owes me money," Keith says, tearing off another little chunk of my heart.

How many days did we work together? How many hours? Exhausting double-shifts that felt like triumphs when the last person left and the door closed and we'd served every one of them above and beyond. Working together in a place that gets packed every weekend is like putting on an amazing show or, I don't know, fighting a fire. Anyone who's worked in food service knows that the right staff, thrown together under pressure, bonds as tightly as a family. I'd trusted Keith, gotten close to him, *cared* about him.

"You call the cops?" Jake's deep rumble cuts through the pain of betrayal.

I shake my head.

"Good. Give me a minute." With brutal efficiency, Keith is dragged outside. The door closes behind them.

I'm left standing stunned in the silent back hall, wondering what, exactly, I'm agreeing to by leaving Jake alone with my ex-employee.

Will he hurt him? Dispose of the body, mob-style? I don't even know what Jake went to prison for. I figure it couldn't have been worse than my brother, since Frank's spent the last decade inside.

Crap. I've got to stop him. I throw open the door in time to watch Keith, bent double, stagger down the alley and disappear into the street beyond.

When I face Jake, he's looking my way, his eyes in shadow.

"What did you do?" I ask, filled with a weird, light-headed trepidation.

3

"He won't be back."

Kitty watches me with those big, tragic eyes and for a handful of seconds, I consider going after the little prick and finishing the job.

"Did you hurt him?"

I shake my head, walk to the door and hold it wide, waiting for her to go through before I pull it shut behind me.

"Did you somehow know he was coming tonight?" she asks. "Is that why you stayed late?"

Another head shake from me. She doesn't move, just stands there in the shadowed hall, craning her neck to look up at me, probably waiting for more of an answer.

"Just fixing the shelves." It's not a complete lie. I'm working on the shelves. But I also stuck around last night and fixed the baseboards in the kitchen. The night before, I installed the extra lock back here. Then when she was about ready to leave, I went out and waited in my car until she drove away.

Her stare moves from me to the door and back. "Did you install that? The dead bolt?"

After a beat, I nod.

"You knew he was coming?"

"No. Figured it'd be good to keep an eye out. I wasn't leaving you to close up on your own."

"I always close up alone."

"I don't like it."

"What are you, my bodyguard now?" She doesn't seem thrilled. She's got that look she gets when people act like idiots. Like when the Circo guy tried to deliver twenty boxes of melons or when a table of frat boys harassed one of the waitstaff. Brow wrinkled, lips pursed. "Seriously. Are you, like, watching over me or something?"

I let my gaze flick down to that pouty little mouth and back up again. She looks soulful. Pissed. Fucking beautiful. "Someone has to."

"Did Frank put you up to this, too? Did he tell you to play bodyguard?" Clearly pissed, she lifts the baseball bat she's still clutching and points it at my face. "That's bullshit. I hired you to cook, not to—"

"You gonna hit me with that?" I don't know why I've got to tease her. Poke her. Make her a little mad just to see what she does next.

"I should," she says, her voice losing the brittle edge.

"Or you could give me a shift drink." I inhale, long and slow. "Shot of that bourbon I smell on your breath."

She blinks and I figure she'll back up a step. We're standing awfully close here at the dark end of the hall. "You never stick around for a shift drink. I thought you didn't do that."

"Don't mind the occasional beer or whatever. Mostly, I prefer vices I can control."

"Vices you can..." Her voice trails off to nothing and ends on a hoarse, "Oh."

I've got no idea why I'm playing with fire like this.

Ah, hell. Who am I kidding? I know exactly why I'm egging her on, tonight of all nights.

But it's a bad idea. For every single reason. Mostly because Frank would kill me if I made a move.

Doesn't stop me from telling her that I'll be right with her. I point up at the light fixture. "Gotta replace that."

"Oh. Thanks. The stepladder's right through..." She looks at my head, which is maybe four inches from the ceiling. "Right. Guess you don't need it."

"I'm good."

Slowly, maybe a little shocky after everything that's happened, she turns and walks away and, though I shouldn't be a creeper, I allow myself a quick sweep of her body.

Fuck, the woman does things to me, messes with my settings, spins everything inside me fast and hard, like a compass at the Pole.

It's not her overblown curves that get to me or all that soft-looking pale skin. It's not even the juicy, ripe mouth I can't stop thinking about or the handfuls of dark red hair I picture wrapped tight around my fist. No, it's her eyes that flipped my switch the first time I saw her—dark, melting, and also somehow catastrophic. Painful to look at.

I grab a new bulb from the supply closet and replace it, check the back door again to make sure that sniveling little pill popper won't be an issue, then make sure the office is all shut up tight. I swing by the head, where I wash my hands, not bothering to look at my ugly mug in the mirror. I know what I look like: big and mean.

By the time I make it out front, Kitty's behind the bar, all business. There's a glass sitting in front of an empty stool.

"Where's yours?" I stay standing.

"I've had enough."

I nod, noting that she's turned off the speakers and all of the many twinkling chandeliers that give this place its atmosphere. As soon as I slug back this drink, she'll make sure we're out of here. Obviously, she's anxious for me to go.

I spin my glass, not ready to pick it up and end this. "You all right?"

"Great. Good." I'm guessing she can tell how little I believe that from the way she cringes at my expression. "A little rattled, I guess."

"Understandable."

"I thought he was a friend, you know?"

"Addiction changes people."

She nods. "Listen, thank you."

"You're welcome."

"But, I didn't ask you to stay late."

"I know." I watch her, waiting for her eyes to meet mine again, for that little zap I get every time.

"I didn't budget for—"

"Clocked out ages ago."

"Well, I can't let you work and not—"

"You know I don't need the job."

"Yeah."

"Any luck finding someone?"

"No." Her shoulders drop under what seems to be a whole lot of pressure. "I don't get it."

"Small town," I say.

"I guess that must be it. Because who wouldn't want to work here, right?"

She holds her arms out as if to show off the space. And it's nice. A lot of old, glossy wood, warm lights set to low, the kind of cocktails you couldn't get when I was a kid. Full of smoke and umami and some shit called shrub. It suits her, though, in an old-timey way. A sort of ageless feel that goes with those bombshell dresses she wears and the bright colored hair. She's somehow classy and sexy and deep all at once. "You tell Frank I'm struggling?"

"Course not."

She searches my face for a second and, apparently satisfied, says, "Thanks."

"Sure." I spin my glass, enjoying the sweet smoke smell without tasting it yet. Enjoying the weight of her full attention. "It's the truth."

Her quiet "Yeah," is doubtful, her narrowed gaze fixed on me. "So, who *are* you? Who is Jake Brand? You met Frank in prison? What were you in for?"

"You haven't looked it up?"

She shakes her head. "Not my business."

"And yet you're asking."

"Forget it." She nudges my drink toward me, the message loud and clear. Drink and get out.

Rather than tower over her, I finally sit on the stool and take a sip. "Maker's." I flash her a surprised look. "Top shelf."

"Not quite." Her smile is apologetic. "Sorry."

"Better than rail."

"You know what? You're right. Hang on." She's shaking her head when she reaches for my glass. "I *should* have poured you the good stuff after what you did back there. It's the least I can do."

"It's fine," I finally tell her. "I like Maker's."

Her fingers wrap around mine. Instead of relinquishing the drink, I let her hold it, and me, for a few quiet seconds.

"You deserve the Knob Creek. Or this local distillery's latest—"

"I'm good." I put my other hand over hers, sandwiching it on the glass and holding her still. "Thanks."

When she looks at me, she's breathing hard enough to move her chest up and down, quick and somehow dramatic, reminding me of those old black and white movies my dad played in the diner when I was a kid.

"Okay."

"Sit and have a drink with me."

She eyes me another minute, her gaze searching my whole face for some answer she seems to find before she gives in with a sigh and a quick, brittle lifting of her lips that looks nothing like a smile. "I could use another, I guess."

I hold off on drinking until she's strained up to grab a sealed bottle from the literal top shelf and blown the dust off, then served a glass for me and another for herself. She keeps the bar between us.

Even if you don't know exactly what I've done, I suppose I can be a scary fucker.

"You all right being here alone with me?" I ask, then watch closely as she considers how to answer.

"That depends."

"On what?"

Her eyes spark in the warm, dim light above the bar.

"On what it is you want exactly."

"What makes you think I want something?"

4

———————

KIT

Oh, he wants something all right. I just can't for the life of me figure out what it is.

But there's something a little too direct about his gaze right now and, suddenly, I can't backpedal fast enough. I'm too shaken and buzzing and more than a little intrigued by this big man taking up more than his allotment of space at my bar. And none of that is a good thing.

"Never mind." I shove the freshly-poured bourbon toward him and grab my own, raise it and wait for him to clunk his glass to mine. "Cheers to another shift down."

"Cheers to you," he says, watching me closely. "Happy birthday."

I pause. "How'd you..." Horror takes over when I realize exactly what he must've overheard on the bluetooth speakers. "Oh, shit."

"Hey. Forty's not that old."

"That's not what I meant, you... Wait. How old are *you?*"

His weirdly light, intense eyes focus on me, a sudden spark of humor heating their depths. A warm weight flips around in my stomach before settling. "What, you didn't memorize my employment information?"

I think back to the papers I copied and filed away. I remember thinking he was young. "You're in your thirties?"

"Thirty-two."

"Must have been young when you met Frank."

"We were convicted the same year."

"But you got out."

A pause. "Yeah."

Neither of us mentions that my brother's crime wasn't one they took quite so lightly.

"He's got a parole hearing. I think early next year."

"He'll get out," he says, although we both know it's not a given.

In the ensuing silence, I latch onto the sight of his thick, corded neck, the hair-rough Adam's apple that moves whenever he takes a swallow of booze.

"How'd you get into this business?"

My startled gaze lifts to preternaturally light eyes. "Oh. Randomly, I guess. Waited tables. Bartended through college. Then stuck around because it was quick money and I liked it and it paid for my husb—" I clear my throat to get that word out of my body. "My *ex's* grad school."

His thick brows rise. "He ever pay you back?"

The answer to that question's caught in the nasty snarl of emotions clogging my chest.

The best I can do is a forced smile and a redirect. "What about you?"

"Me?"

"How'd you get into your line of work?"

"Well, your brother's part of it, I guess."

"Yeah?"

"Frank convinced me not to ruin my life by doing what he did the second I got out." He looks down, gaze lost in the glass of booze for a few seconds. I want to ask so many questions, but manage to hold my tongue. "Helped me find a program for ex-cons. Welding. I was a brawler, you know. Had to do something physical to get it out of my system and working nights down at the plant wasn't gonna cut it."

"You'd lose your soul doing that."

"Yeah. In some ways, it was worse than prison." When he looks up, his smile's very faint, barely a smile, actually, but it's so attractive that the weight turns liquid and slides further south. "Or almost."

I get the feeling, looking at him, that nothing could be worse than prison. I don't let myself consider what Frank must be going through.

"Anyway. I had someone outside, too, who gave a shit enough to take me in and point me in the right direction."

I picture a woman, of course.

"Was that around here?"

"Over in the valley. Guy ran a gym. He..." His eyes flick up to meet mine. "You don't want the full story."

I do, actually, but it would be weird to admit that. Instead, I go with. "Is that where you grew up? The valley?"

"Yeah. Workin' in my parents' diner. On 81. In some ways, I guess you could say the diner raised me."

"Well, you're good."

"I get by."

Staring at the glass of amber liquid in my hand, I suck in a deep, shaky breath, and finally meet his gaze. "Thank you. For taking over the kitchen. And all the other stuff you've done. I didn't realize you were..." My throat goes tight. "And thanks for tonight. I don't entirely get why you're here, especially since you don't need the money, but I owe you—"

"You want the truth?"

Do I? I hesitate, watching him watch me. It's a strange sensation to be the focus of so much attention. I'm not used to it. Can't say whether or not I like it yet. I lick my dry lower lip and shrug with a nonchalance that is eighty percent bravado. "Sure."

"I swung by 'cause Frank asked me to. Took the job because I liked the look of you." The straightforward words shut me up and steal the air from my lungs. I'm still trying to come up with a response when he says. "I heard your messages. All of 'em." His eyes flick up to one of the speakers, quiet now, then back to look at me. "Bad news."

Mortification heats my face. "That was private."

"I know. And I'm sorry." After a beat. "I'll bet it's rough. On you and your new person."

"My person?"

"Your partner. Husband or wife or whoever you're starting a family with."

"I'm doing it alone." I shake my head, hating how defeated I suddenly feel. "Whatever. That's over now.

I'm done." I give him a brittle smile. "I can't afford another round." Aside from his eyebrows going up, there's no reaction. It makes no sense for me to get as defensive as I do. "What? You got a problem with single mothers? IVF?"

"Not at all."

"You sure? You seem awfully—"

"You want a baby?"

"More than anything," I admit, though I don't exactly know why I'm dumping this on the guy.

"I'll do it."

Everything freezes. Me. The air around us. My lungs, my heart, the blood in my veins.

I've heard wrong. I've misunderstood.

I'm suspended, numb with shock. Dropped off a building. In free fall.

"Um. Do what?"

"I'll get you pregnant." He's dead serious.

My mouth drops open. I close it, open it again as I attempt to formulate some sort of reply. It takes an effort to get my voice working again. "Are you... Are you *kidding?*"

He shoves back his stool and stands, takes a couple steps away from the bar. For the first time since I saw this man, he seems something other than steady and sure and firmly planted on the ground. "It's the bourbon talking. Sorry about that. I...I'll take off. Goodnight Kitty." He spins and stalks away.

He's twisted the lock and wrenched the front door open, stepped outside and turned to close it behind him by the time I shake myself free from the shock and get a word out. "Wait!"

He pauses, his hand the only thing keeping the door ajar. Even through the sheet glass of my front window, it's obvious the man's tense.

So am I. I mean, what the hell just happened?

But also—and this is the unexpected part—holy crap, why on earth am I turned on?

My body, which was certainly interested in Jake Brand before he dropped his bomb, is now a live wire. Buzzing, tight, swollen. *Ready.* I'll bet if I shoved my hand down my underwear, I'd find that I'm soaking wet right now.

Slowly, as if I'm not a massive ball of humming nerves, I walk across the dining room, to the door, still wedged open a few degrees by his hand.

"What, um..." No. No, I need to think before I speak. And look him in the eye, not talk through the relative safety of a four-inch gap. I push until I can see his entire face. "Why would you say that? Why...why would you make that kind of offer?" I shut my eyes, grimacing with the unexpected pain of a sudden realization. "Was it a joke?"

"Hell, no."

"Then..." I swallow, force myself to look at him head-on, and say, "Please explain."

He makes a sound of frustration, rubs his hand through his short, almost black hair, and looks around at the dark parking lot, out at the quiet street, maybe searching for an appropriate response to a truly inexplicable situation. Or maybe just searching for a way out of this very weird conversation.

Finally, I guess he lands on something because he turns to me and says, "I've wanted you since the moment I laid eyes on you, Kitty." He looks me up and down in a way I feel to my core.

I'm about to reply when his next words flay me wide open.

"Since the second I saw you, I knew I'd do anything to wipe that sadness from your eyes."

5

———

JAKE

All my concerns about pissing Frank off or scaring the shit out of Kitty fly right out the restaurant's front door when she gasps and bites down on that plump little bottom lip. I think about that lip a lot.

"I look sad?"

"Not right now," I tell her, my usual bluntness probably sealing my own fucked up fate. You can't tell a woman this shit and expect to see her again. She'll probably take out a restraining order on me. "Right now, you look...blindsided. Maybe a little interested." I want to move deeper into the open doorway, closer to her, but until she says different, I'll stay right where I am. Holding myself perfectly still, I ask, "Are you?"

She looks dazed. Lost. "Am I...?"

"Interested."

"I'm—"

A car door slams, jolting her out of whatever spell I somehow managed to cast.

"I'm sorry, this is...I don't know what to say. I've

been drinking and it's a messed up day for me. More than just my birthday, you know? All this other stuff." She shakes her head. "Thank you. For your...weird offer."

"Yeah." I scan our surroundings, watch the car take off, and look at her, hard. "Go ahead and close up. I'll keep an eye out."

"You don't have to—"

I sigh. "It's not a choice, Kitty, I can't *not* watch out for—"

"It's Kit."

"What?"

"It's Kit E. Like, Kit Esteban." She sighs. "The first place I ever waited tables, there were two of us—two Kits."

"That's random."

"Right? Anyway, we were known as Kit R and Kit E. And mine stuck."

"No shit."

"So, it's just Kit."

"Short for?"

After a second's hesitation, she tells me. "Katarina."

The name suits her. Much more than Kitty. Or Kit. "That's right. Your brother's real name's Franco. Y'all are Spanish."

"Half Spanish, half Puerto Rican. And I was named after a German figure skater."

I give the quiet lot a quick once-over, tell her goodnight, walk to my truck, and settle in to wait for her to come out the front and lock up.

When she does, she's got a bright red coat thrown over her clothes. It's long and cinched in at the waist and it makes her look like she stepped out of the pages of one of the old Louis Lamour books my dad used to read 24/7 in the cracked back booth when he was dying. Like a wild west saloon girl or something.

Which works with the whole vibe of her place. It's called Parlor. Frank's never seen it, but he described it to me with impressive precision.

I don't get the impression Frank's aware of her current money problems, though. How the hell'd it happen? The restaurant's obviously doing well.

Something tells me it's the ex.

I watch her step carefully over the gravel of the lot and pause, about halfway to her VW. Slowly, she turns, scanning her surroundings until her eyes land on my truck. To keep from seeming like a total perv, I flick my lights on and off, showing her I'm here.

When she heads my way, instead of to her car, a new purpose in her step, my breathing revs up.

As she crosses to the passenger side, I lean over and shove it open for her.

She stands there, clearly uncertain. "Did you mean it? What you said? Or was that just a...a...I don't know. Like a come-on or something?"

"Some of both." I watch her. "Get in."

After a second's hesitation, she swings into the truck and shuts the door, then just sits there, staring straight ahead through the windshield.

"I don't need a husband," she says, her voice low and tight.

"I wasn't proposing."

I feel the shocked little breath she lets out deep down in my balls. What is it about this woman? Every physical response from her draws one from me. Vague recollections hit me from science class, way back in the day. Newton's law, was it? For every action, there's an equal and opposite reaction? Funny. Here we are, I guess. Newton's theory in action.

"Right. Of course. In that case, would you consider being a donor, without any contact?"

"No."

"Wow. Okay." She pauses, obviously considering. Which is far more than I expected. Not that I expected anything. Hell, I shocked myself when I opened my mouth with the offer to knock her up. "What if...what if... Crap, I don't know. What if it works and then you try to tell me how to raise my child and—"

"I wouldn't ask for shit from you."

"The thing is, I don't sleep with employees."

I give her a look that says *Are you kidding me?* We both know I'm not your regular employee. We also both know that there's a term limit here.

She huffs out an unhappy sound. "I need a cook."

"I'll be out of your hair as soon as you find me a replacement."

"Easier said than done."

"No luck?"

She shakes her head, drops her face, and rubs her eyes.

"Once it's...over, you'll leave town? Stay out of our lives?"

"Absolutely. I'm not in the market for a family." Not now. Not ever.

She nods, her sigh so heavy I feel the weight of it, of everything she carries around on those narrow shoulders. "Why the hell would you do this for me?"

With relief, I let the full truth out: "I've wanted to

get my dick inside you since I first laid eyes on that face."

Her laugh is high, shocked. "You're a real prince."

"Not even a little."

"I'm getting that."

I half turn and let myself loom, let her get how big I am, how it would feel to be crowded by me, show her what it'll be like when I'm up in her space. "I'd make it so goddamn good, Kit. You'd forget there's an endgame."

She shifts and I swear she's squeezing those thick thighs together. Is it wishful thinking or is she as excited by this as I am? "What if...what if once isn't enough?"

It won't be. I know that already. I also see how skittish she is when it comes to men. Not as though she's scared of us, but like she's been burned and figured out through firsthand experience that the best way to avoid it is to cut us out entirely.

"We've got a little less than five weeks to figure that out."

"Right. Right." She turns fully my way. "I make the rules."

I force myself to nod, slow and thoughtful. "Yep. Your rules. I'll provide STD test results and..." I look down at the hard-on already trying to rip its way outta my jeans. "The genetic material."

"Right." I watch her consider, eyes wide as they scan our surroundings, touch on me and then skitter away again. She's probably asking herself if she wants an ex-con for her kid's dad, maybe wondering just how high my IQ can possibly be if I turned to crime as a youth. On the flip side, I'm big and strong. That's gotta count for something in whatever genetic calculations she's running through that sharp brain of hers. "Frank says you're a good man. Says there's no one he'd trust more than you. But this restaurant is my life, Jake. It's all I have."

"I would never hurt you," I grit out, a vow I'll gladly scratch out in blood.

I've counted up to thirty in my head by the time she nods and shoves her slender hand at me. "Okay. Yes."

My cock goes impossibly harder, heavier. It's throbbing where it's trapped between my leg and rough denim. It's takes an effort to do nothing but reach out and slide my palm against hers, grip those delicate fingers, shake.

When she finally pulls away, she's all business.

"Once you get your results..."

"I'll get it done tomorrow."

"Okay. We can do it at my place."

"Probably a good idea."

Her expression changes. "Why?"

"Would you rather do it here?"

"No." Her exhale's nervous or impatient or something. Not impatient the way I am, I figure. I'm thinking about that big, heart-shaped ass. About how she'll smell in bed, how those eyes will look, how her pussy's gonna feel wrapped tight around me. Fuck...going in bare... I swallow. It'll be a first.

Can't fucking wait.

"Things will be the same at work, Jake, got it?"

"Of course."

"You and I aren't...anything."

"Just doing a job." *Ma'am*. The last word's silent, but it's there.

Her laugh comes out, hoarse and high. "Jesus. That makes it sound..." She swallows and shifts in her seat.

Some part of her likes this. I know it. I fucking feel it in the air between us. "Dirty," she whispers.

"That bother you?"

When her little pink tongue comes out to lick that plush bottom lip, I realize I'm in for a world of pain until those test results come in. At least I know they'll be negative.

I haven't touched—or even thought about—another woman since I walked into Parlor and saw Kitty behind the bar. Kit.

No, Katarina.

"Doesn't bother me," she says.

"Me neither."

"You're into it."

I nod. Even without the visible erection, there'd be no denying it. I'm into whatever happens here. Hell, she's pretty much all I've thought about since I first saw her. To get the chance to fuck her raw? "Yep."

"All right." She opens her door, letting in a blast of much-needed air. "See you tomorrow."

She swings out into the lot and pauses halfway through shutting the door again. "Nothing changes. Got that?"

"Of course, boss. Nothing changes." This is a bald-faced lie.

Pretty sure we both know it. But, man, all I can think about is seeing her tomorrow and knowing that soon, she'll be stuffed full of me.

If Frank knew what I was up to, he'd slice off my balls.

6

———

KIT

The thing with Jake is a terrible idea. I need to cancel. Today. I'll take him into the office and tell him I changed my mind. He'll have to respect that, right?

Will he, though? Or will he want me to shell out anyway?

Like I'm something he's owed. Like *getting his dick inside me*, as he so eloquently put it, is somehow his right now that I've agreed to do it. It's a sordid porn.

And here's the worst part. The part that's got me at work way, way earlier than I need to be. The part that made me lose hours of sleep last night because every time I shut my eyes I saw his face, those cool blue eyes taking in details of me that he shouldn't be able to see through my clothes, my skin. Every time I tried, I'd end up touching myself, first at the idea of how he'd push me up against the wall and take me, rough and mean. Wordless. Just fucking me, no emotion, no connection. I've never done that.

He'd use me for his pure pleasure, while I use him for his...*seed*.

Even that word is somehow right and wrong and horny as hell.

Now I'm obsessed with this thing. Obsessed with his desire, which has inflamed my own, drawn it out into the open, made it real and, in doing so, taken away any semblance of normalcy between the two of us.

So, while I cut lemons and pull a fresh keg out of the back an hour earlier than I normally would, trying to prove that this is just work, picturing him taking what I promised, I have to admit that there's a piece of me that wants it that way. Hard and unfriendly, like I've reneged on some promise and he's taking the debt out in flesh.

I am in no way prepared, after these hours and hours of thinking and feeling things I've successfully suppressed since the man showed up at my bar, to actually see him in the flesh when he walks through the front door, the chimes tinkling merrily behind him.

For a few seconds, I lose my bearings at the sight of him—bigger, even, in real life, than the version my fantasies supplied over and over last night—my knife skids across a lime peel and slices through my thumb.

A small hurt noise chuffs out of me, I reach for a bar towel and it's not there. The bev nap I finally grab from the stack is immediately soaked through. "Dammit."

The sting of lemon juice and the sight of all that blood makes me think I've messed up and really cut myself. I'm afraid to look. I've always been this way, scared that it'll be worse than it is. Prepared to pretend it's fine and just running it under water'll be enough. Slap a bandage on and go back to what I was doing.

"You okay?" Jake's behind the bar, leaning over me. He's got a clean bar towel. No idea where he found it. "Let me see."

I hunch over my hand, but he reaches out and gently pries it away from my middle.

"Come on. I've got it. Shut your eyes."

How does he know I don't like to look? Even if the darn thing's cut clean off, as long as I don't have to see it, I'll be fine.

"Good."

When did I obey? I don't remember closing my eyes.

He takes my hand, edges the paper off and turns it over, then presses the towel against it. It doesn't hurt all that much and now that I'm taking stock, his presence is forcing more adrenaline through my veins than the actual pain itself.

"Hold this." He eases the terry cloth into my other hand and stalks off, his footsteps heading toward the kitchen. The creak tells me that the door's swung in and, a second later, swings back out.

When he comes back up to my side, it's his warmth I perceive first. The man's pumping out heat and, with his size, it sort of engulfs me. Lulls me so that when he grabs my hand again and takes the towel off, I'm able to open my eyes and look.

Not at my bleeding hand, but at him. He's bent over, busy cleaning and wrapping my left index finger. From this close, I'm able to see the whorl of his ear, the growth pattern of his fresh five o'clock shadow, the way his nose looks perfect from the side—long, with a bump—but when caught from the front, it's slightly bent.

From a fight, I'd bet.

He's a brawler, he said. Or he was. Maybe whatever he did to wind up in prison also broke his nose.

His proximity sends my body into a fresh tailspin. A dance of a million contradictions. Nipples hard, core soft, wet, everything tight and somehow also swollen. My belly settles into a heavy, liquid ache, while my breathing spins out, quick and erratic.

"Thanks," I manage to say to the side of his face after a shallow inhale.

Aside from a low grunt, he ignores me and frowns down at what he's doing, his utter concentration so single-minded, something awfully close to jealousy rears its silly head.

Oh my God. What is wrong with me? Am I truly jealous that he's paying attention to my hand and not my face? What part of me would I rather he look at, pray tell?

Oh, shut up, Kit. You know exactly what part.

Crap. Crap. I need to stop this. It's absolutely not what I meant when I decided to try for a baby. I didn't want this complicated mess of feelings and I certainly did not want it muddling an already complex work situation.

I'm understaffed. Perpetually working to find decent people, despite good pay and benefits and great tips for the front of house.

But prices are rising and the cost of running a business has gone through the roof and then you've got employees coming back to try to steal from you like Keith last night, not to mention an ex who's prowling around like the vultures squatting the huge tree in my backyard, and after a while, being the sole owner of a place like this becomes too much of a cross to bear and you wonder if having a baby's even feasible in today's market and—

"Simmer down. I'm almost done."

Simmer down? *What?* Is he kidding?

I open my mouth to tear him a new one when I feel the bounce of my leg. I'm grinding my teeth, too, and squirming, perched on the fridge that I don't even recall sitting on. My muttered, *Sorry* goes unnoticed, or unacknowledged. And now I feel like a child. Worked up and chastised and *small.*

I open my mouth to tell him something, like maybe I don't want to do this whole extra-curricular project, after all, because it's put me on edge and made me question things I don't usually doubt. It's also kept me from getting a good night's sleep and—look!—now I'm cutting myself behind my bar. Because of one stupid decision, I've lost every ounce of cool I ever possessed and I can't survive this way. Not with him being so close every day. Not with my body so out of my control. What about after we do it? What about then? Can I just expect all this tension to dissipate or will it get worse?

I'm worried it's the latter. And there's no way I can handle the latter. Not with the crisp tightness at my neck and how high my shoulders have gone. I'll never survive this. I'll put my back out and have to close the restaurant and then it'll all go downhill from there.

I've just opened my mouth to tell him it's off, when a firm hand sets mine down and pats my knee before he steps away.

"Done." He doesn't move farther before looking down at me. This close, I can't meet his eyes so I take the coward's route and examine the neat job he's done on my hand. Bandage and finger protector, both tightly in place. "Be back to normal in a couple days."

I nod, still not looking up.

"Got my tests done today."

My few languorous parts go wild, hitting turbo-speed in a fraction of a second. "Good. Good." I twist, intending to slide off the bar fridge and get some space between us, but he's still too close, boxing me in up here. Getting trapped by his significant bulk sends a fresh blast of hormones through my body, so charged that it's impossible to tell where intimidation ends and excitement begins. Or if they're even separate at all.

"Could you move?" I ask, sounding not nearly the boss I meant to be. "Please?"

"Yeah." He sniffs and stands there for another handful of seconds, then backs up another step.

I'm about to edge my way down and past him when he leans in again and speaks right into my ear. "Thought about you all night, Kit. The way your sweet little mouth opens when you're surprised. The way your eyes get all dark when I'm close like this. Did you think about me?" I breathe shakily through the pause. Still and utterly lost. "You think about how it'll feel, the two of us?"

I want to shake my head, but it would be a lie. And lying right now seems worse than anything, although I've got no godly notion why. Instead, I don't reply at all. Just sit here, staring straight ahead, over his wide shoulder, at the small piece of wall I've been trying to decide whether to wallpaper or leave black.

I'll be embarrassed later when I think of the way my hands tremble and my exhalations come out all choppy. I'll be mortified when I remember the clearly visible goosebumps that take over my bare shoulders when he says, "Decided not to let myself come until I'm deep inside you, Kit." I shut my eyes, hard, and suppress a moan. "My balls are so fucking heavy right now after the night I had, thinking about that ass of yours. So ready to blow." Oh, God. I'm so aroused that if I squeeze my thighs just a little, I might actually orgasm and that's not something that comes spontaneously in my experience. Or at all most of the time. "Figured I'd save it all up—every goddamn drop—for your little pussy, Kit. You good with that? It's what you need, right?"

I nod and then, though it doesn't even start to capture what I need in this moment, I turn and whisper into his ear: "Yes." And then, because I'm apparently not done shocking myself, I say, "I want that."

He lets out a breath and swallows, both sounds way too human for the man who's gone and turned my whole life upside down. "Good." Another exhale, this one warm against the side of my face. "I'll have the results in three days."

With that, he steps back, turns, and walks away, leaving me with nothing but the repetitive squeak of the kitchen door swinging in and out for its usual five beats, and a body that's never once been this turned on.

It's all I can do not to storm into the kitchen and tell him to forget about the test results, follow me into the office and take care of things right now, because I'm more ready than I've ever been.

I didn't survive this far by letting my impulses lead me, though. And I won't start now.

But the rest of the night's going to be hell on my overcharged libido.

7

———————

JAKE

It's been two days since the cut. Three since I told Kit I'd get her pregnant and it sure looks like I've underestimated my body's ability to withstand the constant assault of her presence.

It's early Sunday morning and, rather than sleeping late like I planned, I'm downstairs in Ricky's gym, beating the living shit out of the heavy bag. The door to outside opens and I turn to watch Ricky meander over.

"Did you even sleep?"

I swipe an arm over my forehead. "What do you mean?"

"Drove by last night. Saw the lights on so I swung into the lot."

I snort. "Spying on me?"

"Wanted to make sure Travis hadn't left it on."

"Nope. It was all me." I don't mention that I let the kid sleep on the mats in the corner again. Ricky and I don't see eye to eye about that.

He wants to support the kid, let it go.

I want to have a talk with the mother.

He glances up at the big clock hanging on the bare brick wall. I can't believe the damn thing's still working after all these years. Or maybe Ricky's got a supplier for them.

I turn and throw another punch, follow it up with a left, then another right.

"You working today?" There's a smile in his voice.

"Yep. Brunch." I flick a look his way. "You should bring the lady in."

"Maybe I will."

He won't. Just like he hasn't put the damn gym on the market yet, despite our many, many discussions.

"You talk to the real estate agent?" I send a quick combo of punches to the bag, my bones craving the strike as much as my muscles want the strain of repeated movement and my lungs need to struggle for air.

"She's hard to get ahold of."

"Bullshit."

"Aw, come on!" Ricky's hurt act needs work, which I guess is what happens when you spend most of your time keeping teenage boys out of trouble. "You know I'm busy."

I throw him a grin. "Yeah. Dolores keeping you occupied?"

"She's a full-time job."

"Then let's sell the gym, man. Give her your full attention."

He walks around and catches the bag. "The gym's yours."

"Building's mine, but the business is yours," I say, although really the whole thing was a gift. Repayment for everything the man's done for me in this lifetime. And still, it doesn't even come close.

"It was an investment. You should come in and run it."

I stop, lungs heaving, sweat pouring down every part of me, and let my arms drop to my sides. "I'm not taking over the gym. Told you. I'm not moving back here."

"Then I'm not selling."

Ricky's got one of those faces that's like a map of his life story, carved out one piece at a time. There's the nose—broken a time or two when he was a kid in a local gang, then smashed to a pulp in prison and again, later, in the ring. His mouth's bisected by a long, angry scar, courtesy of his father who, by all accounts was one hell of a piece of work. When I met him, he had smile lines fanning out from his eyes, but now, at over sixty years of age, they're more like trenches, dug deeper by all the years of laughter and yelling and all the other shit that goes on in a place like this.

A place that saves literal lives just by its very existence.

"Wish you'd take over the gym."

"I wish you'd let me sell it and go on the cruise Dolores keeps asking for."

He coughs out a laugh. "Asking? More like demanding. Says if I don't take her this year, we're over."

Dolores, Ricky's long-time girlfriend, has been threatening that for at least five years, but Ricky, no matter what he claims, is no more interested in retiring than I am.

"Let me sell the gym. You can retire."

"Yeah, yeah."

Behind us, the door slams open, hard.

"Fuckin' kids," Ricky mutters under his breath, before turning to yell. "Where are your fuckin' manners, Jones?"

"Sorry, coach."

"Yeah, well, get down and give me twenty."

"Make it fifty," I call out, just to fuck with the kid, who moans a complaint while dropping to the floor.

"On your knuckles!" says Ricky, starting to walk away.

"Call the agent, Ricky," I tell him as I turn back to give the bag one more good thump. "Or I will."

An hour later, showered and shaved, I pull up to Parlor and stare at the white-painted facade, wishing the pain in my knuckles would distract me from the ache in my balls.

My body's not falling for it. Not last night, not this morning. Back at Ricky's gym or up in my apartment, whether I'm pounding the bag, in bed, or in the shower, all I can think about is getting inside of Kit.

I head inside, say hello to Cora, who's prepping the front of house, and catch Kit's eye as I round the bar to the kitchen door.

"You good?" I ask.

She nods with one of those forced smiles she's been wearing since I made my proposal.

Right away, I pull a bin of whole chickens from the walk-in and start prepping them for the Sunday roast Parlor is most famous for. It's a brunch/British pub roast experience that appeals to all kinds of people. Kit puts soccer and rugby on the screens and puts on one of her perfectly selected playlists, and people line up for hours for a table.

I've got nothing but admiration for Kit and everything she's built here, the way she's made a brand for herself that's more than just a fun place to hang out.

The door swings open and the sous-chef comes in, washes up and gets to work. Frida's an older woman—late fifties, I'd guess, maybe older. She's tall and tough and easy as hell to work with. Kit told me Frida took over the kitchen before I got here, but she's got no interest in being in charge. "Wanna get the biscuits prepped?"

"On it," she says. Concise, to the point.

We get into our usual groove pretty quick and have everything ready before the doors open. Throughout the shift, I do my best to ignore Kit's occasional pass-throughs, although not noticing her is impossible when there's so much of her. Curves and presence and competence. It's so goddamn sexy. We're a few minutes from the end of service when one final order comes in and I don't have all the pasta I need. They've got apps, so I put water on and cut through the restaurant to the back hall and the extra dry storage closet I just built new shelves for.

Inside, I grab a couple big bags of pasta, turn, and run smack into Kit, who's just quickly turned the corner.

Steadying her with my free hand, I come to a full stop and look down.

"I need straws," she says, low and husky. Pure sex. Pure sin.

"Have at it."

They're on the shelf right beside her, but she doesn't move to get them, just stands there, looking up at me, her chest rising and falling, quick and shallow.

I don't have to shut my eyes right now to picture the

way she'd look under me, her tits bouncing hard with every thrust.

"Need something else?"

She blinks up. "I... Would you... Can we talk?"

"Now?"

"No. No, after the shift. When..."

When everybody's gone, she means. It'll be Sunday afternoon, edging into nighttime and Frida will take off to be with her wife, the two waitstaff always rush out, too. It'll just be me and her. "Yep," I tell her, unclear from her expression whether this little chat will be a good thing or not. "Better get back. Pasta needs boiling."

"Right. Yeah."

She backs up and I move by her, leaving enough space so she won't feel my pounding hard-on, but if she looks down, she'll know.

I use the pasta to hide her effect on me as I return to the kitchen. Thankfully, Frida doesn't pay me the slightest attention, unless it's to reply when I call orders, and Toni, the dishwasher kid's in his own world, headphones in place, dancing like if he stops, he'll deflate.

It feels like hours later when the last of them leaves. The place is sparkling, pristine in a way few kitchens are after a shift, but I'm an asshole like that. Like Dad insisted on back in the day, nobody leaves until the work space shines.

Finally, anticipation edging into every part of my body, I wipe off my hands, undo my apron, and head out to the front.

Kit

"We need a contract."

"Yeah?"

I shove the papers I've just printed in the office at him and stand behind the bar once again, pouring myself a drink. Wine, this time. I need something tamer than whiskey.

It occurs to me as I take my first sip, that I might not be able to drink by this time next month. Would it be that early? I can't remember when you know, at first. Weeks, right? Nine weeks? No. No, it's less. You tell people at twelve. I'd already told everyone, back then, when I miscarried.

"Pretty detailed," Jake says, eyes still on the sheaf of papers in front of where he's seated at the bar.

"I figured it was a good idea. To be thorough."

"When'd you do this?"

"I had a lull."

"During the shift?"

"Last night and today."

Nodding, he edges the papers aside, his focus on me.

"Want a drink?" I ask.

"You trying to get me buzzed so I'll sign this thing?" His eyes crinkle with a wry sort of humor. "Not sure it'll stand up in a court of law if I'm over the limit."

"No! That's not what I'm trying to—"

"Slow your roll, Katarina. I'm just kiddin'."

Annoyance flares at that easy, good ole boy way of talking. It reminds me of my brother. When we were kids, Frank was always telling me to relax. Stop worrying. Calm down. None of it useful, of course, unless his plan was to get me ridiculously riled up.

"Right. That's just great." I lean to grab the papers, suddenly irritated as hell that this guy has the gall to waltz in here out of nowhere and tell me how to act in my own goddamn restaurant. When we're talking about my body. This is for me, after all, not for him. He's just coming along to get his rocks off. "You know what. Let's forget about it. You're a little too bossy for what I—"

"Whoa, whoa, whoa." He's got the contract in one hand, held above his head, the pen in the other.

I don't want him to sign. To make this bizarre situation real. I want him to disappear and stop confusing me with his too-big-for-this-place presence. Not larger than life, exactly, since he's not loud the way that would insinuate, or overbearing. At all. He's just...too *real*.

I smelled him the other day when he bandaged up my hand and there were none of the things I'd have imagined for him. No cedar or leather or other so-called guy scents. No. Jake Brand smelled exactly like what he is: A man. Soap and skin with the faintest hint of sweat.

The scent wasn't put together in some lab by a perfumer in an attempt to titillate the senses, it was created by nature and genetics and singlehandedly awoke some base, animalistic thing inside me.

In a series of flame-fresh images, I picture myself licking him, running my nose along his biceps, his chest, under his arms, his nape. I imagine touching all that skin and the body hair I've only guessed at from my few glimpses at his corded forearms. I'd taste him with my lips and tongue, test him with my teeth. I'd get to hear the sounds he makes when he loses control. And, now, since he whispered those things into my ear on Friday, I can't stop thinking about how his face will look when he comes.

Decided not to let myself come until I'm deep inside you, Kit.

Two full days of reliving those words in my ear. Over and over.

None of this was part of the bargain.

Which is why I wrote up a contract with clear, concise parameters. Rules.

"We'll do it when you're ovulating?"

"Yep." I nod, working hard to keep eye contact until he starts reading again. "A one-time deal."

"No petting," he goes on, glancing up at me with brows raised. "No licking?" He leans his head back and keeps reading from the papers he's holding out of my reach. "No unnecessary foreplay. Unnecessary, huh? Well, sheeyit. I had my heart set on suckin' those cute little toes and now you've gone and—"

"No *kissing*." I'm breathing hard again. God, why can't I catch my breath around him?

"No?" His eyes glisten under the light of two dozen vintage crystal chandeliers. "We talkin' lips or other places, too?" Like the steady stroke of a hand, his gaze slides over my face, my mouth, my neck, and shoulders, to my breasts, where it lingers.

"No. Kissing. Anywhere." At least I sound firm. A true feat, given that he's turned my insides to jelly with just that look. Which is exactly why I've got to set up firm boundaries right here, right now.

For a handful of seconds, he watches me, a muscle ticking in his jaw, those tendons in his neck standing out with stark tension. Though there's no discernible expression on his face, I'd say that flexing jaw, along with the way his eyes are narrowed means he's pissed.

Slowly, he loosens up, the tension eases, and then, with absolute seriousness, he nods. "All right. All right." I don't know if I trust his easy tone. "You're in charge."

His perusal of me continues, over my belly, my hips, to that hot, aching place between my legs.

The way he's eyeing me—like I'm a steak he's about to eat or, worse, some kind of prey he'll tear apart with this teeth—pushes me to add, "It happens once. One time."

His only reaction is a sardonic lift of his brows. "Yeah?"

Why does this non-response make me think I'm the one who'll be begging him for seconds when the time comes?

No. No, I am resolute on this matter. Once. If it doesn't stick, well...that's it.

I nod. "Once."

"All right. Anything else, boss?"

"Don't call me boss."

His momentary smirk tells me he's needling me. "Fair enough."

"And don't mention this. To anyone."

"I won't."

"My brother never finds out."

He snorts, clearly stunned that I'd suggest it. "That I'm the father?"

"The *donor*," I correct, sounding prissy. But I realized over these last couple of days, that I need these guidelines. Without them, I'm just a woman screwing an employee. With the contract, I can think of this as glorified IVF, with limits and structure and enough fine print to drive him out of his mind. That, I can make work.

We'll both get our way. He can get his rocks off and I'll get the child I want more than anything in this world.

It's simple. A good plan.

He drops the contract, flips to the last page and signs it, stands up, then steps back from the bar. "I'll let you know when the results come in." There's no expression on his face, no inflection in his voice as he says, "Night, Kit," grabs his coat, and leaves.

It's a relief when he steps outside. Or, it should be. He signed my contract, which I am absolutely certain has no legal value whatsoever, but which at least makes me feel like I'm heading into this thing with rules I can abide by. And with a plan. Plans are important.

As long as I stick to them, everything will be just fine.

It has to be.

8

KIT

Ten minutes. He'll be here soon.

I should've had something to drink. It didn't seem like a good idea. Clear-headed seemed better, but now clear-headed feels like torture. My nerves are hopping, my belly's twisted up. If I'm not careful, I'll throw up.

There's a bar downstairs. I could run down. Or call room service and order a shot. Or three.

No. No, this is about keeping my cool, being clear on what we're here for. This isn't about sex.

I can be level-headed.

Shutting my eyes, I breathe deep.

I'm calm. Pretend this is the doctor's office. Pretend the nurse let me into this very fancy room. She's taken my vitals, put me in a robe.

I look down at the high-necked dress I've got on. Bare feet. Bra, no panties.

Yeah. Close enough.

Another breath, counting in, then out. Maybe I'll

meditate. It's worked in the past. After the separation, it was just about the only thing that—

A knock at the door has me jumping out of my skin. I barely manage to suppress a startled scream. *Come on, Kit, woman up already. You're stronger than this.*

I am. I'm strong. A thick-skinned survivor. If I don't nip this in the bud I'll freeze up or something and he won't even be able to get the damn thing in.

Ugh, why'd I have to go and think about that?

Because it's what's about to happen, Kit, you fool.

With another slow inhale, I walk to the door, pause with my eyes closed for three more seconds, and then swing it wide.

Whoa. Oh shit. *Wow.*

He's cleaned up. The man I've only ever seen looking scruffy in leather or denim and chefs' clothes is wearing honest to god suit pants, his white button-down shirt so well cut, I can't imagine it wasn't custom tailored for those muscles. His hair looks slightly damp, like he recently showered, and it takes effort to resist reaching up to test its softness.

I could.

No. No extra touching. Nothing that will make this...*more.*

"Hey."

"Come in."

I step back and he walks in and I smell him, only this time that pure man scent's mixed with cologne or aftershave and it is *delicious.*

Is this how he'd dress for a date? Is that what this look is about?

No. No, this is more like interview wear. Or first day

at the job or, who knows, a meeting with a parole officer or something.

"Nice hotel," he says, taking in the crisp bedding, the thick curtains, the dark furnishings, the tasteful, minimalist art on the walls.

I'm ignoring the issue of the bathroom having no door which would have been a no-go, had I known. We'll deal with that if we need to, at some point. I mean, the toilet has a door. That's what matters. I doubt we'll be taking a shower here today. At least not together.

"Yeah." I nod. "Um, so I was thinking about how we should..." I swallow, shut my eyes and fill my tight lungs again. "Proceed."

He watches me, one eyebrow up. "With the..."

Don't say insemination. Don't say insemination.

"...main event?" He's smirking now, which is worlds better than all the seriousness.

"Right," I release with relief. "That."

"What do you need?"

I blink. "Need?"

"Yeah." His dark eyes flick over my body. "To get ready."

"Oh. Um...well, I, uh closed the curtains."

When he turns to take in the windows, the muscles in his neck shift, stretching the dark lines of ink and underlining just how hefty his frame is. I've never been with someone this powerfully built.

It's intimidating as it occurs to me, for the first time, that I'll have that—*him*—between my thighs. His bulk, his heat, his human scent.

Panic races through me like a chill wind.

"I'd rather do it in the dark," I squeak. "If you don't mind."

He barks out a surprised laugh. "You're kidding me."

"No."

With a sigh, he shakes his head, runs a hand through his short hair and then looks at me. "Fine. What else?"

"No touching at all."

"I remember." His smile's devoid of humor. "It's in the contract."

"Clothes on."

His dark brows lift, giving him a sardonic air. "Gonna be a little tough, isn't it?"

"I can..." I gulp. I'm not a prude. Why is it so hard for me to discuss this like an adult who has actually had sex in her life? "I'm in a dress, so that's easy. And you can unzip."

"You commando under there?"

My face goes hot. "Yeah."

When his only response is another perusal of my very much covered body and a muttered, *Christ*, I get the distinct impression that this man is perfectly up to the task of impregnating me without removing a single item of clothing. Hell, just the way he looks at me feels potent enough. I swear my ovaries are revving up in preparation.

"What else?" he asks, voice tight, jaw rigid.

"Um. Once it's, uh, done. You can just...head out. If that's okay."

"Sure. Your show. Your call."

Why does that easy acquiescence make me almost angry?

Maybe it's just a man thing. They just want to fuck so bad, they don't much care for how it happens.

Right. That's probably it. *Men.*

Clark's easy, cheery smile flashes briefly through my mind, making my feet go cold and my spine stiffen. *Your call, sweetie pie,* he used to say when I'd ask for any opinion relating to our home, vacations, lives. *Your call,* he said, all the while apparently working hard at getting his twenty-year-old barista girlfriend pregnant. The barista from the coffee shop I liked to go to. The one where they put homemade marshmallows on their hot chocolate and there's this cozy back room that's perfect for people with kids. I'd pictured bringing our children there.

"What about you, Kit? What do you need?" His voice, though soft, startles me from my uncomfortable memories.

"Me?"

"How do we get you ready?"

"We?"

When he shifts closer to me, I see that his eyes, which had been as soft as his voice a second ago, have gone dark and ice hard. "What's the plan, Kit? You gonna just spread 'em in the dark and hope I'll fit?"

All the blood in my body whooshes south. Why on earth is that idea a turn-on? Is it the insinuation that he's big? The notion that it'll take work to get his body to slot into mine?

He's closer than I realized, his height and bulk blocking out most of the light from the bedside lamp. "You bring lube?"

"Oh…" Crap, what was I thinking? I am so unprepared for this. "No."

"We've got to get you good and wet then, don't we, Kit?"

I wish he'd stop using my name because every time I

hear it in that voice, it's like he's handling me. Getting me where he wants me without once having to use his hands.

"I'll be fine."

He grunts, clearly not believing me. I don't know why I find that annoying.

"It's good. I've done this before, you know."

"Had clothes-on hotel sex in the dark to get pregnant?"

"No, I mean sex."

"Sure hope so."

"Listen, let's... You just..."

"Go ahead. Tell me what to do. I'm all yours."

There he goes, giving my nerves a work-out again with his words. What is it? Is it the innuendo, intended or not? Is it that it's him? Or is it this weird situation? Would I always be up and down like this, given the circumstances? Skittish one second and half-aroused the next?

"All right. Good." I nod at his pants. "You, um, get ready and I'll...be right back."

I head into the bathroom, lock myself in the toilet cubicle, and lean back against the door. *What are you doing, Kit? Get a hold of yourself. This isn't you, this nervous crap.*

I'm a confident person. I know my mind. I'm not someone who faffs around, trembling for no reason. This is sex. That's it. I've done this more than a few times. I've had a few partners. I mean, it's been years since I've done it with anyone but Clark, but it's just like riding a bike, right? One leg over, ass in the saddle...

After a deep breath in, I walk out, wash my hands, and head back into the room, which is now as dim as it can get without shutting off the light entirely. He's seated in one of the armchairs, waiting.

"Go ahead and get on the bed." I guess he's in charge now. "This dark enough for you?"

"Totally dark, please," I whisper, heading to the bed, feeling like I've completely miscalculated this whole thing.

I sink onto the white comforter, then change my mind and get up to pull it, along with the top sheet back, then scramble onto the middle, self-conscious and awkward, but also tempted to squeeze my thighs together for a hit of friction.

Over the next few beats, Jake heads over to the lamp and shuts it off, the clicking sound final and grim in the quiet. He then settles on the side of the bed, his breathing audible.

Seconds tick by.

"You mind if I get ready?"

"Oh. Go ahead."

The sound of fabric, a zipper coming undone, the dry swipe of skin to skin.

Good lord, why didn't I think of how the noises would be worse in the dark?

A low grunt joins in the unexpectedly erotic sound of the man using his own hand to get himself hard. For me.

Another grunt, raspier, and for some inconceivably ridiculous reason, I want to know what he's thinking about while he does this. Is he picturing the two of us together? Maybe he's imagining something else entirely. A porn or a fantasy situation.

"Are...are you..." I swallow, no idea what I'm going to say, but Jake knows. He knows.

"I'm thinking about those big, soft tits of yours. How they'll bounce when I'm fucking you."

My insides clench up, achingly empty.

"Thinking about how tight you'll be around me, how good you'll feel. Oh, *fuck*."

"Are you... Are you okay?"

He laughs low and private, the sound the warmest thing I've ever heard. "I'm about to get inside you, Katarina. Doing just fine." A pause, filled with the sound of his hand—or hands?—stroking up and down his shaft, squeezing, maybe?

I wish I knew how tight. Why did I need the lights off?

As if reading my mind he says, "Let me turn the lights on, Kit. Forget the rules. I'll make it good for you."

What if... "No."

"Fine. Get ready, then."

It takes me a second to realize I should probably lift my skirt up. "Um. Okay. I'm good."

"Good. Your legs spread?"

"Yes. They're..." I swallow, my throat suddenly dry. "Open."

"That's it. Get them good and wide for me." His hand's moving faster and then suddenly, the sound stops. "All right. Let's go."

9

———

Jake

I kick off my boots. Probably against the rules, since they're an item of clothing, but I'm not fucking her with shoes on. Not this time, at least. Not on a bed.

I reach out, unable to see much in the dark, make contact with one naked thigh, and pull back without allowing myself the pleasure of even a stolen caress. "Sorry."

"No, it's...totally normal."

Not really, but, whatever. It's still somehow turning my crank all the way over.

I edge above her, half pissed off that I'm not allowed to touch and half turned-on by how messed up the situation is. It's hard to resist reaching for her, leaning down to find her lips in the dark.

At the same time, though, there's this thread of perversion or something running through it all that *works*. It's different, so it's a turn on. Taboo, no touching, clothes-on sex. Pretty sure my cock's never been harder. This is clearly hitting all the right buttons.

"You good?" I ask once I've settled my knees between her legs and sunk down over her body. I'm on straight arms, giving her no weight. Almost no contact. Christ, this is weird. Hot as hell, but weird.

"Yeah. Fine. Great. I mean..." She huffs out a small laugh. "You can put your weight on me, you know? I don't see how we'll manage otherwise."

Breath held, I ease slowly down, more to get my bearings than to get right into it.

My aching cock lands on her pubic hair with a thud. Fuck. I screw my eyes shut.

"You okay?"

"What? Yeah."

"You're just, um, breathing kind of hard."

Now, it's my turn to do one of those voiceless laughs. "Yeah, well, this feels pretty good."

Her breathless "Yeah" stops me mid laugh.

Fuck. "It does?"

"You feel, um...big, you know?"

"I am."

She snorts. "All right, show off. Just, you know, stick it in already."

Nope. Hell no. Not so fast. If this is the one time, I'm enjoying every goddamn second of it. I need something to take back to the spank bank. And, so far, though this is pretty novel, it's also nowhere near the fantasies I've built up of this woman in my head. She's so lush, her body so full, so beautiful, there's something almost tragic about not getting to see her.

To put my hands all over her.

"You wet?"

"I... Should I check?"

"No. I got it." Putting my weight on one arm, I grasp

my shaft, brace myself, and nudge the rock-hard head between her legs.

The first swipe is dry. Not good. The second splits her open like a ripe fruit. I edge deeper and...oh yeah. She's wet. Not soaking, but damp.

"Oh. Oh." Her voice goes a little squeaky. Good. I want her to lose the control she's got herself so tightly wound up in.

"Good?" I ask, just to hear more of her voice.

"Yeah. I think."

Nice. Just *great* for my ego.

I slide my dick down, dragging her wetness with me, then back up to hit her clit. The whimper she lets out is gratifying as hell, so I stay there.

No touching was the rule. With my hands. Might be cheating to use my cock. Pretty sure I don't fucking care.

Lord knows I've never been all that keen on rules.

"I...I... *Oh.*"

"Good," I tell her. "Almost there." Another slick sweep down, coating myself in her. Every move loud. And, fuck, she smells so goddamn right. The exact flavor of sex—of woman—I've been aching for. I nudge her opening and ease back up. Down and up a few times until we're both gasping from the contact.

"You feel that?" I speak to the side of her head. "You feel how hard I am for you?"

She nods.

"Good. I want you to know how hot you are. Even in the dark, Katarina."

"You're...you're talking."

"No rule against it."

Her half laugh devolves into panting when I nudge my tip just into her opening. "This what you want?

Huh? You want this fat cock inside you? You want to be bred?"

"Oh, god. I can't... Don't..."

I pull slightly away. "Just tell me and I'll stop."

"No!" She grabs my arms with both hands, hard. "No. Stay. Do...what you need to."

"Good." I dip down and tease her some more. "That's good. You're so fucking good, Kit."

She shivers at those words. I save that little tidbit for later.

"You ready?"

"Yeah. Yeah, I'm ready."

"Good. Good. Just...stay just like that." I line up with her opening and press in, slowly.

She pants, light and quick. I pause. "You all right?"

"Yeah."

Does she realize she's holding me? One hand on my shoulder, the nails of her other pressed into my back. I want those hands everywhere.

"So goddamn good," I tell her, trying with difficulty to press in.

She's gone stiff as a board.

"Breathe, Kit."

"Oh. *Oh*, sorry."

I pull back and give it another try. Not quite wet enough. Shit. "I don't want this to hurt."

"It's fine."

"Mind if I use spit?"

Can't tell from her shaky inhale if she likes the idea or not, but her whispered, "Fine," is consent enough. Putting my weight on one arm, I spit in my hand, reach down and coat my dick with it, then do it again.

This time, when I line myself up and push in, I slide

easier. Not as well as I would if I'd made her come first, but it'll do.

I nudge deeper. "You feel that?"

"Oh, god. Oh, oh…" I feel her little whimpers in my cock, my balls, in my chest, where there's no reason for any of this to reside.

"Yeah. Fuck." Finally, I bottom out. "You feel how deep I am?"

She whimpers, clenching around me.

"You take my cock so nice. Don't you, good girl?"

"Please, Jake, I don't…"

"I'm gonna come in this pussy. Fill it up."

Another sound, this one lost, and her hand clenches in my shirt, twists it up.

"You want that, Kit?"

"Y-yes. Oh, God."

"Good. Told you I've been saving it up for you."

She groans and I pull back and slam inside. Not too fast. Not gonna come yet. Already, she feels fucking amazing.

"My balls are so goddamn heavy right now. You know why?"

She moans.

"'Cause of you. In those sweet dresses you wear all the time. All curvy and in charge behind the bar. Every time I head out front and see you, I think about it. This." I tighten my ass, make her feel what I'm saying.

Another whimper makes me pull out, then plunge deep and twist. Her little cunt clenches up around me.

"Oh, yeah. You like that, don't you? You like that?"

She doesn't reply beyond a wordless whimper that I'll be thinking about in my own bed tonight. Christ, how did I think once would be enough?

"I wish you could feel how tight they are, baby. All full and ready to unload inside you." Fuck, I'm getting close. It's the way she responds when I talk in her ear, the way she can't seem to clamp down on her noises, although she's clamping just fine on my dick. And where she wasn't quite wet enough before, right now, she's dripping. "You want that, don't you? Tell me. Tell me what you want from me."

She barely hesitates before responding. "I want..."

"Say it. Go ahead."

"I want you to come inside me."

"Yeah. That's a good girl."

I'm thrusting faster now that she's replying, moaning, meeting my hips with hers every single time. Regardless of the clothes we've got on, we're working together now, our rhythm seamless, our bodies perfectly in sync.

"Such a fucking good girl." Her pussy tightens at those words, which is a wild thing to know about your best friend's sister. "Such a good girl letting me fill up this pussy."

"Jake."

"That's right. Begging me for my come."

"Oh, god, Jake, I can't."

"Yeah you can. Do it."

"I..."

"Tell me."

"Oh god," she whimpers. "I...I need you to fill me up, Jake. Give me a baby."

With a grunt, my cock hard as nails, I set to work to do just that.

10

———

KIT

No. No way. No.

I'm about to come.

This wasn't part of the deal.

I don't want it. I don't want this to be the best sex I ever have.

"Hurry," I force out between embarrassing bouts of moaning I'm completely incapable of stopping. "Please."

"Yeah? You want it?" His breath is warm on my face, his lips so close to mine, they're ghosting me.

"I want..." *You.*

No. No, no. Stop it.

"Hold on. Wait."

He stops moving immediately.

"I want..." No. I don't want. This isn't about sex. It's about the end result. In the dark, so full of him I can't move, can't breathe without sucking in his smell, his taste, can't think without wanting something I'm not supposed to have, it's impossible to work it all out.

"You okay? Want me to pull out?"

"Yes," I say, immediately regretting it when he leaves my body, sits back on his haunches, and gives me space. No way we'll accidentally kiss now. No way he'll skim my breast or lean down, overcome, and put his mouth on my nipple. His face against mine. That won't happen with him over there, our bodies separated. I can't smell his sweat like this or consume the deep rhythmic grunts that permeated the air with every insistent pump of his hips. "It's too much."

"Shit, Kit. Did I hurt you? Are you okay?"

"No. No, I mean..." I need space. Breathing room. "Could you get up?"

He's up and off the bed like a shot. "Kit, just tell me what—"

"From behind," I interrupt with a blaze of inspiration. Behind's better. It's anonymous. Geez, why didn't I think of that to begin with? Instead of all this close, body-to-body, in your face business? I won't come if he's behind me. "It's better."

Feeling so empty now, and aching for more in a way I'll have to unpack later, I get up and turn onto hands and knees, then crawl down to the edge of the bed.

He's right there, smoothing my skirt up. "I'll have to touch you. A little. For this."

"Fine," I concede, sinking to my front so I can bury my face in a pillow. "Do whatever you need."

"Good."

His hands are all over my ass now, pulling my cheeks wide. For a handful of seconds during which neither one of us moves, I wonder if he'll bend down to lick me there. I shut my eyes tight and deny that part of me is wishing for it.

Instead, I almost whine when one of his hands

disappears. The sound of him spitting again sends a flashwave of desire so hard it arches my back and presses my bottom into his rough palm.

"Yeah. Be patient. You'll get it."

I hear chafing. It takes me a second to figure out it's the hand he's just spat into, stroking up and down his shaft, lubing him up again. Why oh why did I ask for pitch black? I could be watching Jake Brand jerking himself off right now.

"You can probably go ahead," I urge, still pretending there's some dignity to this. "I think I'm wet enough."

He hums, the sound weirdly doubtful and somehow bossy, too. It's a *you'll be wet enough when I say you are* hum and it turns my insides into warm syrup.

Yeah. Yeah, I'm in trouble here.

"Here we go."

I brace myself, as if that will change a thing. It does no good, of course, when his tip dips between my lips, notches at my entrance, and then he slams inside, so hard, I'm shoved up the bed. The hand he's got on my ass shifts to my hip and tightens, then goes loose. "I..."

"What?" I lift my head.

"I need to hold you... Um." A quiet huff of air. "On my dick."

How can I not smile at that?

"Permission to, uh, hold your hips, boss?"

I groan, this time not with pleasure.

"*Please* don't call me that." Why on earth is my face flushing hot in the dark? Like what even is the point of blushing when no one can see?

"Sorry." He's clearly not. The jerk.

But, hey, at least I'm smiling now.

"Go ahead."

"Anything...off limits?" he asks, as if he's not already balls deep inside me.

"What?"

"Can I touch your clit?"

And then everything goes still as I remember the thing I've tried over and over again to forget. The time I got pregnant, early on in our relationship, before Clark insisted he wasn't ready. In a waterfall of images, the last ten years of my life rush down on me, taking me, for a handful of seconds, from this room and throwing me back into the hospital, the house, the baby's room, then finally, by myself. As alone as a human can be.

"Stop!"

He pulls out. "You okay?"

"I need you to..." I gulp back a mess of emotions I've spent a decade dealing with in the safe confines of my therapist's office, and concentrate hard on speaking. "Just...jerk off, okay? And then...put it in."

He huffs out a sound. "Seriously?"

"Listen," I start to turn. "You can go if you want, this was a terrible ide—"

"Fine." His hand's back on my ass, spreading me open again for a second. And then those erotic skin to skin sounds. "I'll do it. I'll finish."

There's something ominous about those words. Half threat, half return to that clinical setting I'd hoped for. At the same time, the emotion's still whirling inside of me, along with a fresh dose of something that feels a lot like guilt. For leaving him in the lurch, I suppose.

He's working himself hard, the sound a dull clap, his breathing a rhythmic panting. I tamp down all desire to look and touch and smell, and concentrate hard on thinking about my ovaries. My uterus.

Cold and clinical. That's the goal. I can do that.

Or I could, if he didn't grunt occasionally, or mutter *fuck* under his breath or reach out with the lightest touch against my butt, as if to make sure I'm still here. Not even a stroke or a caress, just a feather light landing, just checking.

My ass moves, the hard curve of my back entirely unintentional. I go still, tamping it down. But then I notice how my inhalations coincide with his, how my pussy's suddenly almost painfully empty, how I'm spreading wider, my insides needy and wanting, how I'm straining to catch every little sound.

It's physiological, I decide. Like seeing porn, like rough fabric against my nipple.

"Fuck, Kit. It's coming."

I bite back a moan and arch deeper, presenting myself to be mounted like an animal.

"Yeah, I'm coming. I'm coming."

The backs of my thighs go warm as he moves in, splits me open again and, without ceremony, shoves that monster cock inside me.

Oh, god.

My eyes screw shut. It's big. Huge. I'm so full. It takes every ounce of willpower I have not to move with him.

"Fuck, yes. Here it is."

A sound escapes me. I bottle it up.

He pulls halfway out to stroke his erection with only his tip lodged inside me.

"Deeper," I tell him. Obviously not for sex reasons. For pregnancy reasons only.

"Oh, yeah. Yeah, you're so tight, baby. Fuck, it's so good."

And it is good. It is. Too good. So good it's all I can do not to sob.

His shaft is throbbing with each jet shooting inside me and, despite my efforts to stay detached, I'm clenching him.

"That's it. Take it. All of it." His hands grasp my hips, tight, and pull me onto him, the slap of his balls to my clit sparking every nerve in my body. Even through my bra and top, I feel the rasp of my breasts against the sheet.

I shut my eyes and work hard to ignore my body's response, loosen my muscles, go elsewhere.

He's slowing now, his thrusting deeper, less controlled, each one punctuated by an animal grunt.

"Every fucking drop is for you, Kit." He shoves deep and bends so his body's covering mine, warm, but not quite touching. "I'll give you everything," he says in a strangled whisper I'm not even sure I'm meant to hear.

It takes every ounce of effort I can muster not to orgasm on his still hard cock.

11

———

Jake

Fuck. Me.

Biggest orgasm of my life. In the dark with a woman who's using me for my come.

A cynical smile twists my lips as I gather my last few functioning brain cells and ease out slowly, then turn and collapse onto the bed with an old man groan.

"Sorry, just need..."

"It's fine." She rolls away and scoots up the bed. I picture her getting into some specific conception pose and then imagine laying a hand on her leg, stroking it, picturing how it would feel to stay inside her, go hard again, and start the whole thing all over.

Hell, I could go for hours with this woman, especially with how pent up I've been since we decided to try it. Since she agreed to let me breed her.

Jesus, have I developed a fucking *use me* kink or something?

For Katarina Esteban?

The problem, right now, is that I'm already hoping

once won't be enough and though it's shitty as hell of me, I hope it takes many, many tries and I hope every one of those takes place on my cock.

"You can, um...go anytime. I mean, sorry, I'm not kicking you out. I'm just..." Her uncomfortable laugh makes me want hug her. "Going to lie here for a bit and..."

"Hope it takes?"

"Yeah." Another awkward laugh.

"All right." With a groan of effort, I sit up and roll out of bed, conveniently dressed, except for my shoes. I tuck myself back into my pants and have to try three times before I can get my zipper up. With a hard shake of my head, I feel around with my feet, grab one boot, and then struggle to find the other. "Any chance I could turn the light on? Can't find my shoes."

"Oh. Oh, sure. Yeah. Right."

I edge back against the bed and lean over to the light, flicking it on to the sound of rustling fabric. Once my eyes have finally adjusted to the brightness, I slide my foot into the second boot and bend to tie them both before standing.

I scrub my hands through my hair and turn to see her lying on her back, legs curled against her belly, the white hotel sheet drawn up literally to her neck, as if me seeing some portion of her would ruin this somehow.

For the first time, a wave of something like resentment flows through me, unfounded as hell. Not to mention pointless.

None of this was about me. I've got to remember that.

It's for her. Like a gift.

I swallow hard.

"All right." I can't look at her, lying there after letting me fuck her raw, hiding all that glorious woman-scented heat under a hotel sheet. "You need anything?"

"I'm good!" The chipper thing is definitely an act. Pisses me off.

"See you at work." It takes effort not to drag my feet on my way to the door. I want to stay, goddamn it. I want to wrap myself up in that sheet with her, bathing in the scent of us, and play with her beautiful body.

Better get out of here.

"Yep! See you tomorrow. Bye, Jake." I'm halfway out the door when she adds a low, "Thank you," like she's not sure she should say it or not.

And, honestly, I don't know either. On the one hand, yeah, it's a favor. On the other, we both know I asked for it.

I asked for it.

Now, all I can think about is getting more.

Kit

I almost came. Oh my god. I almost came during actual sex, without involving my hands or his or a vibrator or anything.

After the door clicks shut, leaving me in this bed, alone with my knees up and my dress bunched around my waist, that near-orgasm is all I can think about.

I've never gotten off from penetrative sex alone. Not once in my life. But today...

Ugh. Why?

Why now? Why this man instead of the man I was

married to? Actually, never mind. I'm glad I never came with that asshole.

But...Jake?

I mean, yes. One look at the man and you know there's not a single unsatisfied woman in his past. He's probably given more orgasms with that massive thing between his legs than I've experienced in my entire lifetime.

I reach down and feel the wetness—his, mine. My fingers slide easily through the sticky mess and glance against my clit, sending pleasure zapping through me.

Without thinking about it, I let myself play, down and up, again, again, then circle my clit with the precision of habit. Oh, wow. Wow. I'm so close.

A few mindless circles and I orgasm, quick and tight. My whole body clenches, my eyes, my toes, my abs. I turn and stuff my face into the pillow, willing the pleasure to last, while already steeling myself against the familiar infusion of guilt.

Tears rush up the back of my throat to crowd my sinuses, burning hot as acid. I manage to hold them back.

Pleasure wasn't the point of this.

For him it was.

For me, it's supposed to be... What? Penance? Punishment? A life sentence?

Throwing back the sheet, I roll to standing, walk to the chair where I left my things, and slip on my underwear and leggings. I won't shower until later. Maybe tomorrow morning.

Already, his come's sliding out of me and I can't for the life of me figure out how this makes me feel, aside from blindsided.

Quickly, I finish getting ready—not daring to look in the mirror, given my inner turmoil—and head out. Once on the road, I find myself turning toward the restaurant instead of home.

Avoidance, my therapist would call it. Working my ass off instead of facing the issues at hand. Scrubbing and cleaning until my body's aching and my brain's no longer swirling with possibilities I can't for one second contemplate.

Yeah, well, avoidance it is.

I've been there for all of thirty minutes when there's a knock at the door.

Shit. No. I can't face anyone right now.

Another knock. *Dammit.*

I stand from where I'm cleaning out the inside of the bar fridge. Something that feels an awful lot like anticipation runs through my belly when I see him through the glass door. As if it could be anyone else.

Maybe he forgot something here. Maybe that's it. Or maybe he's like me and needs work to distract him from what we did in that hotel room.

Yeah, right.

Whatever the case, I unlock the door, avoiding his gaze as he comes inside. It slams closed. We stand here.

"You okay?" His light eyes search my face.

I nod. "Yep. You?"

"Yeah. I thought I'd..." He indicates the kitchen and then stops, arms dropping at his sides. "You think it worked?"

By *it* he obviously means the pregnancy. I know it's not meant to be sexy, yet my body seems to think it's unspeakably hot. Every time we talk about it. Every time he comes close, I'm turned on.

"There's no way of—"

"I know that. But I've heard people just *know* sometimes. Like an instinct or something."

After a second's consideration, I shake my head. "No. Nothing."

He nods, shoves his hands in the back pockets of those hip-hugging trousers, and looks over the big dining room. "You're ovulating, right?"

After a shocked initial reaction, I nod. "Yeah."

"Let me know when you're ready to try again," he says, innocuously enough, though his expression's pure fire.

I nod.

With that, he opens the door and walks back out into the night. Tattooed perfection in custom-cut clothes.

I don't allow myself to watch him stalk to his truck or drive out of the lot. It's a problem, I guess, that I want to. I can imagine his long-legged stride well enough: the solid, wide back, the way his thighs fill out pants that were not conceived to contain so much muscle. He's all heft, all brawn, and yet, walking back to the bar, I concede that there's another side to the man. Under the tattoos, the scars, and the hard bulk I've now felt the weight of, there's a person who's got just as complicated a history as mine. Maybe more.

I stare down at the shiny bar, towel in hand, for half a minute before it occurs to me that we both just insinuated we'll be doing it again, which is absolutely against the rules. My rules, dammit.

Once, the contract said. *One time only*. And now...

I pull out my phone to text him that it's not happening again, but end up opening my fertility tracker app instead and the first thing I see is the ovulation symbol, big and fat and happily smiling at me from the calendar.

Maybe...maybe I can change this one rule, to up my chances of getting pregnant. Just the one.

Instead of the cease and desist message I'd planned on sending, I tap out a quick: ***Tomorrow, same time and place,*** hit send, and shove my phone away like it's dangerous.

Immediately I pull it back out and type: ***One time only. No more changing the rules. We have a contract.***

Sure, he replies. I can't tell if he's being sarcastic or straightforward.

Quickly, I reserve a room, wishing it weren't quite so expensive, although it's nothing compared to the cost of IVF.

I select my payment information, hit the Confirm button, and stare down at where it says the reservation's nonrefundable.

This is a bad idea, isn't it?

Yeah. It's a terrible idea. But nonrefundable means there's no going back now.

I do my best to ignore my excitement.

12

The room's dark when I arrive.

I shove back the prickle of unease that comes over me as I swing open the door and step inside, hit by that sterile hotel room smell. Like the smell's an aphrodisiac, my body immediately primes itself, hot and ready. Who knew the scent of air freshener and bleach would make me hard as nails?

"On the bed." Her voice is high, breathy. It sounds nothing like her.

"Kit?" Figure I'd better check.

"Yeah. Come on in."

When the door slams closed behind me, I take a moment to allow my eyes to adjust. There's a faint frame of light around the curtains, a dull glow from the bathroom. That's it.

"Straight ahead," she says. "Same as last time."

Amazing how much opposing nonsense the human brain can provide in a few short seconds: I don't want the same as last time. Also, bring it on. Give me dark.

Give me anonymous. No. No, give me that mouth. Or her eyes. I just want to see her eyes.

I shove the key card into my pocket, suck in a deep breath, and pause, hands poised at my fly. The musky scent of her filters through the air. "You get started without me?"

"No talking either."

"There an addendum I should sign for that?"

"I just..." She lets out a long, weary sigh. "It's easier this way."

I disagree, but I know enough to keep my damn mouth shut.

Slow and careful, I make my way to the bed, stop when my knee hits the mattress, and ask, "You on your back again or—"

"On my front, like last time when you..."

"Filled your warm cunt with my come?"

"*Jake.*" Her shaky voice sends a deep wave of satisfaction running through me. If I can't make her feel good, I can at least make her feel *something*. Annoyance, if nothing else.

"What?"

"I said no talking."

"I thought you meant dirty talking. While we're doing it."

"I meant..." An annoyed huff. "You know what I meant."

"Might want to spell it out." Who the hell knows why I push her buttons like this. Maybe it's to get a rise out of her. A rise is better than this whole big load of nothing she's trying to turn this into.

"I meant no dirty talk. At all. Period."

"That wasn't talking dirty, Kit."

She snorts. "Right. Sure. Then what the hell was it?"

"Facts." I'm close enough that I hear every breath now, every slight shift of her body on the sheets. Her smell is the perfect amount of savory sweet. My mouth's watering to taste her.

Fuck it. She wants this to be like a job? I'll give it to her how she wants it.

Doing my best to ignore the anticipation and treat this like a job—the way she wants—I unzip just as my jeans-clad leg nudges hers, pull my rock-hard dick out, and bend at the knees to center myself between her thighs.

She gasps when my cockhead nudges her slick lips open, and moans when I sink right the fuck in, my belly filled with this messed up combination of want and need and frustration that's somehow, in no time at all, become the biggest turn-on in my arsenal.

"Oh, god," she whimpers.

"That's right." I plunge deep as I can get and hold tightly to her hips, not moving through the first few seconds of mind-erasing pleasure. The shock's like diving into cold water. Finally, I shake my head. "My cock's all the way in, Kit. You feel that?"

"We're not... You said..."

"Facts. Just stating facts. Nothing dirty about the truth, is there? Fact: I'm taking you bareback right now." I draw out, slow and explicit, my dick aching with how good it feels, then slam back inside, satisfied at the almost violent expulsion of air from her lungs. "That is a cold, hard fact, Katarina. No more, no less."

Another, long, slow slide, and then a thrust, rough, to the hilt.

She grunts. I join her. "I'm filling this tight little pussy with my cock. Fact." When I pull out this time, it's quick, purely functional. The penetration is anything but. It's an invasion, a taking. If she won't watch me fuck her, I can at least make sure she feels every goddamn inch, good and deep. "Using this little hole the way you're using me." My own words shock me, then a second later, feel so right. So *fucking* true. "Seems fair, doesn't it?"

I withdraw and pump back in. Over and over again, the slap of our skin a violent staccato beat. "You like it like this, Katarina? Deep? Rough?"

Her only answer is a groan.

I stop, lodged halfway inside her and, out of breath, whisper, "You okay?"

"I'm fine." She's breathing hard. "It's fine. Just keep going."

She didn't say finish. She said keep going. I latch onto that distinction, clasp her hips harder and pull her back onto my dick. Again and again. Every time, she grunts and gasps and pants, each sound a gift I've had to earn with my body. "That's it, Kit. That's it," I say, my own orgasm approaching like a runaway train. I shove it back. "Fuck, you're getting tighter."

"I'm...I'm...oh, god, I'm gonna..."

Gonna what? Is she coming? Christ, I want that. My eyes screw shut as I force myself to hold off, needing the feel of her climax before I'll relinquish my own. Only fair. Only *fucking* fair.

"Do it. Come all over my fat cock. Do it."

A high whimper, her pussy flutters around me.

With any other woman, under any other circumstances, I'd fall forward and wrap my arms around her, maybe, if she was into the idea, grab her hair or her throat. Or something softer: a tender stroke, a kiss. I don't have those options with Kit. I follow that urge to bend, but have to settle for latching my hands onto her shoulders, startled to feel them covered in fabric, and yank her back onto me.

"You feel my balls against you? All high and tight? Fuck, Kit, they're so full for you. So ready to give you what you want."

"What I *need*," she corrects, the words punctuated by the smack of my hips to her ass. Fuck me if her bossiness isn't the hottest thing I've ever heard.

Bossy Katarina and her heavenly pussy.

Hell, this is it. Right this second, I can pinpoint the birth of a new fetish. Only it's not about being told what to do. Hell, no, that would be too straightforward.

What I want, when she orders me around like this, is to do it right back, to make her change her mind. Make her want whatever I decide to give. I want to scrap, not dominate.

Kit doesn't like to be told what to do. That's been obvious from the first time I met her. It's my own response to it that surprises me. Makes me want to boss *her* around—here, at least—manhandle her until she succumbs and then take some of the load off her shoulders. Force her to accept what I give. There's a weird power play involved, but I get—even as wound tight as I'm feeling right now—that she won't just give up control. She needs it wrested from her. A hard-fought struggle.

And who doesn't love a good battle?

"It's what you need, isn't it, Katarina?" I slam her

back onto me, bottoming out inside her. "Say it. Tell me."

"I need it," she whimpers.

"Need what?"

"Your...your come."

"*Fuuuuuuck.*" Excitement gathers at the bottom of my spine, building fast and hard. "Yeah. You'll get it." I piston into her, quick now, too close to the end to take my time. I feel my rhythm breaking down, my lungs starting to seize.

Through the haze, I notice her backing into me, her whole spine arching to give me that extra depth. I hear the way her moans and grunts have turned needier, higher, more out of control than before. It's the little, "Oh, gods" that hit me right in the gut. Or maybe the sudden clenching of her cunt around my shaft. It might be the way her front end collapses onto the bed, like she's lost the use of her limbs, swamped in all this pleasure.

"That's it," I mumble, right into her ear, my lips so close as to almost—*almost*—be touching. "Take it. Come on my cock and take my seed. Fucking take every goddamn dro—"

I lose it entirely as the orgasm hits. Pleasure that snaps and singes, burns out my inner wiring and shuts down essential synapses. My arms have wrapped all the way around her, pulled her up tight against my crotch, so she's not on the bed at all anymore. I'm half standing, half-squatting, pulling her down onto my clenched thighs, fucking up into her, and I swear to god I lose some brain cells along with the load shooting deep inside her.

Each spurt comes out hot and hard and it takes

every bit of my restraint not to reach down to cup where I'm planted inside her, to explore her, to feel where we're connected. To stay like this. As deep as a man can get.

It's too much. Too *goddamn* much.

I'm groaning when my brain comes back online and I realize I'm disobeying at least one of her cardinal rules.

No Extraneous Touching. That's the one. Not entirely broken, but cracked. I want to smash it to smithereens.

Rattled, I drop my knees to the mattress and let her settle there, push inside her one last time, and force myself to pull out.

I don't wait to see how she's doing. I don't stop for anything. I tuck my aching dick inside my underwear, zip up, and pat my pocket to make sure the keycard's inside before stumbling to the door. After one last inhale, I leave.

The door slams shut behind me.

I squint down the hall for one off-kilter moment, trying to get back my bearings, and finally go left.

That's it, I decide in the elevator going down. No more breeding Miss Kitty. Twice was more than enough.

I've got to get the hell out of here.

13

———

KIT

It's been a week. Well, six days. Tomorrow will be a week since I masturbated in a hotel room and waited in the dark for a man to come and fuck me.

And not just any man. *That* man, over there. Jake Brand. The guy my brother referred to as one of the best people he's ever known. Hands down.

He'd trust Jake with his life, Franco said.

Loves him like a brother.

I can't think about that right now.

I'm pretty deep in denial these days. Not exactly the best place to be, but certainly better than facing facts head-on.

Facts, as he reminded me the other night. Cold, hard facts, like the way his body felt inside mine. How he sounds when he comes, more animal than man.

They didn't feel like facts when he said them in the dark, his voice rich and rough, wrapping right around my throat, leading me into a midnight dream of desire and a heap of other things I'm not allowed to have.

I cringe right here in the kitchen, thinking about how hard I came, how tense I got fighting it, how hopeless it was even trying. The man managed to do with words and that one bodily connection what no one has ever accomplished.

I never stood a chance against Jake Brand, with his filthy mouth and talented body and the way he looks at me even now across the line.

"How we doing on the shrimp?" I ask, as coolly as I can in an attempt to douse the flames eating me up inside.

"Two minutes," he replies, his gaze snagging mine for a perfectly acceptable interval. He could look at anyone here for that long and it would seem normal. Yet, in that brief span, he manages to share something so raw, so explicit, that I can't possibly be the only one who sees it.

Except, I realize when he turns to bark something to Frida about table twelve, it's all one-sided. Me, imagining things that aren't there.

Yeah. My imagination's gone absolutely hog wild this week.

Reality? Totally normal. Like none of it ever happened.

The first day back, I was sure he'd do or say something at work, but he's been nothing but professional. Hellos and goodbyes and order ups and behind yous and eighty-six the fried trout and all the other shit you say at work and none of the things my body's geared up for. None of the phrases I think about over and over, like *Filled your warm cunt with my come* and *Using this little hole the way you're using me.*

Using me.

Using me.

Oh god. What am I doing? I can't stand back here staring at him. I turn and shove through the door into the dining room, where service is starting to slow down. Cora walks up to the bar and tells me she needs an Irish for twelve. With relief, I swing away, happy for something to do with my hands. I grab one of the cute insulated glass mugs I purchased for just this occasion and start pouring.

"One spicy shrimp." Startled, I turn toward the voice I can't stop thinking about.

"Oh." I sound out of breath. "Great, thanks."

"And a slice of cake."

I look at his hands.

"I didn't order cake."

"No. But you looked like you needed some."

"I did?"

"I've seen the way you look at my cake." With a wink, he leans in, hands me the plate, and looks around. "Where's the shrimp going? I'll take it."

"Oh, you don't have to—"

"Don't mind. Everything's gone out."

"It's for Taylor, right over there." I indicate one of my regulars at the far end of the bar. She's a gorgeous twenty-something blonde who brings her laptop and has dinner nearly every week. Writing a book, apparently. I've watched her get chatted up by the businessman beside her for the last few minutes, wondering if and when I'll need to step in and run interference.

I take a bite of a ridiculously delicious pistachio cake Jake made this afternoon and catch his eyes on me. The second I look his way, he grabs a roll-up and circles the bar.

Oh my God, this is *good*. Caught in a weird sort of ecstasy consuming another one of his gorgeous creations —the man makes a lot of good cake—I watch him set the cutlery and plate down. Taylor gives him a smile brighter than any expression she's shown her neighbor. She says something and Jake responds, leaning between her and the businessman.

I put the plate down on the bar, the cake suddenly too sweet in my mouth, too cloying. I turn and grab a rack of glasses and a clean towel and start polishing, my back to the room.

Taylor's closer to Jake in age than I am. She's twenty-eight, I think? Younger? And she's interesting. Writes books and articles, travels for work. She's creative and talented and gorgeous, with the kind of long, lean body I always wished I had instead of this overblown hourglass I was gifted with at adolescence.

They'd be perfect together. He's big and tall and dark and she's slender, strong. Smart as hell. And sweet, too. I mean, I really like her and I'm not easy to please.

My phone buzzes in my pocket and I pull it out.

There's a text from an unknown number. I open it and read.

Kitty. This is Clark. I've had to resort to going through someone else's phone, since you've apparently blocked me. I wanted to do this amicably, but you're making it impossible. I've talked it over with Lily and the lawyer and everyone agrees that we can't settle as is. The restaurant's too valuable and we're not finished here until the assets are re-

evaluated. Please, let's have a chat. That's all I'm asking. Call me on this number.

I shove the phone away. Asshole. *Asshole.*

He's "giving" me the restaurant in the negotiations. Big quotation marks there, since I'm the one who built the place from the ground up. He'll be demanding half my grandmother's house next. I put him through fucking grad school, supported him through the PhD, and his lawyer's still fighting for more.

Clark was so mad back when I got pregnant. He accused me of all kinds of things I'd never consider doing. The miscarriage, for me, was hell. Clark, though? The bastard was relieved.

Now here he is, all excited to be a daddy.

God, *god*, why did I stay with him?

Despite myself, I let my eyes lift to the antiqued mirror behind the bar. Unerringly, I seek Jake out. He's still there, bent toward Taylor. Gorgeous, young, easy-going Taylor. Her body language is a full 360 from what it was with the disappointed-looking tech bro. She's got a hand in her gleaming hair, her lips half pursed, half smiling, eyes wide as she stares up at him. And who can blame her? Jake looks almost unreal with how big he is, how wide and solid, striking with all that ink crawling out from under his chef's coat. And then there's that face. A living challenge. A fascinating map of too many years packed into too little time.

I'll bet *she* wouldn't make him do it in the dark.

He turns slightly and, like the coward I am, I immediately look down at the champagne glass I've now polished to within an inch of its life. But the glimpse of his profile I caught in the split second before I looked away has given me something close to heart palpitations. How can he be so beautiful?

Which is not a word I use lightly. The man's looks are soul-crushing, gut twisting. And I don't mean his frame or all that strength. The way I feel after that millisecond's glimpse is the way I remember feeling when Clark and I went to Yellowstone on our one and only vacation—planned, organized, and paid for by yours truly. I woke up one morning in time to see the sun rise over the misty mountains and I remember crying tears, actual tears, at how wrenching a sight it was.

Jake, like that landscape, is made up of contrasts. Towering mountains and lush greenery, harsh boulders swathed in silken mist. Only he's warm flesh and thick, rounded muscle, built on a framework of cartilage, tendons, and bone. He's human, but...is he really, with how gorgeous he is?

Oh my god, what am I doing? Why am I thinking like this when there's clearly nothing between us?

I'm just a mess with Clark breathing down my throat, as if I'm the one who owes him something. That's all this is.

Frantic, I look up again, straight into the mirror, where I see my own face, broken up, the smudged eye makeup only highlighting the bags I can't seem to get rid of, my lipstick too bright against my haggard skin. Unerringly, I glance his way.

Our gazes clash with somehow a million times more impact in the mirror than they would have had real life. I feel the jolt like lightning down my spine. My body's in instant battle between taut and liquid.

In the glass, I watch, helplessly ensnared by his gaze,

as Taylor's hand lands on his forearm. It's a casual move that could be interpreted any number of ways, but I'm familiar enough with the woman at this point to get that she's interested.

In Jake.

He turns to respond to her, releasing me from his hold, and I'm left boneless behind my bar. The one place where I'm in charge and know my power. Only, right now, I don't feel any of that. I feel awful. Weak. Sad.

Just as I put the glass I've been polishing away, Cora walks up. "Mind handing me the whip?"

"Oh, yeah." I grab it and head over to finish her drink.

"What's this? Cake?"

"Yeah," I tell her. "Grab a fork. Jake made it for us."

"Yum, god, why's he so good at this?"

I concentrate on pouring coffee and topping the drink with whipped cream and a dash of cinnamon.

Mouth full, Cora leans close. "Think she'll finally get him to go home with her this time?"

"What?"

She rolls her eyes. "Taylor. She's been working Jake for a while now. I mean look." She nudges my arm, lifting her chin to the other end of the bar. "Seriously, people, get a room."

Swallowing back the nervy wave of nausea trying to work its way into my throat, I do my best to put a smile on my face and shake my head. It's all I can manage.

Cora shovels more cake into her mouth. "Oh my God. Is she going to kiss him? Hol-y shit. Werk, girl."

I won't turn. I won't look.

He's not mine. What we have is the farthest possible

thing from a relationship. He owes me nothing. *Nothing*. Taylor's perfect for him. Right age. Right looks. Right situation in life.

"I um..."

"Christ, they're gonna go at it right there? I can't tell if she's whispering in his ear or, like, licking it. Man, you might want to shut that—"

"Sorry, I have to go to the..." I head out from behind the bar, straight to the back hall and bathroom. No. No, there's someone in it. My office. Crap. I need keys. Scrabbling at my pocket, I pull out my set, shaking so hard it jangles like bells, shove the key in and stumble my way inside. I shut the door behind me and sink onto the sofa, hands over my face.

What am I doing? I keep thinking, over and over and over. *What I am doing? What am I doing?*

I don't know. I just have no earthly idea. And no matter how many times I ask myself, I can't come up with an answer that makes sense.

14

JAKE

"What are you up to tonight?" Taylor asks, doing that thing where her eyes flick up to mine and down to my mouth. She's twisted toward me, one finger toying with her lip while the other hand's running through her hair. If my inner alarm bells hadn't rung when she breathed right into my ear, they most definitely are now.

"This," I tell her as I ease back, arms folded, and glance toward the bar.

It's empty.

"You get off soon? You must, right? Kitchen's closing."

"Staying late. Got a project in back."

Taylor's eyes look over my shoulder to where the hall disappears at the end of the dining room and looks up at me, voice low. "The back? Need any help with that?"

The guy seated behind me mutters something and shoves up to standing, bumping me with his stool in the process.

"I'm good, thanks." I tap the bar. "Have a great one, Taylor."

"Hey," the guy asks, a little unsteady on his feet. "You know where the barmaid is?"

"Barmaid?" I force my hands to unclench.

"Yeah, you know, the one with the—"

"What do you need?" I swear, if the fucker mentions Kit's chest, I'll lose it.

"Just want to cash out and get out of here." He casts an angry look around. "Place is dead."

I nod. "I'll get her."

After a quick check of the kitchen, I head to the back. There's no one in dry storage. The restroom door's open. Empty. I get to the office, reach for the handle, and hesitate. After a quick inhale, I knock.

"Yeah?"

"You're needed."

Silence.

"Kit? You okay?"

"Yeah. Be right there."

I wait. Nothing happens. I grab the doorknob and pause. This isn't a woman whose space you encroach on.

Fuck, though, do I want to encroach. After a few seconds, I force myself to turn and head back out. At the bar, I tell the guy she's coming and give Taylor a curt goodnight, then return to my kitchen.

My kitchen. Right. Best knock that proprietary feeling out of my system right away. I've got about as much claim to this line as I've got to Kit. Meaning none.

She's hiring someone to replace me and I'm heading to Norway.

Norway's easy. Rig life's straightforward—cold as

hell, but that's not a bad thing. Then brief periods of land life. Sex that's straightforward, women who want exactly what I'm looking for—physical relief. Huge bonuses. Hell, maybe I'll stay there past the contract or move on to Aberdeen. There's good beer in Scotland.

After that, hell, maybe South America.

"What's the date, Frida?"

"Uh, seventh. No, eighth.

Fuck, I've got three weeks left.

"Any sign of a replacement for me?"

Frida shakes her head, scrubbing her station with her usual calm competence.

For the first time in forever—years—I feel unprepared to move on.

It's the gym. That's why. Got to sell the damn place.

Fuck. Ricky and I need to talk because his woman's getting pissed and he's digging in his feet and it's time for me to move out of the area. Permanently.

Just standing here, wiping the counter, my gut's suddenly twisted so hard I'd swear I was sick if my stomach wasn't solid as a rock.

I reach for a pan, burn myself like it's my first time in a kitchen, and pull back.

"All right, chef?" Frida glides by with a pile of dirty dishes, which she stacks neatly in the sink beside Toni.

"Yep."

The look she gives me from behind her steel-framed glasses is quick and assessing. "Seem distracted."

I shrug. "Nah. I'm good."

"Course you are."

Ignoring her, I turn back to the line, make sure everything's shut off and start breaking it down. It'll be an hour, at least, before I'm done and even then I won't leave. Not until Kit takes off.

I'm on my way back from the walk-in fridge when the kitchen door swings open with a bang to show Cora, out of breath. "You gotta come. Hurry."

I drop my shit and take off. "What happened?"

"Douche canoe at the bar ran without paying. Kitty took off after him."

"Shit." I knew that asshole was looking for trouble from the second I laid eyes on him. It's why I got so close to Taylor. She did that subtle woman thing of letting me know she needed help without actually saying it out loud.

Nothing in this world is worse than a man who thinks he's owed something. I put on the speed and streak through the dining room, ignoring the shocked faces of the last few customers and a flustered-looking Taylor, out the door. My eyes take in the lot. There. The Audi. Door open.

Fuck. Fuck.

Something switches in my brain when I see that he's got her shoved up against the side of his car. I've lived through this before and the change that comes over me is not the wild, out of control adrenaline rush you'd expect. A soft calm lays itself over my body. I'm wrapped in cotton. Unreachable. My vision's hyper focused. Those are his hands. On her neck. Her pale throat. One hand grips her arm. She's fighting him, trying to shove him back, but she's trapped and her face is all tight and pissed and scared and—

He's a dead man.

I know it with a bone deep certainty. I'll fucking kill him.

He's touched her and now he'll pay.

The equation's simple.

Before he's even noticed I'm here, I'm on him, ripping her out of his hold and pummeling. My fist connects with his nose and there's that pop and crunch of cartilage and bone and the warm spray of blood.

I've been here. I know this. Before prison. In prison, too, when everything was on the line every second of every day.

Thanks to Ricky, I knew how to fight before doing time, but Frank's the one who taught me the quick, efficient jab, jab, kick to nose, nuts, knees.

Then, it's liver, hand, and liver again.

All the shit wreaking havoc with my insides boils up and over and this...this...*this* is what I need. Something solid. Something clear to take it out on. Good versus bad.

"Jake!" That's Kit's voice. I hear it, from far off. It's tinny and weak, not throaty and warm like when we fucked in the hotel. When she laughs at something Cora says behind the bar. When she tried the flounder I fried up for staff meal tonight.

I've got him by the clothes, my grip twisting fabric as I drag him away from his car. There's yelling. I hear it. It just doesn't sink in. Doesn't matter.

"The fuck are you doing, man?"

The guy's scared. Shaking. Bleeding all over his expensive suit.

"You don't fucking touch her, you get that?"

"Stop it, man!" He whines, arms thrown up to protect his face. "Stop. Please. *Please*."

I pause, blinking, staring down at him, still seeing

only a man who'd hurt a woman. And not just any woman. Katarina Esteban.

"She's *mine*," I mutter into his face.

On one plane is his breath—onions and garlic that I cooked—the chilly air, loose gravel beneath my boots. The instant, sharp pain in my knuckles. On another, deeper level is hunger and hate, the need to hurt. To punish. It doesn't feel separate from me at all. It's not emotional, it's essential. Basic and true. A part of my being. Like someone's cracked my bones and it's seeping up and out of my marrow like lava that's laid dormant all these years. Violence, as deeply woven into my being as blue eyes and an affinity for tough, soulful, thick-thighed women.

I'll fuck him up. Punish him. Teach him.

One fist in his shirt, the other cocked, knowing this kind of man will never stop hurting women. A third punch to that liver and he's down, in terrible pain, bruised and fucked for days.

A hand clasps my fist, tight. "Jake."

Her voice, Christ, it's a key turning. A lock open, tightly woven fibers loosen inside me.

"Jake. Leave it. Stop. Please."

"I'm calling the fucking cops," the guy says, only to realize, when I shove him back against the car that maybe talking's not the best move here.

"It's not worth it, Jake. Leave him. Let it go. You don't want to get arrested." That last sentence sinks in.

Right. Right.

Prison.

I've been here before.

I shake the bloodlust from my head, squint down at the guy's overgrown frat cut, not quite balding at the crown, the sweat mixing with the blood on his upper lip, and his expression...pure fear. Deer in the goddamn headlights, rabbit caught in a trap terror. Because of me.

With a whoosh all the rage floods out.

"Take off," I say, forcing my limbs to loosen when what they really crave is to give him one final shove. Something that'll hurt. Something he'll remember.

Punishment.

Fuck. Fuck, no. That's not who I am. Some avenger or vigilante justice warrior like Frank.

This guy's weak. Look at him. Shame swirls sick and heavy inside me, alongside that hefty dose of anger and contempt.

The second I give him space, he scrambles into his car and locks the doors, starts the engine and takes off, spitting gravel.

"Can't wait to read his yelp review." Kit slides up beside me, watching the taillights disappear.

"He'd better leave it alone." Distance hasn't rid me of the adrenaline yet. Not for a single second. "If he knows what's good for him."

From the restaurant, loud voices ring out as the front door opens and a handful of curious customers come out. At least one of them's got their phone up, filming. They seem worlds away from what just happened out here. From what's still happening. But shame at the idea that my violent outburst got caught on camera edges in.

"You okay?"

I turn and let myself look at Kit. Her beauty hits me the way it always does, only more. So much fucking more with adrenaline making everything bigger, deeper, brighter. More alive.

There's a red mark at her throat and, right away, the

shame's replaced with pure hatred. Men who hurt women and children deserve nothing but hell. It's that simple. The man's life isn't worth a thing in my eyes.

Yeah, it's extreme, I guess, but I've got my reasons. People talk of shades of grey, but sometimes, there's black and there's white and that's it.

Kit's close enough that I could lean down and kiss her right now. Wouldn't have to take a step. It'd be so fucking easy. She's watching me, her expression serious, wary. One touch and I could get that look to slide right off her face, replace it with the expression I imagined both times we did it in the dark.

She moves, which I don't expect. Reaches out and grips my hand. Just that, with a low, quiet, "Thank you."

And fuck if that doesn't mess me up more than anything else she could've done.

Thank you. Goddamn thank you. Again. Thank you for your service, Jake.

I look down at my knuckles. They're scraped raw.

With a nod, I gently disentangle my hand from hers and step back. "Any time," I manage with a cheesy smirk as I set off, ironically saluting our audience at the door. "Better close up." I head back inside to clean up and finish off my shift.

Thank you, thank you thank you.

It's a drumbeat in my head.

Good work, Jake.

Work. *Work?*

Yep. That's exactly what it is.

Fucking work.

Blood, sweat, tears. Semen.

All just part of the job here at Parlor.

Suddenly, I'm real fucking tired of her contract, her rules.

The woman wants to get knocked up and that's exactly what I'll do.

Except starting right now, it'll have to be on my terms.

15

______

Kit

The staff's gone except for Jake. I'm jittery and weird after everything. With the asshole at the bar going after me in the parking lot. With Jake.

I took a photo of the creep's license plate. I could call the police.

But the last thing I want to do is get Jake into trouble, which is a real risk given his past.

I watched him walk back inside earlier, saw the way his back stiffened when the few remaining diners stared. Taylor said something to him which he ignored.

Right now, he's in the kitchen, scrubbing the place like it's punishment. I'm behind the bar, washing a rack of martini glasses that looked streaked in the low light.

If he doesn't quit soon, I'll go and tell him it's time to take off. Knowing he's back there—feeling his presence —the antsiness is killing me.

The song I've got blasting through the speakers comes to an end. It's a slow anthem of lost love, sung by a deep-voiced woman who knows what she's talking about.

The first few notes of the next sad love song slide into the air. The kitchen door creaks open.

Every cell in my body goes on alert and somehow I can't move. Can't turn or look.

"Mind if I grab a drink?" He's a few feet away.

I shake my head, elbow deep in suds and caught in this flash-frozen state. "Go ahead." After a second. "Help yourself to top shelf."

His footsteps pause.

"Top shelf, huh? As a thank you?"

I nod.

I think he's watching me. I won't look. I can't.

"What if I don't want top shelf?" He moves in, closer. "What if I want something else?"

"Something else." The words aren't words, they're sounds I'm repeating. Meaningless huffs of air and pressure from vocal cords that have lost all power.

"Yeah." Another step brings him so he's right beside me.

Finally, my head swivels enough to look his way and I immediately recognize my error. This sacrosanct space might be my territory in civilized times, but this isn't a man I'm currently facing, it's a beast. Giant and wild. The light in his eyes isn't rational. It's hovering at some halfway point between cagey and hungry, watching me like he's some massive, sleek creature hidden deep in the jungle and I'm an intruder he's considering making a meal of. There's a danger to that liminal place.

"What if I want another go?"

Everything inside me goes liquid, hot and loose and

syrupy thick. My body doesn't even pretend not to know what he's talking about.

"Would that work for you, Kitty?" A final step brings him right up against my back, not quite touching, but there.

Here. Right here.

"It's against the rules. The contract—"

"I don't give a shit about the contract, Katarina."

"Well, I do. We agreed this would never happen at work."

"Yeah?" His bulk shifts, tilts, close enough that he barely has to voice his next words. I feel more than hear them against my ear—a warm puff of air, a cold shiver up my spine. "Stop me."

Is that a dare? A request? I can't tell. Can't move. Can't, apparently, meet the challenge at all.

The fabric covering my butt shifts. Is he...touching my skirt?

He is. Oh, God, he's pulling it up, slowly, a panther playing with its food.

I should tell him not to.

"Spread your legs."

After a few seconds' hesitation, I obey, giving tacit consent.

What rule is he breaking right now?

No doing it in the restaurant. That's the rule I'm letting him break by widening my stance.

Just that one move. The rest of me is immobile. The rest of me *wants* the rules. The contract. The framework. Guidelines to make sure this doesn't get out of hand. I need them. They're essential to absolutely every part of my life—my *existence*—and yet, I can't for the life of me find my voice to make him back up.

"Good girl."

Oh, those *words*. They settle into my marrow, warm me from the inside out as cool air hits my thighs. He's dragging the skirt up and up and up and then...

Behind me, Jake expels a low, grating sound. It's my thong, I imagine. Probably. It's not meant for seduction, which I'm sure he wouldn't believe. I wear them because my ass is big and I'll wind up with material inching up between my cheeks anyway. At least like this, it's minimal. My choice.

"Fuck, yes," he mutters, like I've somehow done something right.

I haven't. I've done absolutely nothing. I haven't lifted my hands from the water or straightened my spine. I haven't mentioned our contract or the one—well, two—time restriction.

As I stand here, not for one heartbeat denying him, I can only thank god that I locked the door before closing out the till for the night. Though if anyone pressed their face to the front window, they could see us. My reputation is on the line here. My business.

After a pause that is too long and too quiet for comfort, during which I shamelessly will him to touch me—anywhere he wants—I finally hear the slow slide of his zipper, the rustle of denim, cotton.

I shut my eyes, tight. Tight tight tight.

He grips more of my skirt and wraps it up into a ball at my waist, pulls my thong to one side, and pries one of my ass cheeks to the side.

Slowly, almost teasingly, his thick, hot cock slides between my legs.

Every hair on my body stands up, every cell goes molten.

The moan that escapes me is pure, unadulterated pleasure, born so far inside me I couldn't keep it in if my life depended on it.

"Fuck, baby," he whispers. "Fuck, look at that little pink asshole. *Fuck*."

A long, slippery descent—both literal and figurative. When he bends his legs, the backs of his thighs cradle mine. Hair chafes my skin. My waterlogged hands move of their own volition to grip the rim of the sink and with my next breath, he's in, deep.

Oooooooh.

I'm stock still, sizzling with shock at the fullness, the pressure, the very slight thrill of pain.

For a handful of seconds he keeps himself fully seated inside me.

Neither of us budges.

It feels... There's not a word for it.

Like nothing. Like everything.

Right.

I'm wet, which would be a surprise if it weren't the way I always am now when he's near. Even so, that first thrust was hard enough to jolt me, deep, deep inside, the friction rough and explicit.

His next series of moves is purely practical—getting me wetter, opening me up—and every one of them turns me into his rag doll.

His grip on my skirt tightens, his other hand presses down on my upper back before grabbing my hip. When he pulls out, it's with excruciating slowness. I hate him, a little, for taking his time. For the undeniable, hot friction of every inch of him.

Another deliberately slow penetration. Another leisurely slide out. There's something about the way he's doing it that doesn't feel the same as before. I can't see him. There's no mirror out there that will show me how he's covering me. So silent, this time.

But that's it. That's just it. With every advance of his body into mine, he's saying something, staking a claim, without uttering a single word.

I can't help how my back arches toward him when he moves impossibly closer, his bulk over me now, around me.

He plunges inside me, hard, harder, and I collapse fully forward, my soapy wet hands struggling to find purchase on the edge of the bar and then his hands are there, caging mine in. Every smack of his hips to mine winds me tighter, so my spine's a taut bowstring and my insides clench and then—oh god—then he bends, right up against me, hides his face in the side of my neck. There's the heat of his breaths, the slide of a tongue I'm not even sure he's just used and finally, with a sort of rightness that is absolutely wrong, he opens his mouth and bites me, right at the junction of throat and shoulder.

I come. Harder than I've ever come. The pleasure a thing separate from me, alive and writhing from my center to places I've never felt. He's tearing me open, fucking me like this. Like he's a primitive creature and I am one, too. Like this isn't a bar in a civilized city, and we're not doing this with any objective in mind.

Behind my closed lids I see nothing but his feral, hopped-up eyes, so I open mine and stare at where his hands grip the wood, caging me in with their scraped, bloodied knuckles and the ink there. The words...

Love. On his fingers. It says that: *Love*. And *Hate*.

How did I never notice that?

His teeth hold me in place, never breaking the skin, but keeping me where he wants.

Pleasure bursts open so hard it hurts. A high whimper leaks through the tightly closed dam of my lips. My knees turn to jelly. The only thing stopping me from going face-down into suds is the thick arm that wraps around my middle.

I'm ruined, I realize, as he pumps deep and clamps me to him with his teeth and his hips and those raw-knuckled, love-hate hands. He's gasping like he's run a race and, it *is* a race.

It *was*. But it's over and he caught me and I'm *fucked*.

"That's one rule down," he whispers against the place he's just bitten. "Or is it two?"

"What?" I gasp, my mind pure mush.

"Restaurant sex. That's one," he lists off, sounding as out of breath as I am. "And biting." He gives me a nip as if to prove his point. "Was that even in the contract?"

The answer's no. No, it wasn't in the contract. But it should have been. Because now, along with everything else I told him we couldn't do, it's on my list of things I want more than anything.

Which just confirms that I am, indeed, totally, royally *fucked*.

16

"Here." Kit hands me a sheet of paper almost as soon as I walk in the next day. "Schedule."

"Thanks." I don't look at it, focusing instead on her face. "You good?"

"Yep." Her smile is wide and plastic, which tells me only that she's uncomfortable. It fritters a little when she gets a good look at my eye. "What's that bruise? What happened?"

"Nothing to worry about." I shove the paper into my pocket and turn away from the sudden annoyance on her face, heading into the kitchen to start setting up for the shift.

My knuckles are a mess from last night, not to mention this morning's activities.

When I woke up to the sound of fists against a heavy bag this morning, hitting someone again seemed like just what I was missing. Only sanctioned hitting this time.

I'm an idiot, I guess, but I needed something, anything, to get all this ramped up shit out of my veins.

Problem is, no matter how hard I work my body, the antidote to what ails me can't be found in the ring.

A while later, Kit comes back into the kitchen. "Hey, you mind adding a person to tonight's staff meal?"

"No problem. I made more than enough." I always make more than enough now that I know how often Kit likes to give food away.

"We sometimes have guests," she told me the first time. Now I just add the extra portions automatically.

Guests, in this case, turns out to be a party of one, a kid who can't be more than twelve or thirteen and looks enough like Toni, our dishwasher, to be related.

"Hey," Toni says to me. "Thanks."

"Anytime." I set two steaming platters of mushroom risotto on the ten-top we typically eat at. Cora and Riley get flatware and plates and Frida follows up with a green salad. I point my chin at where Kit's filling a water pitcher behind the bar and say, "You should thank the boss."

"Jake, this is my sibling. Raf."

"Nice to meet you, Raf."

Raf gives me an inaudible hello, clearly too timid to dig in.

"Raf, um, eats here when our parents kick them out."

My brows fly up. "That happen a lot?"

Raf shrugs, which I'll take to be a resounding *Yes*.

Before sitting down with the others, I mosey over to the bar and grab a stack of glasses.

"Wasn't it a different kid a couple days ago?" I ask under my breath.

She nods, eyes on what she's doing.

"You take in all the strays?"

Her shrug is almost defensive. "I'll feed whoever's hungry."

"That's one way to run a business."

"That's the *only* way."

Her gaze meets mine and my stomach clenches, though I can't exactly say why.

No, that's a lie. I know exactly what it is.

This brings me back to when Dad used to give coffees to the homeless guys who stopped by every morning and sent whole meals home with the couple who came to clean the diner at night. I remember Mom getting pissed because, as she put it, these little gifts, "Ate into the profits," but in the end, Dad's funeral was a packed, loving celebration of his life and, well, I don't know what happened at Mom's. I couldn't make it that day.

I'm about to go back to the table when she looks up at me, her expression changing when she catches sight of my full face. "You okay?" she asks.

It takes me a second to realize she's staring at the bruise beside my eye. "Oh, yeah, just went a little rough at the gym this morning."

Her eyebrows lift. "Are you a boxer?"

"I fight occasionally."

"Fight." The air around her fizzes. She's probably thinking about last night.

"In a ring." I give her a smirk. "With a referee. Not always in back alleys. Or parking lots."

She looks over at the gathered staff and lowers her voice even more. "So. Um, hey. Did you, uh..." Is she blushing? Fuck, she's pretty. Those big warm eyes—grey-green-brown—that sweet, wide mouth. I can't stop staring at the little dips above her collarbones and up, up to where I see the faint red imprint of my teeth. Fuck if the sight of it doesn't make me want to bend her over the bar again. "Did you look?"

"Look at what?"

She steps closer to whisper. "At the schedule. The one I gave you."

Confusion settles over me until I remember the paper she handed me at the start of the shift. A schedule. I did something with it.

Where is it? Slowly, I set the glasses on the bar, reach back and pull the paper from my pocket.

It's a calendar. A bunch of dates are marked with big Xs. Not a work schedule, I'm guessing.

"Jake, you know what, maybe this wasn't..."

Fuck. *Me.*

It's a goddamn sex schedule. A whole three weeks of it. Spaced out so there are two per week. Near the end, there are five days that say PERIOD in block letters.

My cock's instantly hard.

I swallow. "No. This works." A quick glance at her rosy cheeks, her bright, skittish eyes. "You do that stuff where you, uh, take your temperature? In the morning?"

"Yeah, but..." She won't look at me, not directly. "You can get pregnant any time. Even during your period." She points at the paper. "I blacked those days out, though. I know guys—"

I've never considered it before, but I open my mouth and say, "We'll see."

Her thick, dark brows lift in surprise. "Oh. Okay. Yeah. TBD, then." She takes a shuddering breath. "Might already be pregnant, anyway. But, if not, when you get a chance, maybe just confirm which of these dates you can—"

"All right," I tell her, folding it more carefully before putting it away. "I'll let you know."

"Wow. That's...great. Um, so, about the hotel, it's kind of expensive and—"

"I'll take care of it."

"What?"

"I'll pay for it."

"Oh, no. That's not what I meant. I should be paying *you* for this, not—"

"Getting paid to fuck you might be a little weird."

She looks horrified. "Oh, right. I'm so sorry. I didn't mean—"

"I was kidding, Kit."

"Okay, but if you need anything—"

"Like money?" I dead eye her.

"Yeah."

"No." I heft the glasses and water pitcher.

"Right." She lets out a loud, exhausted sigh. "So, do you mind my place? For the..."

"Event?" I'm smirking. The woman's fucking cute when she's embarrassed.

"Yes."

"Your place is fine." I glance over at the staff table and catch Frida's attention on me, then on Kit, head tilted, eyes narrowed, then back to me. One grey eyebrow lifts in question. I turn back to Kit. "Better go eat."

"Right." She nods and scoots out from behind the bar, as awkward as I've ever seen her. Makes me want to wrap my arms around her and pull her up against my chest, tuck her head right up under my chin. Makes me want to promise shit I've got no business thinking about.

I'm putting it all out of my mind this very fucking second.

But then I remember the way she bit her lip just now, the way she didn't for one second protest my fucking her behind the bar last night, not to mention the fact that she just handed me a goddamn sex schedule, and decide that with three weeks left, bending the rules is *exactly* what this situation calls for.

Kit

The phone rings just before the doors open. I pick it up.

"Collect call from the State Penitentiary Facility."

With my usual excitement at hearing from my brother, I press the button to accept.

"Frank?"

"Hey, sis. What's up?"

"Not much. You okay?"

"Yeah. Yeah, got some news."

"What's that?"

"So, there's a parole hearing coming up."

"Right. Next year."

"Yeah." He pauses. "Listen, don't get your hopes up. I'll let you know how that goes, okay?"

"Yeah. Please do. I'll come and speak for you and—"

"So, you meet my buddy Jake? He stop by to see you?"

My mouth stays open, mid-word. "Um... Uh, yeah."

Frank's low chuckle comes through the phone. "Yeah? That's all you got to say? What, you didn't like him?"

"He's, um, cooking here, actually. While he's in town."

Silence.

"Cooking, huh? For you?"

"Well, not for me. For the restaurant. But, yeah. He's good at it."

"Don't doubt it." He sniffs. I push the phone to my ear and concentrate through the music and rattle of flatware on the prison background noises I've grown used to. The murmur of voices, the occasional yell. Something banging with a hollow thud. As it has every time I've talked to my brother in the last fourteen years, my throat closes up and tears try to press their way out. "So, does that mean he's planning on sticking around?"

The question sends an unexpected wave of something through me, some uncomfortable emotion that I can't quite look at head-on.

"Oh. No. He's going to the North Sea, I think."

"Hm. Okay. That's too bad."

"Is it?"

"Rather have him there with you."

"I can look out for myself, you know, Frank."

"D'you know he does underwater welding on those platforms he works at?"

"Oh. No, I didn't."

"It's the most lethal job in the world. Literally, more people die doing that than any other work."

"What? Why does he do it, then?"

Frank lets out this condescending half-laugh that's always annoyed me—as I know it's meant to. "'Cause he doesn't give a shit. 'Cause he's got nothing to go home to. Might as well take the big risks and rake in the big bucks."

I can think of nothing to say to that, nothing to feel but a sort of low, thumping shame that's like a second pulse in my throat. After a few moments of silence, I ask, "You, um, you okay, Frank?"

"I'm good. Great," he says in that over-the-top way that makes me think life in prison can't be anything but miserable.

"I wish…" I start and then stop myself. There's not much to say really about what I wish for at this point. I can't turn back the clocks and make Frank not take it upon himself to punish that man.

If I could do that, I'd wish that the man hadn't hurt Evie to begin with. I'd wish Frank hadn't had to find out his friend had been sexually assaulted by the minister from her youth group. I'd wish, at the very least, that the police had put the pastor away for it so my righteous-minded brother hadn't decided to go off and do something about it on his own.

I'd wish a lot of things. For me and Frank. For Toni and his sibling Raf, kids who don't deserve to be kicked out for how they feel in their skin. I'd wish Jake hadn't done prison time, too.

"Don't bother wishing, Sis. It's a waste of time."

I don't tell him again that I wish he was home. It only makes him feel bad.

"You get those cookies I sent?"

"Sure did. Thank you." I can never tell if he's lying, but I figured out a while ago that the best thing I can do is pretend I believe what he says. He gets comfort from that, I think.

And that's the only comfort I can offer since he refuses to let me visit.

"I love you, bro."

"Love you, sis." A beat. "Tell Jake I love him, too."

Those words send a little shock through me. It takes me a second to realize it's because I've never heard my brother say that about—or to—another soul.

"I will."

"All right. Have a good night. Make lots of money."

I force a smile into my voice and say, "Sleep well," since I can't think of another thing to wish a man who's got another five years in his sentence.

The phone rings again a couple minutes after I hang up and, for some silly reason, I think it'll be him again. "Parlor," I say, expecting the collect call message.

Instead, I hear. "Kitty. We need to talk."

Oh, God. It's the ex. The last person I want to talk to. Honestly now or ever.

"We're open, Clark, this isn't a good time and you know it."

"Listen, you just need to listen. It's important."

"Actually, Clark, one of the benefits of no longer being with you is that I don't have to listen to you anymore. Goodbye."

I jam my finger to the button to end the call and stand there, out of breath, for a few minutes.

When I look up, Jake's at the end of the bar, watching me. "You okay?"

I nod. "Great."

"That your ex?"

"It's...it's fine, Jake." When he doesn't move for a few moments, I walk over to him, voice lowered, and say, "I'm *fine*."

"You don't seem it."

"He's an asshole."

"I got that."

"Frank called."

"Yeah?"

"He says he, um," I swallow back a weird wave of emotion. "Says he loves you."

"Okay." Jake goes still, his eyes doing a quick search of the room behind me before he looks at my face again. "I guess, next time, uh, you could tell him I love him back. If you don't mind."

"Sure."

He nods. "Thanks."

After he's swung back into the kitchen, I look up and smile at a handful of diners being seated, say hi to a couple regulars, and serve a few cocktails for Riley's big group of raucous women who come in once a month to, I believe, bitch about their home lives.

All I can think about, the whole time, is how my brother apparently loves Jake enough to tell him so, which is a big deal for men like that.

He loves Jake and Jake loves him and here I am, using the man as a sperm donor.

17

Jake

"You need me to bandage those?" asks Frida a half hour into the night.

"Nah. I'll be fine."

"Sorry. Let me rephrase that. Sit down so I can bandage your hands, Chef. Nobody wants that near their food."

With an eye roll, I pull out a stool and sit down, surprised to see that she's already gotten out the first aid kit.

"Hope the other person looks worse than you do." She smirks, wrapping my hands with the kind of efficiency only someone who spent decades as an emergency room nurse can have. "'Cause you look like shit, Jake."

"I'm fine."

Giving me an eye roll of her own, she tuts and glances toward the door to the dining room. "Told you I'm immune to toxic masculinity." She smirks. "It's like the *opposite* of Kryptonite for me. Macho shit just makes me stronger."

"Good thing I'm a feminist then, isn't it?"

"Mm-hmm." She glances again at the door to the dining room. "She see this yet?"

"What's that?"

"Boss know you're moonlighting as an extra in our local Fight Club?"

"I'm not—"

"You two gonna make it official or what?"

"How did you know we were—"

"I didn't," she cackles. "But now I do!"

I pause, shut my mouth, and sit back on the stool, staring at her for a handful of seconds while she very purposefully does not look at me, instead focusing on getting my knuckles wrapped nice and tight before grabbing the pair of gloves she's already set aside.

"There's nothing to make official."

She snorts, giving me the kind of look my dad used to give me when I lied right to his face. "At least you're not insulting my intelligence by pretending you don't know what I'm talking about."

"Wouldn't dare."

"That's what I like about you."

"Just that?"

"One of the many things I like about you, Jake." Frida's got this stare, man. Dark and sharp enough to cut right to the heart of a person. If she points it just right, I'm pretty sure it'll do permanent damage. "But I'm gonna give you a word of advice."

"Please don't. I'm not in the market for—"

"Yes you are, now shut up."

"Geez. All right. Give it to me."

"Kitty's all hard on the outside. 'Cause she's had to be. Had some rough setbacks. Especially recently. In fact…" Frida hands me the gloves and drops her hands in her lap, her eyes losing their focus as she goes back to some place I'm not convinced I want to know anything about. "It's how we met."

My eyebrows fly up in surprise. "You didn't meet here?"

She shakes her head, her mouth going so flat it almost disappears in the network of wrinkles around it. "It's not my story to tell, but I met her at my last job."

Shit. Okay. Shit. She won't say it out loud, but I'm pretty sure she means the hospital.

"And Kitty's strong as hell, okay? But she's not your kind of strong."

"What kind is that?"

"You've got a strong core."

I snort. "What makes you say that?"

"What was your childhood like?"

A bunch of images—moments—take over like only memories can. I'm hit with the smell of coffee, bacon, and apple pie, as if the whole thing's right here in this kitchen, freshly brewed and fried and baked. Mom sashaying through the diner, slinging plates full of food, belting out *You're Beautiful* and *Somewhere Only We Know* and all those other sentimental songs I haven't thought about in ages. I'm doing homework at the counter and I…belong. I'm happy and I belong.

"It was good," I say, without looking up. "It was great." Until it wasn't. But that's not something I'll be getting into anytime soon.

"Kitty's was rough. You know she lost her parents early on? Car accident?"

I nod, slowly, trying to piece together what exactly Frank had said. "Yeah. Frank told me."

"Those early years matter. They give you the inner strength you'll need to deal with the shit life throws at you from then on out." She tapes up one hand and moves to the other. "Wherever you acquired your toughness, Jake, I figure it was built on a solid inner core."

Not sure how the woman perceived that, but I let it go and continue to listen.

"Kitty, now? She's all bark. Just layers and layers and layers of it. So frickin' tough, you know? Doesn't let a damn thing inside." She sighs and stands, stretching before grabbing her stool and folding it to put away. "Problem with all that protection is if something gets inside, you got no way to...to handle it. She doesn't let herself feel anymore. Too damn painful after that prick..."

"What did he do?" My voice is ground glass.

"Nothing you need to get in a tizzy about."

"Look, Frida, just tell me what the man—"

"Just dude shit, okay? Just shitty men being shitty." She shakes her head. "Nothing you need to get all violent about. The guy was a selfish prick and, far as I can tell, he continues to be one." Her eyes narrow on me, possibly measuring me up against the man. "Did you know that married women live shorter lives than those who don't have husbands?" She finishes up the second hand.

"Well, Frida." I stand. "It's been a blast hanging out, but—"

The door swings open, thank god, cutting me off mid-sentence. "Eight's done with apps." Cora drops a pile of plates at the dishwashing station and heads back out again.

Frida and I jump into gear.

My body's moving slow and calm, the way it always does behind the line, but inside, there's a whole lot of discomfort.

I turn the oven heat up for the soufflé. "You warning me off her?"

"Hell, no." Frida doesn't look at me while she chucks a few oysters into the fryer and spoons seaweed and sesame garnish onto the plates, her body moving with the quick efficiency of an expert.

"Then what's your point?"

"My point, Chef, is to keep doing whatever it is you're doing." She flashes me a grin, showing a set of teeth that're slightly crooked and yellowed with age, then goes back to prepping her plates. "'Cause she's looking almost relaxed."

"Jesus," I say, wondering if Frida's got any idea what Kit and I have been getting up to together. With my next inhale, something eases open in my chest. "You think?"

She grins. "I know." And then, because we've gotten to be friends, I guess, and she's hell bent on having this awkward moment with me, she leans in and says, "Just be careful. I like you both." Frida uses a forefinger to trace an up and down in the air between us, as if she's outlining my body from top to bottom. "Plus you kick ass in the kitchen." Before I have time to brace, she finishes with, "I'd hate for whatever y'all are doing to backfire and ruin my stable work environment. You're here for three more weeks. Don't fuck it up. Order up!" She yells in the exact same breath. She reaches out to ding the bell and turns to let Toni know he's slacking on the pots and pans, leaving me on my own to fire table nine's mains in a weird, half shell-shocked limbo.

It's almost closing when I head back to dry goods to grab flour. I'm baking a cake. Ostensibly for tomorrow's dessert special, but it's really for Kit.

The woman loves cake with a passion that turns me way the hell on and, like Frida, I really like seeing Kit happy.

Kit

I trail Cora and Toni to the door at the end of the shift and lock it behind them, then turn around. The dining room's dark, the many chandeliers—twenty-six to be exact—are all currently off, leaving just the warm light behind the bar and the rim of white around the kitchen door.

He's back there, probably still scrubbing away at dirt that nobody else can see.

Which means it's just the two of us.

Again.

Just knowing that he's there revs me up. This is the last thing I want, after my call with Frank and the realization that I'm doing something I might not be entirely comfortable with.

At the same time, it's undeniable, this pull. Stronger than me. I feel guilty and ashamed and, right there, braided in with those two is this low, thumping excitement.

The door swings open, startling me into jumping.

He steps into the room and pauses while the door slaps shut behind him.

He'll say something now, make a move. He'll tell me to spread my legs and I'll do it. I'll take it.

"That thing always screech like this?"

For a few seconds, I can only blink. "Oh. Um, I guess? I don't notice it with the music and people talking and so on."

He nods. "Be right back."

He disappears into the kitchen, leaving all this nervy anticipation to burn off into nothing. God. Oh, *god*, I'm a mess. On tenterhooks. Waiting. Hoping. Afraid at the same time. All of this unmet expectation feels like sitting alone on a seesaw, my weight holding me down, while the other side's flying up, empty. I'm anchored here for half a minute, unable to move. Unsure of where I was headed or what I'd planned to do next.

Just as I start over to the bar for a final sweep before shutting everything down, he comes through the door again, sending my insides tumbling around like clothes in a dryer. He bends and oils the bottom hinge, then does the other two, tests it, adds a bit more oil, and tests it again. Muttering something under his breath, he disappears into the back again and the second he's gone, it's like my frozen limbs are freed from their paralysis.

Quickly, I swipe at a surface, grab the keys and my bag, and turn back, ready this time to face him as he swings back in, in all his massive, tattooed glory.

"Here." I look at the plate in his hand. "Cake."

My gaze rises to his. "What for?"

"It's for you."

"It's not my birthday."

"No. But you like cake."

"How do you know this? Why do you keep feeding me cake?"

He grins, not answering my question.

I accept the plate and a fork and take a bite, moaning with pleasure at the rich chocolate, the thick buttercream frosting. "Jake. Oh my god."

He growls, low, the sound entirely inhuman.

"Mm?" I look up, mouth still full of the most scrumptiously rich blend of sweet and salty and slightly bitter chocolate.

I go still when I see the way he's watching me. My heart's thumping hard in my chest.

"Something wrong?" I wipe at my cheek, sure there must be something there.

"Watching you take that first bite's always a fucking pleasure, but the second?"

What about the second? What do I do? What does he see that no one else has ever commented on? "What? What is it?"

He leans in. "The sound you make when you take that second bite? It's the exact sound you make when I first sink into that soft pussy." Slowly, his gaze moves from my mouth to my eyes. "We on for tomorrow?" I can't move. "Your place?"

For an extended moment, the power of speech evades me. "Oh, uh, yes. If you don't mind."

He chuffs out a sound that's half-laugh, half snort and slips his coat on over the cotton T-shirt he strips down to at the end of every shift. "Mind?" He looks up, his eyes snagging mine again mid-air. "No, Kit. I don't mind the idea of fucking you raw again."

I swallow that second biteful of heaven, everything

suspended as I wait for whatever he'll say next. For what he'll do.

I want him to do *something*. Walk toward me like that caged lion, grab me, take all the difficult choices away.

"Give me your address."

I blink. "Oh. Oh, right." I rattle it off.

"What time?"

"Maybe, uh, five?"

He nods, slow, thoughtful, his eyes doing a quick up and down inventory of my body, my face. "See you then, Kit."

"See you." I'm breathless, waiting while he stands there.

"I'll walk you to the door."

"You don't have to—"

He looks at me balefully and my mouth snaps shut.

"I don't need you to watch out for me." I buss the empty cake plate, shut off the last light and head to the front with nothing but the parking lot lights to guide me.

"I know that."

"You're stubborn," I tell him, opening the door and holding it for him to walk through. I can tell he wants to be the one to hold it, but that's not happening. No absurd chivalry tonight.

"So are you."

I freeze. "If you're trying to sweet talk me, this isn't the way to go about it, you know."

"Not trying anything." His shadowed smirk is slow and would be almost creepy if he weren't so damn handsome. "Don't need to try with you, do I?"

My belly goes unpleasantly tight. "*What?*"

"You're a sure thing." He pats his back pocket. "Got the schedule right here to prove it."

"Geez, Jake. That's real nice."

"It sure is." The smirk turns to a full-on smile as he throws his keys into the air and catches them, turns to scan the lot and then slants a look my way. "I'm like a kid at Christmas."

With that, he takes off across the lot, his boots crunching over gravel as he goes.

I watch him for a few seconds, then catch myself staring and follow, only registering once we get close that he's parked literally right beside my car today. In fact, I think he's done it every day recently.

I unlock and get in, start my engine without looking his way, and finally ease out so as not to spit gravel at his windshield when I leave.

He pulls out after me, which I ignore, but when I turn right out of the lot, I give in and lift my hand in a goodbye he probably won't even see.

I won't let myself wish he'd follow me home tonight instead of waiting for tomorrow.

Like Christmas, he said. He sounded sarcastic, but still.

Maybe for him it's something to look forward to. To get excited about.

I can't remember the last time I was excited about anything.

Except that's a lie, isn't it?

I'm excited right now, alone in my car at the end of a long, busy shift. The first couple of times, I was too nervous to be excited and last night...well, that was different.

But right now, the anticipation I feel scares me more than anything else I can think of.

For the first time, I almost wish this whole thing didn't have an end date.

Almost. Because along with that anticipation is something a lot closer to fear. The fear knows that I could fall hard and fast for this guy.

And that's the very last thing I want.

18

Jake

If blue balls were a real diagnosis, I'm pretty sure I'd be in treatment for it by the time I roll up to Kit's place the next evening. It's only been two days since I lost it and took her behind the bar, but, given that I think about it every second of every day, I don't know how I've survived without rubbing one out at all.

It's probably just the blue balls talking, but I almost lost it when she gave me a literal fuck schedule.

Pretty sure she'd hate it that I think of what we do as fucking and not, say, fertilizing or donating a sample or whatever, but as I've made very clear, this isn't about that for me. It's about sex, plain and simple. Scratching an itch that's too persistent to get rid of.

The problem with some itches, though, is that they only get worse the more you scratch. I had chicken pox as a kid and I remember that first hit of nail to skin was absolute bliss. Until I scratched myself raw and my whole body was covered with the damn things.

That's what this is like...except sexy.

Now that I've heard those little gasping noises she makes and felt her come around my cock, I want her more than ever. Exponentially.

There's also a very good chance that all the withholding she's done has only made it worse. Who doesn't crave forbidden fruit?

The only solution at this point is to get her out of my system.

I've got less than three weeks left to do it before I move on.

The stone walkway up to her little house is overgrown with weeds and grass. The roof looks like shit. I don't imagine she's got a whole lot of time to take care of anything but the restaurant. The house itself is cute. A pale yellow bungalow with dark shutters, their paint peeling so bad it's hard to tell if they're meant to be brown or grey. I'd probably throw a coat of black up there and on the door to make the whole place just a little sharper.

Not that she's asked for my opinion. Nor is she likely to. Katarina Esteban is a woman who knows her own mind. She's got boundaries—and rules—for days.

I head up the steps, bottle in hand, lift the knocker, and barely have time to drop it when she's there, opening the door.

My lungs empty. Christ, I thought she was gorgeous at work, all done up, her face put on, in those tight-waisted dresses or jeans that hug her curves, but this look? The soft, no makeup, loose top, comfortable pants look? She's a dream.

"Hey," she says, a shy half-smile on pink lips I've only ever seen in bright red.

Cute is the only word I can think of and I know for a fact she'd hate it.

"Howdy." I hold up the bottle. "Figured this couldn't hurt." In my pocket, I've got lubrication of a different sort. Just in case.

"Oh. Yeah. Right. Thanks." She steps back without taking the bottle off me. "Come in."

I walk in and look around while she closes the door.

"Um, so, that's funny, because this is for you." There's a shallow silver tin sitting in the palm of the hand she's holding out.

I stare at it for a second before picking it up. "What's this?"

"It's for your, um..." She points at the bruise on my face. "Your bruise and knuckles."

"Yeah? What is it?"

"It's some salve I whipped up. My grandmother used to make it and I figured...it helps. It really does."

I nod. "Okay. Thanks."

"Here, let me..." She takes the tin and unscrews it. Rubs her finger over the top of what looks like honey or a creamy, hard wax. "Oh." She pauses, up on tiptoes, her finger right next to the cut on my face. "You mind?"

Out of words, I shake my head.

She pats the stuff on with a touch so delicate, I barely feel it.

"Smells good."

"It's lavender and calendula and aloe and a few other things." She takes the bottle I've brought and sets it on a coffee table, then awkwardly looks at me. "Could I...your hands?"

I put them both out, an almost familiar tightness back in my chest again, and watch her face while she dabs it on my messed up knuckles, so fucking gentle, it hurts everywhere but where's she's touched.

"There." She shuts it and holds it out, all business now. "Booboo balm'll make you better in no time."

"Booboo balm?" I laugh.

"Yes. What? That's what Grandma Esteban called it. It's great for skinned knees and..." She motions vaguely at my hands. "Other stuff."

"Thank you."

Clearly embarrassed, she turns and sees the champagne bottle, picks it up, reads it. "Wow. You got the real stuff." She looks up from the label. "You didn't have to."

"You don't think so?"

"You know what I mean." Her smirk's got that sharp edge I can't get enough of. "Like you said before, I'm a foregone conclusion."

"I'd never really assume that."

"All right. Well, good, because, um..." She stands there, looking smaller than I'm used to, paler, too, with an awkward edge that makes me want to, hell, build her a nest or some weird shit, wrap my arms around her and hide her from all the crap the world can throw at her. "Actually, I, um..."

I go still, watching her.

"I think we should call today off."

I can't think of a polite response.

"You know, it's just...my house isn't the right place and, I don't feel... I guess I mean..." The sentence fizzles off into a frustrated exhale.

I grab the champagne she's currently waving around in agitation. "How about we crack this open?"

She pauses, blinks down at the bottle we're now both holding, and nods, quick and tense. "Yeah. Yeah, okay." She looks at my face, takes in my smirk and rolls her eyes. "Stop it, okay?"

"All right."

"This is hard. I don't know how to—"

"Doesn't have to be hard, Kit."

"Sure. Whatever."

"You nervous?"

"What do you think?"

Pretty sure she's jumping out of her skin almost worse than the first time, although I know better than to point that out. Instead, I follow the urge telling me to step into her space and use my bulk to edge her up against what's probably a closet. I relinquish my hold on the bottle and plant my hands on the door, boxing her in. "I think you need to come. Quick and hard. That'll relax you right up."

"Already tried that."

My brows lift and my cock gets heavy and thick. "And?"

"I was close, but..."

I lean in and inhale the warm woman scent of her. "Wasn't enough."

"Look, Jake, this isn't what we're doing."

"What isn't?"

"Seduction. It's not the point."

"I know that, Kit."

"Then why are you bothering?"

"If giving you an orgasm helps get you to your goal—"

"Not to mention yours." The words are a quick, sarcastic reminder that she's not usually this hesitant. Kit Esteban's a boss, with guts for miles and a brain that's razor sharp. I'll bet she's used to doing the pursuing. Yeah. That makes sense. But some instinct keeps telling me she wants this—to be cornered, chased down, taken. Hell, what happened behind the bar just proved me right.

I smirk. "Making you come will definitely get me closer to my goal."

"This wasn't the deal." Her eyes are huge, pupils blown wide. Her chest moves up and down like she's run a race and that image—her running, me going after her—lodges in my mind like a splinter I can't get rid of.

"Deals change." I get closer, hem her in tighter and, in response, her eyes drop to my mouth.

Fuck, she wants it. She wants the dirty, animal sex I picture every time I look at her face, her throat, her ass. She just doesn't want to want it.

"Why are you doing this?"

I could lie and tell her I'm just a good guy and all I care about is giving her the baby she wants so desperately, but I've never been one to take the easy road. Also, I've never lied my way into a woman's pants and don't plan to start now.

"I'm doing it, Katarina, because when I get in bed now and close my eyes, instead of a good night's sleep, I toss and turn thinking about how your pretty face must look while you come on my cock. But I got one big problem."

"Wh-what?" She's panting, cheeks rosy, her bottom lip shiny right where her tongue just slid.

"I need something to work with." I move in, run my nose over the soft skin of her cheek, her ear. Is there a rule about touching her with my nose? Didn't see one. "See, when it comes to you, my imagination's got nothing on the real thing."

"I don't...I don't understand."

"Remember when I fucked you?" I whisper, a secret just for us. "That first time, in the hotel?"

After a moment's hesitation, she nods, barely.

"You felt so damn good, Kit. Better than any..." I'm about to say woman, but the truth slides out instead. "Anything."

Her exhalation is a harsh sigh that presses her chest almost to mine.

"Figured that was it. One and done, right? But then we did it again, you and I." I huff out a laugh that's zero humor and more than a little resentment. "See, you keep giving me that sweet pussy and not letting me see your face and, Christ, Katarina, what am I supposed to do with a challenge like that? Back off? Turn around? Walk away without getting a taste of that holy grail?"

"Oh, come on, you can't truly—"

"I can. I do. See, you let me in there and you showed me what I was missing and now I want it all. Every piece of it. I want to see you, hear you, taste you. You ever think about that? My mouth on you? My tongue in that hot little cunt? I have. Over and over again."

"This...this wasn't supposed to be that."

"Right." I nod, frustration making me feel like a teenager again. A kid without skills or language. With just his hands and his body and a desire to punch through anything that got it his way. "Christ, Kit, why the hell don't you want to feel good, huh?"

Her mouth drops open, like she's about to reply, and then goes still, blinking. It's fascinating to watch her expression morph from initial shock, through realization, to annoyance and then—God, she's gorgeous—a decisive certainty.

When she looks up and meets my gaze now, her chin's jutting out at a stubborn angle. "Fine, you can make me come," she says, like she's the one doing me a favor. I fucking love it. "Just...make it quick."

I can't help but grin as I shift my weight onto one arm and make a show of stretching out my fingers, one at a time.

She rolls her eyes, but I don't give a shit. Because this is so much better than doing her in the dark. And she hasn't brought her annoying rules up once.

Course I'm the one who has to go in and do it, I guess, because I open my mouth and say, "What rule are we breaking now?"

"I don't...I don't know."

"Touching. That the rule?"

"Yes."

"I'll just use one hand. How's that sound?"

"Fine. Good."

"Yeah. Now, open your legs for me, Kit." I put my face close again and whisper, "Let me get this little pussy ready for its breeding."

19

Heat washes over me.

I'm on fire. A molten river of hot, velvet lava.

And the bastard hasn't even touched me yet.

This is fine. Just fine.

Leaning on the door of my coat closet, a bottle of cold champagne clutched in one hand and Jake Brand's huge, callused hand sliding into my underwear with the kind of efficiency that comes from vast experience.

Where he'll find me wet and ready. The way I am every time he's around.

It's a Pavlov's dogs situation by now. Jake walks into a room and I turn to mush. And that's before he went and mentioned his tongue inside me and all those other things I really, really didn't want this to be about.

Now, as he edges one thick, rough finger under the waistband of my high cut cotton granny panties, all I'm capable of doing is leaning my head back against the wall and doing my best to look unaffected.

I don't know why this is important, but it is.

It's essential that he not know how much my body wants this.

Maybe it's because I've never felt like this—not with Clark, not ever. My libido's gone haywire for Jake and my body feels like it's been trained like those dogs. Aching and edgy and constantly, constantly ready any time he's around.

"There we go," he mutters in that dark, slightly southern accent, his fingers fanning out over the pubic hair I told myself I didn't have to shave for a man who wasn't my boyfriend. At least he won't see it this way. In the shadowy hall with my yoga pants firmly in place.

Yeah right. Who am I kidding? After that whole speech he gave me a second ago, there's no way in hell he'll give me a chance to hide again in the dark or under clothes. The man's thrown down the sexual gauntlet and if I choose to take him up on his challenge, he'll be calling the shots from here on out.

A shiver runs through me.

"See? That wasn't hard, now was it?"

I growl.

"Just hold still, Katarina." He gives my mound a little slap and I immediately obey.

"Oh, baby. Look at all this," his mouth oozes words beside my ear. "Fuck, Kit, you little liar."

It's because he's slipped down between my lips and found out just how wet I've gotten in these last few minutes.

"I didn't lie." I sound like a bratty teenager. "I never said I wasn't turned on."

He snorts in disbelief while the hard callused edge

of one finger explores parts of me I've mostly ignored these past few months. Hell, even before the breakup, because Clark never spent much time down there or even worrying about how sex felt for me at all.

My eyes shut hard on the pleasure of Jake there, sliding over my stiff clit and down to a place he knows intimately, but has never once seen.

When I think of it that way—when I take my feelings and fears and everything else out of the equation—it does seem unfair, somehow, that I've kept him from touching, looking, tasting.

That one finger feels huge this way, with his big body hemming mine in and his breath so close to my face.

Between the cold champagne bottle in my hand and Jake, I'm trapped here, which is a relief, somehow. If he's making me do this, then I'm entirely absolved of responsibility.

I shudder when he rubs back up and nudges my clit again, sending pleasure racing through my nerves.

"You're such a good girl, Kit, getting all swollen and wet for me like this. It'll feel so good when I fuck you," he whispers.

"*Jake*," I admonish, embarrassed as hell by his words.

"Sorry. Should I be telling you to hold still?" He huffs out a humorless sound. "Grit your teeth? Shut your eyes while I administer a dose of medicinal fingering before we move on to the main procedure?"

"That's not what I meant."

"Yeah, well. Forget the no-talking rule." He shakes his head and shifts closer, glides his hand deeper again to gather my wetness and draw it up to where he's concentrating his energies.

My entire body curls in on itself at the spark of rough fingers to stiff clit.

"That rule," he breathes, the words coinciding with the slow swirl of his fingers in a way that makes the whole thing bigger, harsher, brighter. "Wasn't in the contract, was it? In't that true?"

It's true. It's true, it wasn't in the contract. We talked about it, mentioned an addendum, but it was clearly a joke and now, here I am, being talked dirty to in the hallway of my house while Macon's chihuahua barks up a storm next door and Mrs. Kreighton's probably throwing all her weeds over the fence into my yard and I don't care. I don't care about anything but this. "I guess," I manage to eke out, since he's clearly waiting for a response. The truth is, I've got no idea what we're talking about.

"And this, what I'm doing here?" His head bends, bringing his nose not quite against my cheek. "Fingering your tight little pussy like this? There's actually no rule against that, is there? No mention of finger-fucking in the contract, was there?"

When I shake my head it brings my skin against his, presses his words into my cheekbone, imprints him there like it's where he's meant to be.

"It was touching or...unnecessary foreplay," I remind him, ever the good student.

"Oooooh, that's it. Right. Well, that's gone. Dust. You and your sweet little, soaking wet pussy decided to forego that rule, didn't you? You're a bad girl, actually, Katarina."

"No," I moan, truly upset, for some inexplicable reason.

"You are. 'Cause now that we've blown through it, it's gone. That's how this works. You get that, right?"

"Oh, god."

"Yep. Better pull up the contract so we can scratch out some of those rules. What do we have so far?"

"I don't...I can't..."

"Was there a rule about licking? Hmmmm, can't quite recall now."

My eyes fly open as I turn quickly to protest, but his body's there to staunch the flow and box me in again. "Shhhhh, shhhhh, don't get bent out of shape over nothing, Katarina. I'm not licking your little pussy right now, so calm the hell down."

He's right. He's not. But he's introduced the idea and that's as good as.

"I'm not sucking this little clit." His deft fingers surround what feels like the nucleus of every active nerve in my body and pinch, hard enough to make me gasp. "Christ, that looks good. You know how much I've wanted to see you when you're like this, huh?" Another pinch makes me try to bend double. Of course he stops me with that body. The bastard.

"Let me sum up, though, what we're crossing off the menu, huh?"

"Okay," I whisper, half hating myself for agreeing and more than half turned on that he's calling it a menu.

"Restaurant sex: Check. Biting: Check. Unnecessary foreplay: Double-check."

I hum while he caresses me deep and firm.

"Is this petting? Huh?"

I shake my head, still somehow fighting to maintain a boundary or two.

"Every expression on your face, Kit, is so goddamn perfect." His sharp inhale sounds hollow in my ear. "Like now. When I slide in between your lips like this." He eases down, separating me smoothly, explicitly. "Sweet, silky soft, fluttering open for me, like a flower. Like petals."

I work hard to give him a bitter half-laugh. "You a poet now?"

"Can be."

"When it…suits you?"

"Sure. I could tell you how the swell of your bottom lip makes me think of biting ripe fruit, my teeth sinking in."

I can't help a moan at the idea, the way his hand's working me while his words wind me up.

"Yeah. Hell, yeah. Look at that mouth. Plump and plush and prime for the picking."

"That's…nice alliteration."

"Fuck, I love when you talk in big words for me, Katarina. So smart. So fucking hoity-toity and well bred."

"Don't…"

"No? Too much?" Another easy skim down, down to breach me, deep and slow and we know—we both *know*—that he's taking his time with this. He's making it last. And the only thing I can't figure out is if there's a power thing happening here or if it truly gives him pleasure to watch me writhe. Maybe both. Definitely.

The point fritters away to irrelevance when a second finger joins the first and his hand twists to an angle that no one's ever used before and suddenly what felt languidly sexy becomes an urgent need to...

"I'm gonna come." I sound shocked—I *am*. At once somehow begging him to stop and to make it happen and hurry up and I don't even know how or when my free hand wrapped itself around his wrist, but it's there and it's holding him and my fingers don't even span his width there and that...that...that...

His size, his smell, the way he nudges closer with his nose and tells me how good he'll suck my pussy when I let him. Not if, when. How his tongue and his hands together will make me come so hard I'd see stars. How I'll beg for his cock. How he'll get on his back and drag me on top of him and split me wide open on his face and just feast.

"Stop, stop, stop talking," I whisper against his chest while my insides screw tighter and the ache gets deeper and I tug at his wrist, and it's not to pull him off me, but to press harder, drag him closer, more.

More. Please, more.

His thumb's strumming me, fast, and his fingers press deep and if I let myself suck in his scent I'll be nothing but animal pleasure and want, and want.

"Should I stop?" He grates out, low and mean. "Stop telling you how you smell like sex and I'll bet you'll taste like goddamn sugar? No? Yeah? Should I not say that I'm gonna come so deep and so hard inside you today I'll be leaking out for hours. Tomorrow at work. And then, Kitty, you know what I'll do?"

I shake my head no, though the words are almost meaningless against the swelling tide he's conjuring between my legs. It's almost too much and also nothing, nothing could stop me from bearing down and seeking out this thing he's hell bent on giving me. "What?" I gasp as if I need the answer as much as the climax.

"Tomorrow, I'll take you in the supply closet. You head in there for bevnaps or straws or some shit and I'll shove a box against the door and bend you over and use this perfect little hole to empty my balls into. It's what you want, isn't it? What you asked for? You want to be bred, right?" He's fucking me hard with his hand now, and, oh god, how does he do it so well? The motion of his fingers like a *come here* is somehow pressing on the part of me I didn't know needed pressure and it's twisting me higher and higher, making my insides feel tight and full enough to burst. I've got to pee for a second, but not. "In't that what you wanted me to do? Fuck you full of my come and fill this belly up so it's huge and tight and your tits..." He groans and I realize his hips are moving with the cadence of his hands. My entire body is moving with it. Dancing to the rhythm he's forced on me. "Christ, you'll look so good like that. You want that? My come overflowing your pussy every second of the day?"

I clench, *too tight*, at the crassness of his words. I can't... I can't... "No," I mutter, though I've no idea if it's in response to the dirty way he speaks or the idea that he can take me at work—again—and I'll just let him. Or or or it's something else. The way I want exactly what he's offering. Promising. *Threatening*.

"Yeah. Yeah, you'll take it like a good girl." A grunt. His, I think. Or was it mine? "My good girl. My sweet, good girl."

Oh god, oh, god, oh god, every word is punctuated by a deep thrust of his fingers. I'm up on my toes, straining. Stretching, arching. Trying to escape it, while every cell reaches toward it.

"That's it. Fuck. Fuck. Fuck, baby. That's it. That's it. I've got you. Oh, Katarina, sweetheart, I've got you. I've got you. Let go, yeah. Fuck. *Fuck*. Give it to me." His voice, those words, the *thump thump thump* of the door, all of it disappears in the supernova blast that takes over.

"I got you," I hear one more time, and then I'm gone.

20

———————

JAKE

Shit.

Shit. Shit shit.

I snag the champagne bottle with one hand before it drops to floor and catch the woman with my body, lean up against the flimsy wooden door, and just hold her.

"That's it," I whisper when she takes her first deep breath after what was one hell of a detonation. "That's it, baby."

I reach down to tuck a stray lock of dark red hair behind her ear and just look at her—face flushed, handful of freckles scattered across her nose and cheeks. That stubborn jaw loose, her lips wet from where she licked them, and so goddamn soft I want to test them with my own.

"Wow," she whispers without looking up at me.

I squeeze her. "Think that'll do the trick?"

Her reaction is a light, unselfconscious laugh that I want to hear again as soon as it ends. Slowly, though, tension creeps back into her body, her breathing slows, she nudges me away and peels herself off the door.

"That was..." She casts an embarrassed glance up at me and to the side, her cheekbones a dark, angry pink. "Thanks."

There she goes again. Thanking me for services rendered.

Hell if I know why it annoys me so much, when I'm the one who offers, every damn time.

Now, here I am again, standing here like a dick, hard as wood, and aching for more.

"Should we go to the bedroom?"

She stiffens instantly.

"Or not."

"Sorry, I could use a break." She throws me a side-eye. "You've got skills."

Shutting down a fresh blend of pride and exasperation, I hold up the champagne, and take what feels like my first ever look at something besides her. "You got glasses for this?"

After a brief hesitation, during which I can feel her trying to figure out my mood, she leads the way through the living room, back into the kitchen.

"This matches the outside," I remark as she opens a yellow-painted cupboard and pulls out two shallow champagne glasses.

"You mean the paint job or the time period?"

"All of it."

"Needs updating."

"It's got its charm."

"Only so much charm you can squeeze out of chipped Formica and this monstrosity." She kicks an oven that's got those electric coils on top.

"See this?" I show her an old scar on the meaty part of my thumb. It's a faint dark ring now, barely there, but just the sight of it sends a shudder through me. "Had a run-in with one of these stoves when I was a kid."

"Oh my god, Jake! That must've been bad."

"Yeah." I don't mention that the run-in involved my stepdad. I edge away from the stove. "It was an antique even back then."

The smile she gives me feels like a prize. "It's an ancient artifact now."

"Guess with everything you got going on a new kitchen's not a priority."

"Not really." She shrugs. "Divorce is expensive."

"Restaurant doing okay?"

"Actually, yeah. Better than ever. But there's also..." She looks down at her belly, flushing hard, and finishes up polishing the two glasses. In silence, she reaches for the champagne.

The entire kitchen smells like sex and that lavender balm. My cock's aching, hard and ready.

"I got it." I tear off the foil, relishing the fresh spark of annoyance in her eye. The woman doesn't like to be coddled. If she could do everything herself, she would. Including the obvious. How messed up is it that her irritation turns me on almost as much as those pink lips and her heart-shaped ass. Not to mention the musky scent of her pussy on my fingers. "IVF must cost a bundle."

"You have no idea."

"Mind if I ask you a question?"

"Shoot," she says, sounding doubtful.

"Why do you want a kid?"

Her eye avoids mine. There's a pause, like the room just breathed, and then she meets my look. "I want a family. Other than that, I'm not sure I can explain it." Her sudden smile's lopsided. "Not right this minute anyway."

"Fair enough." I ease the cork out with a light pop and pour golden liquid into first one then the other glass. "For what it's worth, I think you'd be a good mom."

"Yeah?" Her gaze goes still on mine. There are little brown dots in the hazel-green of her irises. No, the dots are yellow. She lifts her drink and I realize they're the exact same gold.

Her eyes are warm and expansive. Sweet and so fucking sad it's all I can do not to drop my fancy etched glass and take her in my arms.

"Definitely."

"Thanks." She reaches out for a toast. "To, um... To getting it right this time."

I can't bring myself to agree to something that would end these sessions for good, so instead I tap my drink against hers and say, "To having fun trying."

Her unexpected laugh—uncomfortable though it may sound—makes me wish for things I've never once considered.

I shut it all down quick, slug back the drink and set the glass on the little chipped, green-painted kitchen table. The pockmarked wood makes me think of farm kitchens and potting sheds and growing things. Settling down. Family. Kids, warmth. Love.

Fuck. What am I even doing working this hard to seduce this woman when I'm the guy who doesn't stick around?

Ever.

This is Frank's sister, for Christ's sake. The way he

talks about her, she's a saint or an angel. At the very least, a holy virgin.

And I'm the creep who pushed her up against a door and made her come so hard she saw lights.

Frank would kill me. And it's important to remember that killing, for Frank, isn't just theoretical.

With that thought hardening my insides, I look around, knowing damn well that I should go.

"Show me your room," I say instead. I've got to get this woman out of my system, once and for all. "Let's do this."

Or maybe I've just got a death wish.

21

―――――

Kɪᴛ

I blink up at him for a few heartbeats before comprehension sets in. Bedroom. Now.

Let's do this.

I guess it's time.

He holds his hand out.

Okay, then.

I slurp the last of the bubbles, wishing I could drink three more glasses, and work hard to make the switch from bubbles to business.

He watches me as I drink, blue eyes gone completely opaque, dark and hard. Unfriendly, almost, in a way that tickles my tummy and straightens my back. Sends my blood boiling south again, even as a fresh hint of unease slides through my veins. It's just the two of us here in my little, girlie cottage of a home. My grandparents' cottage. The hotel was different, though it's hard to pinpoint all the reasons why.

He's huge, first of all. I mean, I knew that, but I

didn't think about how he'd take up all the space—not to mention air—when standing in my house.

I hand him the glass and point out the way to my room, not for one second allowing myself to wonder where he's going after this session with me. Does he have a date he doesn't want to be late for? A night out with the guys? Will he tell them about how he came straight from an impregnation?

A *breeding*, as he so gallantly put it.

My skin flushes hot at the thought. No way. This man doesn't tell anyone anything. It's one of the things that both intrigues and concerns me about him. What kind of person keeps their secrets held so tightly to their chest, bares so little of their insides to the outside world?

Unless there's just nothing in there. That's possible too, I guess.

Yeah, right. If anything, I'd say this man is too complex. Rife with complication.

Then there's the fact that I've not mentioned this whole set-up between us to a soul.

He pauses beside my door, waiting for me to enter my room before following me in and that strikes me as such a strangely gentlemanly move from a man who looks like a thug that I pause, suddenly flummoxed.

Aside from his crass mouth, he has been a gentleman, every step of the way. For some inexplicable reason, that knowledge lodges in the narrow hollow at the base of my throat.

I almost tell him to leave the door open.

What must he think of my place, this man with the violent past and the nomadic present? He's got money now, despite his misspent youth. He can probably afford to stay in nice places when he travels. Does he notice the cheap plastic blinds I didn't bother changing out when I got the house? The bedding, clean, but rumpled, because no matter how hard I try, I've never been able to make a straight line or perfectly smooth out a sheet in my life. The little striped rug on just my side of the bed, bought because I keep the heat low to save money and I hate cold feet in the morning.

There's none on the other side, of course. Why bother, right?

Looking at it now, it's painfully obvious that this is a one-person bed. A one-person home. A one-person life.

For the first time, I wonder what his place is like. Though he gave me his address when I hired him, I've got no idea where he lives. Is it a dump, a swank bachelor pad, maybe a lonely little house like mine, in need of TLC?

No. It's impermanent, I know that much. Even if it's a place he owns, it's probably a crash pad. Simple, utilitarian, that's what I'd guess knowing him now.

"It's um, it's not fancy," I say, immediately annoyed at myself for feeling like I've got to explain my bedroom.

"It's nice."

"A little too bright in here."

His dark brows lift. "Okay."

"I...I don't know how to do this." If we're looking at each other, I mean.

"How to do it? You did it the other night just fine." A wicked little half-grin. "Not to mention out in the hallway just now."

I let out a frustrated groan.

He's already unbuttoning his plaid shirt, revealing a white T-shirt beneath, a smattering of dark chest hair visible at the neck, and it occurs to me that I'm about to see him naked and that's way, way more than I'd bargained for when I agreed to this.

"You, um, you shouldn't," I tell him, indicating the shirt.

He looks down, then back up, those eyes burning dark. "You want me to just unzip and pull out my dick like the other times? Glory hole style?" He casts a glance around my room. "You want that *here*?" And then. "After what just happened out there?"

"I..." I blink, stunned by his crass honesty and a little lost at the sight of his arms, the skin covered in layers and layers of ink. "It's against the rules."

He snorts, a muscle ticking in his jaw. "You actually want..." He lets out a frustrated grunt.

"Want what?"

"*Shitty* sex?"

It's all I can do to keep my jaw from dropping. *Shitty?* There was nothing shitty about what we did in that hotel, no matter how hard I tried. I've thought about him—*this*—every minute of every day since the first time we did it. Actually, since he first mentioned the prospect. Since then, it's only gotten worse.

"Was it...was it *bad* for you?" I whisper, against every ounce of good judgment I have. My mouth is dry suddenly and my head's sort of light and weird like the one time I passed out in my twenties. Shaken, I take two stumbling steps over to my bed and sit, let my head fall into my hands. "I...I'm sorry. That wasn't my intention."

I should have known, though. Clark was obviously so unsatisfied with me that he had to go and get a younger model.

"Hey." His weight sinks onto the bed beside me, forcing me to lean into him. When he pulls me in against his side, I can't help the way my entire body loosens at the contact. The smell. The warmth and physical closeness. "Come here."

His other arm wraps around me and he drags me up onto his lap sideways. After a second's resistance, my head drops to his chest, and he tightens his hold and it feels amazing.

More than amazing. This closeness feels somehow necessary, like air or water.

Oh, god, I've missed it so much.

Hugging. That's all we're doing. I think I might cry.

Oh, dammit, here it comes. My eyes are leaking and this isn't what this is supposed to be about. None of it. Not the closeness, not the sexiness, the attraction.

The *humanity*.

I want a turkey baster, dammit. A Petri dish. I want black and white images on a screen and lab coats, not this warm, close feeling of being with a person. Of needing. *Belonging*.

The fact that it's a farce—him and me and any semblance of belonging, just makes the tears prickle more painfully in my sinuses, press harder to the backs of my eyes.

"Hey. It's fine. It'll be fine." He tightens his hold and I burrow deeper and it's so freaking wonderful to feel this way, if only for a few moments, that I give in and let it wash over me. "*It was so fucking good, Kit.*" The words may be whispered, but that doesn't lessen their effect. You can cover your ears against a shout, but a whisper? It slides in, sinuous and silent, through pores, up spines, along nerves. It's a million times more undeniable than screaming.

I'm compelled to hear his words, the way I had to

accept his quiet destruction of me in my hallway.

He's a master of whispered words and small movements. His Trojan horse ways get him inside my shell-shocked walls before he obliterates everything with the battering ram trifecta of dirty talk and orgasms and telling me what a good girl I am.

His head drops to the top of mine. He hums against me and that's more comforting than any sound I've heard in ages. We sit here and breathe. I pull back a little and feel the heat of his exhalations against my cheek, my ear. I really, really want him to kiss me.

But I can't go back on that. Kissing is the one thing that would break me open right now. Turn me inside out. And, honestly, my insides aren't something I need to give anyone a close look at.

Then again, look at me. Already broken. Already wishing I'd said no and wishing I weren't doing this at all and also, if I'm being fully honest, a tiny itty bitty bit of me wishes that this were something else. Something it's absolutely not and truly shouldn't be. Not with who he is and who I am and—hell, he's not just my brother's long-time friend, he's my employee, for goodness' sake.

For now, but still.

I draw in a last, shaky breath and force myself to look up at him. What I see makes me want to hide my face again. Instead, I make myself absorb it.

His expression is worried, possibly, but that's not the thing that bowls me over. It's the intensity of it. The... the...the *craving* I see there.

Unless I'm misinterpreting.

I probably am.

"Sure you don't want that kiss?" he whispers and, the fact is, I do. I really, really want it.

22

———

Kɪᴛ

The last person I kissed was Clark.

I remember the last time he kissed me.

It was a quick kiss, distracted, granted mid-sentence, while he grabbed his stuff to run out the door for an early class. He asked me to pick up more of the coffee pods he loves—the only stuff he'll deign to drink, aside from what he gets in coffee shops—which were, of course, only available at the grocery store on the other side of town. So, since I didn't have to work for a few hours because the restaurant doesn't open until later and he had to be on campus early, I made the trip for him. It never once occurred to him to pick the damn stuff up himself, say, after work.

Now, of course, I know that after work, while I was running a restaurant, he was fucking her in my bed. Giving her the baby he'd refused me for the last decade.

Ugh. I'm a mess.

I swallow back the memories that still feel too raw, too new, and shake my head. "No. We still need rules."

He doesn't nod or respond at all. I'd say he's unconvinced, but it's hard to gauge now that he's blanked his face out. "Time to renegotiate."

"Look, that's not a good idea. If we start with—"

"One." He edges me off his warm, surprisingly comfortable lap and stands, reaching for his last shirt button. "I take my clothes off."

"Oh. I..." It's not a lot to ask, I suppose. If it makes him happy. He's doing all this for me. "Okay."

"Thank you, ma'am."

"I'm not your boss here. You don't have to—"

"I know, Kit." His gaze snags mine with annoying ease and holds it. "I *know* that."

"Good." I have to turn away from that stare. I look down at myself, wearing an old pair of yoga pants— which I'll never see the same way again since the hallway incident—and a soft, long sleeve cotton shirt. A comfortable bra underneath. I chose my ugliest cotton briefs, too, thinking I wanted to make myself as unsexy as possible. I want this whole thing to be clinical.

At least I did.

Now, watching him go back to peeling off his shirt and shucking the black molded tank before getting to work on those worn jeans, I don't know how I possibly imagined this could be anything but carnal. I've also got to face the distinct possibility that giving in on this one rule isn't about pleasing him so much as it is about finally getting a look at his body.

Which, given everything, seems immeasurably selfish.

Can I do this? If we get physically close, the way he's demanding, can I really continue to make it about fluids and nothing else? It doesn't have to be intimate or loving. It can be bodies, doing this one thing they're designed for. That's it. Mechanical and necessary. A means to an end.

Right. Like that *purely functional* orgasm in the hallway.

Oh, god. I'm an idiot.

Straightening my back, I start on my pants, working hard not to notice the way his skin's so tightly-packed full of muscle and sinew. The wide mounds of his shoulders, his lightly furred chest, the slim cut of his hips and heft of those thighs, not to mention what's between them, covered now in nothing but the dark cotton of his boxer briefs. Everywhere I look, I see nothing but intimidating strength. Well, that and loads of ink.

He looks up to catch me staring and a succession of expressions cross his features: surprise and then satisfaction and then intensity as hot as fire.

Flushing hard, I turn away and roll my pants the rest of the way down my legs, kick them off and stand there in the least sexy lingerie I could find. My body's an angry mash-up of guilt and annoyance and desire, despite every attempt not to want this. Or him. Or anything.

It's wanting that leads to heartbreak.

He sits on the end of the bed in that perfectly-molding underwear and watches me, his erection obvious enough that I don't have to look down to know he's big. I wouldn't have to anyway. I've felt that monster inside me.

"What do you need?" I ask him, wishing his gaze wasn't quite so heavy or warm, wishing I couldn't see the admiration there.

"Come here," he says, casually adjusting himself

through the cotton with one large hand. "Let me just... look at you." He flicks his gaze up to my face, eyes narrowed in challenge. "That allowed?"

"I guess." My attempt at a laugh is sickly. "Not like you can help but see me in daylight." Swallowing hard, I walk over to where he's made space for me between his spread legs, and stand, feeling awkward and pale and absurd.

"What if," Jake says, taking in my half-clothed body with lascivious interest. "I said I wanted the shirt off?" He leans back on straight arms, body hard and somehow lazy all at once. On display, too, which I think might be purposeful. There's so much of him that I've got no idea where to look.

"It's against the ru—"

"Is it?"

No. He's right. I didn't put clothing in the contract.

There's an evil light glinting in his eyes. Like he got a plan and wants to play. "Contracts get renegotiated, right?"

I pause, breathing quick and light through a mouth that's slightly open. "Um. Yeah?"

"What do you want in exchange for taking the shirt off?"

"Nothing."

"I'll take a pay cut. At work. Twenty-five percent." His eyes narrow to shiny slits.

"What? No. Stop that." As I start to step back, he grasps my hand and holds it, lightly enough that I can break away if I want. I don't. "No, that would involve money and that's not...I'm not. No. That's firm."

A hint of humor lights up his glare.

It takes a second for me to realize that his hold on

my hand's changed. No longer intent on stopping or holding me, but slowly, imperceptibly caressing my thumb, my knuckles.

"Take off the top." His voice has gone hoarse. "Show me those tits and I'll...fix that front walkway outside."

I try to pull away and he tightens his hand again. "No! God, that's so—"

"Nice? Handy?" His hold shifts so we're palm to palm, then he eases his fingers between mine. "A good way to make sure you don't trip and fall coming home from work late at night?"

"I don't want anything from you. I'll just do it. Okay?" With an irritated huff, I drag myself away from him, reach for my top and yank it up and off. "No trading. None of this—"

"Tit for tat?"

A surprised laugh forces its way up and out of my throat and before I know it, I smack him with my T-shirt. He *of course* gets a hold of it, wraps it in his fist and pulls me toward him in a slow tug-of-war I haven't a chance in hell of winning. I let it go and continue undressing, ruing my choice of a sports bra when he has to help me untwist it and wrench it over my head.

Suddenly, I'm half across his lap and we're both in nothing but our underwear, breathing like we've just run a sprint. His hair-rough thighs are doing things to my sensitive, naked breasts.

"There." There's that lion playing again, in the depths of his gaze. "That wasn't so hard, was it?"

Which certainly can't be said about the erection prodding my belly. The desire to bear down is almost stronger than me. Which is exactly what prompts me to jump back up to standing.

But of course, this is way worse, because now I'm here, planted in front of him in nothing but my underwear, on display with my breasts out and my thighs in full view.

It's a body I love. A body I'm proud of. But nobody has seen this body naked—aside from my asshole ex—since I was in my twenties and, truly, forty is a whole new ballgame.

"Jesus, Katarina," he whispers, while those wildcat eyes eat me up.

I guess Jake likes it.

If anything, his erection's more prominent than a second ago, his cheekbones flushed darker. "Touch 'em," he says, staring at my chest. A chest I'm fine with, but my boobs are big and heavy and always—*always*—hoisted up by underwire.

My brain's running circles in my skull, but somehow my body's bypassed all these doubts. I swear my hands were locked and loaded before he uttered a word. Every argument I might have come up with seems to have disappeared into thin air and I'm touching myself in no time, the feel of doing this under the heat of his gaze like nothing I've experienced in this lifetime.

"Looks so good, Katarina."

I shiver at the sound of my name and tweak myself harder.

"See? We don't need those rules. The rules weren't helping."

"The rules," I hiss, as contrary as a human can be while touching her body for the pleasure of a man. "Keep this civilized."

"Yeah?" His gaze focuses hard and bright on my face before returning to where my hands have fully repudiated my brain's jurisdiction. Nothing civilized about the way he looks at me there. "That how babies are made? Over fucking tea and…whatever those little cakes are."

"Scones," I say, using both thumbs to toy with myself. "Crumpets. Iced fairy cakes? Hot cross buns?"

"Fuck. That's it, Kitty. List off snobby British food while you show me how sexy you are." He swallows, the sound a dry counterpoint to my rushed breathing. We're both almost smiling. Almost, because being this turned on is a serious business, I guess, and there doesn't seem to be room inside my tight skin for both mirth and the way he makes me feel.

"Harder," he orders and, my god, my body's into that idea. I can't help the slight forward press of my hips when I lift my own breast and squeeze, pull at the other nipple, then hold them both up and together, as if offering them straight to his mouth. "That's good. Yeah."

That's when I notice that he's reached down to grip himself through his shorts. His eyes flick up to my face and back down, then up again. He dips into his underwear and pauses, looking me dead in the eye. "Nudity's on the table. That rule's gone, Katarina."

I shut my eyes at the overwhelming flood of pleasure I get from no longer being in charge. He's ripping down my walls, one flimsy rule at a time.

"I *know*," I say, sounding snarky as hell.

I've never once been this turned on. Well, aside from the last time. From every time. The hotel, the restaurant. The hallway.

And this is so much more, I think. In my home, my room.

He's going to fuck me on my bed. On my clean sheets. In broad daylight.

No. No, not fuck me. If I start thinking like that, I'll be done for.

Oh, shut up. We both know it's too late.

With obvious eagerness, he yanks the waistband down, baring the thickest, longest cock I've been in a room with.

Oh. My. God.

My mouth drops, along with the heavy weight in my belly. It takes everything I've got not to moan as my eyes take him in, as ravenous as the rest of me. I don't think I'd have let him fuck me if I'd seen him first.

Now, when he starts stroking himself, it's with rough, quick movements. I know this because I'm staring, rapt. I know it, too, because I've heard him do it in the dark. I've pictured just this. My imagination did not do him justice. The whole picture, the full naked man, is a thing of wild, unrestrained—and frighteningly unrestrainable—beauty. The sight is decadent and scary. He's too thick, too strong, too hairy, his eyes too hot, his hunger too obvious. My vision dims.

A single drop of clear fluid gathers at his slit and starts to roll down the head where his palm catches it on its way down, rubbing it into his skin.

As if it has a mind of its own, my tongue slides out to lick my lower lip.

He sees me and stills. Dead serious, he looks me straight in the eye. "You want a taste, Katarina?"

23

———

JAKE

Kit swallows. She wants it. The way those nipples bead, hard and swollen and bright red from her own fingers, the way her mouth hangs slightly open, the blown-out black of her pupils, eating up those whiskey eyes. All of it tells me she's turned all the way on.

But she's stubborn as hell—so damn appealing—and that means it'll take more than an invitation to coax her mouth to my body.

And hell, when I said taste, it didn't have to be my cock. She can sample any part of me she wants. The lengths I'd go to in order to get her to cave on one more little rule.

"I...I don't know."

Instead of words, which seem to get her back up, I use my hand and my cock to convince, twisting at the top, squeezing on the way down, so tight my scarred knuckles go white. To stop my other hand from reaching for her, I slide it down, over abs that have gone tense with want, to cradle my aching balls.

The noise she makes urges me to look up at her again, but that, I intuit, would be a mistake. No direct eye contact. No more mention of that fucking contract.

Then again, now that we've gotten past the first few rules, I magnanimously don't mind the contract quite as much. If the idea of it makes her feel safe enough to stand there half naked watching me get my dick hard in order to breed her. Probably more than anyone, I get that some rules are meant to be smashed through with an iron fist.

I've never once regretted breaking most rules. Not the other night. Not today. Not back when I thought I could make a difference to the person who mattered most.

What's one more set of restrictions to bust through, right?

I weigh my balls the way she hefted those big, beautiful tits, and let the pleasure ooze out of my mouth into the quiet room.

"Would it..." Christ, listen to her panting. "Would it *help*?" I glance up to see her indicating my cock and hell if that doesn't make another thick drop of pre-come gather at the tip. "If I..."

I give a pained nod. Not quite a lie, although *help* in this case is relative. Will I blow in her mouth? No. No, it'll be tough, but I can manage to hold on until I've slid inside her. I can do that.

"If you sucked me?"

She gulps, nodding a quick response. "I mean, if you *need* it, you know, to get ready?"

It's almost comical how ready I am right now. Which she can damn well see. But my Kitty's finally letting her libido bend her own rules.

"I'm pretty fucking hard already." Well, look who went and grew a moral code. I'm an idiot.

"Oh." Is that disappointment?

What the hell is wrong with me that I can't lie to her in a moment like this? Lead her on, play her own game? Let her think I need her mouth to do the job I was more than ready to do the moment she came on my hand?

"Maybe I could use a little help," I finally say, feeling so fucking dirty as the words come out. "Might be good to see your tongue on it."

"Yeah," she whispers and I swear she doesn't believe in this myth any more than I do, but who cares?

I think we both know there's more fantasy than reality in this dialogue.

Slowly, I kick off my boxers and stand, legs wide, dick held tightly in one fist.

"Sit down." I step back so she can take the spot I just vacated.

The way she obeys, a good student following instructions to the letter, makes my guts twist up tight. I sink into the sensation, point my cock toward her waiting mouth, and nudge it down. Then, because this whole thing's rewriting my permanent fantasy playbook in real time, I give in to my dirtiest urge, reach out, and gently grasp the bottom half of her face.

"Open up, Kit. Get this dick good and hard now so it can breed you."

Her bottom jaw drops. In any other situation, I'd bend and take her mouth with mine, show her with my tongue what I want her to do to my cock. Without that option, I grab my dick at the base and move straight into her space.

What happens next—fuck, I'll remember it 'til the

day I die. Kit's pink tongue peeking out to lick the drop of precum glistening at my tip. She opens wider at my hand's urging and I flex my hips and then the whole head of my cock's inside.

My eyes roll to the back of my head at the shock of pleasure, the absolute soul-drenching bliss of her hot, hot mouth, so soft and slick and...

I'm humming low, electric and just...alive.

For a handful of seconds, there's only that—warm mouth, achingly hard cock, the flick of her soft tongue at my slit. And then, Christ, with a moan that's too low to hear, but I feel clear to my toes, she eases forward another inch, shuts her eyes, and reaches up to grab her own tits.

The sight of her—deep in the throes of the kind of bliss I've only ever imagined on her face—flips a switch inside me. My fingers twine into long, silky hair and go tight, preparing to take this deeper, harder, faster.

Her eyes open, vague and lost, so goddamn beautiful, and a warning light goes off in the far reaches of my brain: Get out or go feral.

For a suspended handful of seconds with her head in my hands and my dick sitting on her tongue, the possibility remains. I could take her like this. I could make this rough and wild, get off and get her off and turn it into something she never asked for.

Though she kind of *did* ask, in a way, didn't she, when she took me into her mouth? Look at how she wants it. Look at how...

Fuck. I can't. I'll come and then there won't be any pretending that this is about knocking her up.

"Let's go," I manage, still holding her, cock lodged between those lips for a handful of seconds before I manage to pry myself away and move back. "On the bed."

"Oh. Was that okay?"

"Did the trick," I bite out, nudging my chin toward her pillows. "Get up there."

"Good. Right. Um..." Her hands flutter up to the waistband of her underwear. "Could you just put it in? Like last time?"

"Hell, no." I mutter, losing parts of my control I hadn't even felt break away. "We both blew right through that Unnecessary Foreplay rule today. What was that? Rule 4 or 5?"

"I don't know."

"Nudity's what? Rule 6." Her annoyed hum wipes out every last bit of humor. "Go ahead. Take those off," I order, hoarse and rough. I want to last. Please make this last. Make it good for her.

"Oh. Okay. Right." She looks around like she's never seen the place before, drags her panties all the way down and scrambles up the bed. Despite our age difference, she's so young in this moment, a little lost. There's a tenderness to the way I feel that I've never experienced.

Better lose that.

"On your back," I tell her, gruffer than I intend. "Legs spread. Like the first time." Only better. Because I can see her. Taste her. Touch this gorgeous skin. The rules are dropping around us like flies.

She flips to her back and spreads out. I'll think about how eager she is later, but right now, I need inside her.

"Good." I crawl over her. "I'm touching you, Kit. Rule 2 is history."

"Oh. Oh. Yeah." She nods quick. "Sure. If it'll help."

Help. *Right.* Christ, this is some fucked-up charade.

I look down at her tits, then hold back a desperate groan as my hand lands on one. Fuck, she's soft. Big. More than a handful, like her ass and the curved belly she highlights with those fancy dresses she wears to work.

When she arches up to meet my touch, my cock spurts out a fresh dose of lubricant and if I don't slide inside her quick, this game'll be over long before it's even started.

Which, I have to remind myself, *again,* is absolutely not the point.

The point is getting her pregnant. Which...she could already be.

My body stutters to a halt, I blink down at her, images racing through my mind and they're not just of her big and pregnant, they're of a kid that looks like her. Or like me. My dark hair, her warm brown eyes. Both of them on a porch swing out front, laughing. She's singing. The kid's—

No. Fuck.

I focus on her, concentrate.

Make it last. Make it last.

Could be the last time.

Slow, slow, I let my eyes roam over her body, then, because I can, I follow their path with my palm.

She goes a bright, pinkish red, the color crawling from her chest and up to crest atop her cheeks. "Fuck, Kit, look at you." Hip, waist, breast, throat, shoulder, I shove the tenderness back and stroke and measure and knead all of her, eating up the way her body responds— like a live wire.

Make it last.

"You ready? Wet enough?"

"Oh...oh, maybe." Her hands hover like she wants to touch me but doesn't quite dare.

"Should I..." I clear my throat, shut my eyes against the pleasure, and decide to push the button again. "Maybe check you? Make sure I'll slide right in?"

With a shiver and a dry sounding swallow, she nods quick and eager. "Probably."

"Yeah." Easing my weight onto one arm, I slip one finger through her lips. She's soaking. No surprise. I slide it inside her. "That okay?" At her quick nod, I let another finger join the first. I ease them deep, curve them toward me, and enjoy how blissed out she looks when her eyes go to that half-mast point and her mouth drops open. "That still fine?"

No words, but her response is good enough for me. A quick series of gasps to punctuate each press of fingers to G-spot.

"See? Foreplay's a good thing, isn't it?"

"Y-yes."

"Fuck, you're gorgeous. Look at you."

Her face scrunches at the compliment. Discomfort warring with pleasure on features I wish I were an artist just to paint. I'd put her on a fucking chapel ceiling and share this devastating beauty with the world.

My insides go weird at how I'm being. All the thoughts taking over my head. Beauty and painting and how I don't, for one second, plan to let this moment end. To let any of this end, not now, right here in her bed on a bright Thursday afternoon. Or the next time.

'Cause there'd better be a next time.

Fuck, I want this.

"Your cunt's so tight. You clamping down on my

fingers like this. Makes me so excited to fuck you again, harder this time. Can't stop thinking about it. How you feel around my bare cock."

"I don't..."

"Never fucked anyone else bare, Kit. You know that?" My fingers play with her, slowly. I go deep and then ease out, use her wetness to slide up and stroke her clit, then down again.

"You want it again?"

She doesn't respond, although I can't tell at this point if it's because she can't or some vestige of modesty is telling her not to.

Fuck that. I'll bust right through the modesty, the hesitation. Over and over again, if I have to.

I'll make this body—this woman—crave me the way I crave her.

Painfully, inevitably.

Hell, I'd stop if I could.

No. No, that's a lie. Because it's gone too far, now. Or maybe it was already too far the second I saw her, met her, told her I'd give her what she wants.

I look down at her face—flushed and lost and so fucking beautiful I am crushed beneath the weight of wanting her—and admit to myself that I've badly miscalculated...well, just about everything.

24

"Yeah," I gasp as Jake works me close to that orgasm point again with irritating ease.

"Good girl," he says, mean and growly above me. "You're so fucking good."

His body's huge, taking up more than his share of the bed, claiming space the way he keeps claiming my body with just two fingers and a presence I can't ignore.

He should stop all this talking and touching and get to it. My pleasure's secondary here.

"You...you...you don't have to..."

"What?" He's right there, above me, in my space, his breath warm, his body the kind of fragrant I am inexorably drawn to. Soap and aftershave and that combination of pheromones that feels right.

"I don't have to finger you in your sweet little bed? Huh? I don't have to make you come again before planting myself inside you and giving you my seed? You don't want that? You don't want the pleasure? Just the pain? The chore of having a baby? That what you're saying?"

He draws out for a second and I'm incapable of stopping the way my body tries to hold on to him. When he swipes my copious wetness up and uses it to rub my clit, I feel something close to gratitude. He knew. He knows. I need this, more than all the rest of it. I need the pleasure. The good ache to steal a little space from everything else.

"I've heard," he says darkly, leaning in to speak beside my ear like he's sharing a secret, "that if you orgasm, it might increase your chances of conceiving."

Oh, god. Is this sexy? *Is it?* Talking about this? No. No, it's not. Or it shouldn't be. But then he sinks those fingers back inside me and pulls forward like he's calling me to him and says, "Also, you'll remember that my dick's pretty fucking big and I don't want to hurt this poor little pussy when I slam inside it and fill it up."

"Okay," I gasp. "Yes."

He smirks. "Thought so." I'm watching him watch me now and my mind balks at the strange infinity mirror effect of seeing him admiring me, wanting me, feeling the way my body wants him and, if I let myself admit it, my brain, too. I don't see myself reflected in his pupils, but I feel the attraction.

It's a pull stronger than any I've felt before. Animal in its magnetism.

"Oh, god," I wheeze. "I think it's..."

"Yeah. That's it." The intensity, the fierceness, as he pumps those fingers inside me, heats my skin. It would scare me, I think, if I were more lucid. Instead, it eggs me on, lifts my hips, arches my back, squeezes my lungs until I'm wailing. "There you go, beautiful. There it is.

Fuck, look at you coming on my hand again, you gorgeous, sweet woman. Look at you all needy and hot. This cunt's gonna feel so good around me. You've got no idea how hot you are. How quick it's gonna be once I'm in there, stretching you out and giving you every drop of what I have."

Oh my god. I'm lost. Burned up by his words. Intense and crass and too much, just too much for this reserved person I am or have become or, maybe always was.

I don't do all this emotion. I don't succumb to hormones. I don't let things hurt or feel. I can't.

Which is why the orgasm, when it hits, takes me by complete surprise, twists up my insides, and spits the rest of me out. It shouldn't be this strong after the hallway.

The sloppy wet noises of his fingers keep going until I groan from the nervy zap of too much sensation, and grab his wrist, yanking to let him know I can't take anymore.

He won't leave it at that, I realize, once he pulls out of my wasted body, puts his fingers to his lips and paints my essence all over them before licking them clean.

"You're the hottest fucking thing I've ever seen, Katarina Esteban. Ever tasted." He leans over me now, intent, a deep, dark threat in his eyes. Following the path of his gaze down, I watch him grab his shaft, then feel the hefty slap when it lands against where I'm still quivering with the final aftershocks of the climax he's wrenched from my body.

The sound of it slipping through all my wetness is frankly pornographic. A little embarrassing. It's too much. I turn to hide my face, but he reaches for me, urges me to look up. "Watch, okay beautiful? Will you do that?"

"Yeah. Yes." Whatever he wants. Anything. Everything.

"Watch me fuck you raw. Watch while I fill you up, Katarina. Give you what you want. You know how hot that is?"

"Yeah," I pant, wanting this more than I ever thought I would. "Do it."

"Fuck, yes." He runs the plump crown of that cock up and down my slit, giving me just a taste of what he's about to feed into my body. It's too big. Like a forearm, the head enough to fill my entire mouth.

Which is a detail I wish I didn't know.

"I've got so much to give you." When he looks up and snags my gaze, I'm caught in those dark eyes of his. Trapped. "Been saving it all up again."

"You have?" I ask, aching to rub his back like he's been so good. Like he deserves praise for all the good work. I just barely keep myself from doing it.

"I promised, didn't I?" His expression is a compelling mix of excited and mean. The frown, the tight jaw, the compressed lips, directly contrasting the way his eyes flick from my face down over my splayed breasts to where he's lubing himself up between my legs, teasing me, and likely himself in the process.

Every sweep of his tip to my entrance makes me tense up, waiting, wanting, and every time, he coasts over it, bypasses it, gives me nothing but a hint of the pleasure to come.

Something like misgiving skitters up my spine when I remember that none of this is supposed to feel good. He's doing a job here. I'm doing a job. There is an end to our means, no matter how much we may forget it and, for a handful of seconds, I'm cold at the realization that this isn't real. It'll end.

It has to.

That's the deal.

It always was and that's not something that can change.

If only it didn't feel quite so...tragic all of a sudden.

25

JAKE

Something passes over Kit's face and I go still, hating this feeling of holding back, when what I want more than anything is to plunge inside her, take what's mine and give her what I've promised.

Mine being a relative term, I guess. But this shit racing through my system, testosterone or some other aggressive hormone, it's telling me to take and mark, to claim. To own in a way I've never allowed myself to do. Never wanted to, if I'm being honest.

Whatever's going through her mind, she seems to get a grip on it at about the same time she decides to get a grip on this situation and reaches down to line me up where she wants me.

"Go on. Do it. Do what you came here to do."

"Sure, Boss." I give her a lazy smile. It's the complete opposite of what's happening inside when I shove back her hip and press it to the bed. "Hold off. Give me a sec."

"I want you to do it. Come on. Now."

A muscle in my jaw flexes as I meet her look, head on. "You'll wait."

Her inhale is quick, surprised, and either very turned on or so pissed off she's about to haul off and smack me.

"I'll give you what you want. In my own time." I loosen my hold on her hip when I'm sure she's not moving up to try to fuck herself onto my dick again. And then, because the rules have definitely changed, I slowly rub my knuckles along the plump underside of one breast, then the other. Her skin's so soft. Daring her to protest, I hunch down and take one of those fat nipples in my mouth, lick and then suck hard enough to make her moan my name, loud and clear. "Licking rule's officially been broken." She whines. It's a minor protest. "Sucking, too."

"Jake."

"What?"

"Come on."

"My good girl's begging, isn't she?" I give her nipple a little nip and move up to watch her as I press inside. "*Now*, you'll take my cock."

"Yes. Yeah," she whispers. "I'll take it."

While I slowly, so slowly push in, my hand luxuriates in her satiny skin, first gently and then with a rough kind of ownership I know I'm not supposed to feel.

I've got just over two more weeks of this.

"For two weeks, this is mine." I stroke her tit, her side, reach down and take a handful of the ass I can't stop thinking about.

"Oh. Oh, god."

"Lie back." As if she's not already prone and spread-eagled waiting for just this. "Legs wider," I order just to be a prick, which isn't something I need to unpack right now.

There's no earthly reason for resentment to flood me while I take full possession of her body.

No fucking reason for my jaw to clamp down in anger while I drill deep and hard. Or for every bit of tension I've been holding to feed this powerful need to mark her with whatever tools I've got.

No fucking reason except that I can't get enough of the sight of her and she's got her eyes screwed shut.

And that pisses me off.

"Look at me," I tell her.

My hips pound with the loud slap of skin on skin, bedsprings bouncing, Kit gasping for air. With every thrust, it strains my muscles, pulls my tendons, hardens my bones, makes me want to fuck us both right into oblivion.

"Look. At. Me, Katarina."

Like a sullen teenager, she sets her jaw and stares up at me, defiant as fuck and, hell if that isn't a whole fresh level of turn-on.

"That's it. That's it." I slow my hips, despite my body's urges, and make her feel every explicit inch of me inside her. "Feels good, doesn't it?"

No reply. Of course.

I push deep and hold, claiming every inch of her body, circle my ass and nudge deeper. "Feels so fucking good, Katarina. Goddamn heaven inside you."

Her eyes start to close again and I pull out until just my head's inside her. "No. Baby, no. I need you to look at me. I need you to watch what I'm doing to you. My cock, my face. See how it looks while I..." I swallow because Christ this whole thing turns my crank so hard. "Put a baby inside you."

"God, Jake." She squirms at those words.

"That's right. You like it. You fucking want it. Get yourself ready."

"Jake." My name's a long, drawn-out whine. A complaint, which I don't mind when she grips my ass in her hands and drags me tighter against her hot, hot center. "Come on."

"Fuck, you want it. You want every drop."

"I do," she gasps, giving in a little more to this game that's not a game, but isn't real life either. "I want it."

"That's right." A deep thrust, a long, slow withdrawal. "You want it bad."

"Yeah."

"So bad."

She gasps through a handful of rough thrusts and then, because at heart, I'm just a selfish prick who gave up on loving anyone else a lifetime ago, I make her say it again. "You want me to fill you up with hot come, don't you? Every fucking day."

Her only reply is a grunt.

"Empty my balls into this willing hole. Give you a baby. Fuck, that'll be so sexy. If you were mine, Katarina, I'd keep fucking you the whole time. Keep you pregnant, keep you full of my spunk."

"Oh, god."

The image—and her reaction—revs me up until my body's about to fly over the edge and give her all the things I'm describing, but the idea that this could be the last time is unbearable.

She whines and twists her face away, eyes shutting against my crass words. I'm so far gone for this mess, my brain and body a knot of lust and need and want. So much want.

I withdraw from her entirely, deeply pleased when she reaches for me like she wants this as much as I do, then I grasp both of her thick thighs and press them up and back until they're against her shoulders, opening her up to me.

She's caught like this, trapped, her face visible, her pussy on display.

Like the dick I am, I make her wait like this and just stare, take in her addictive, earthy smell—our smell—and when I'm ready, palm her calves, line myself up and slowly, so goddamn slowly, sink back in.

"You've got to look, Katarina."

She shakes her head.

"No. No denying this. You look or I stop." Pretty sure we both know it's a lie. "You watch me breed you. Watch."

My body slows, muscles tensing with each obscene invasion of my dick into her pussy. I make a show of it, give her a version she'll remember forever. Something to take to bed with her at night.

"You like that?" I meet her eyes head-on.

Something in my chest twists unnaturally.

She nods, but we both know it's not enough. A part of me's broken open and I'm on a rampage now. I'm forcing her to admit things, to give things she's got no intention of sharing. Hell, I don't even want anything from her. Just this. This.

"Say it. Tell me."

"I...I like it," she grits out. It's an effort, I guess, when you're folded in half and getting fucked so hard you're bouncing halfway off the bed.

"I know you do." The grin I give her is unhinged. "I know you try not to. I know you want to be all prim, all business, don't you?"

"*Jaaake*," she starts to complain, but I won't let her. I can feel how tight she's getting, I see her neck straining and feel the scratch of her nails on my back, my biceps.

"Beg me," I tell her, so close to coming now my balls are high and tight, the zing of orgasm building low in my spine.

"What?"

"Beg me. For my come. Do it."

"Jake, I—"

"Fucking beg, Katarina, or I'll pull out and come all over your tits."

With a groan of annoyance, she strains up—head, neck, hips—then releases back and says, "Fine. Fine, I want it. I want your come."

Just those words send a flush of endorphins or some shit through me. It feels so damn good. "Yeah. More."

"I want you to fill me up."

"That's fucking right."

"I want to to to feel it. I want to..." She swallows. "I want to to to..."

"Be my little come slut."

"No!" So outraged. Like she hasn't thought it.

"Say it. Say it, Kit."

"I want you to to to give me a baby." A pause while she screws up her face and keens. "Give it all to me. I'm your...oh, god, I'm...I'm...your..."

Pleasure rushes me, hard and fast, makes my brain malfunction and my tongue spew nothing that makes sense.

"Oh god," Kit's moaning. "God, fill me. Fill me. I'm...I'm I'm..."

"You're my sweet little come slut and I'll give it to you every day. Every fucking drop I ever have. All yours. All yours. Always."

Which is what I do. With every deep, frantic shunting of my hard body into hers, all the nerves and rules and duties scatter and we're nothing but bodies. Fucking hard. Taking. Giving.

Wanting.

Wanting.

My ability to speak gets lost in the mindless mix and before I know it, before I can stop it, everything's gathering in my gut, my spine, my balls, building, building, the pressure an ache, a pain, a steel piston, driving hard and then—

Detonation.

Eyes screwed shut, vocal cords raw, every cell straining, stretched taut.

A shockwave. Another.

Numb. Quiet. The pressurized vacuum.

A roar tears from my lungs, scrapes its way through my throat and out. Out.

When I come to, what feels like a lifetime later, my spent body's wrapped tightly around hers, my half-hard cock still buried inside her. My weight's probably stifling the life out of her.

I start to move, ready to get up and leave—too destroyed to think this could possibly be the last time—and for a handful of seconds, her arms refuse to let me go and she's warm and soft and solid and feels exactly like home.

This is what I want.

"That was…" She swallows, turns and presses her face into my neck and whispers, "Thank you, Jake."

Fuck. Those words are a hard punch to my gut. I lose my air.

I squeeze my eyes shut and breathe through the pain.

Thank you. *Again.* High class Katarina Esteban dismissing the lowly help.

For the space of a few breaths, I feel defeated. Empty and sad.

I'm an ex-con. A roughneck. A nomad, between jobs. I can cook, but she'll replace me as soon as she can.

I'm a fucking gigolo, now, too.

Humming, she works to move me off her.

"Sorry." I pull out, lift up and back, sit on the edge of the bed and watch the relief take over her face when she lowers her legs back down again. "You okay?"

She nods and smiles and stretches, looking warm and happy as a cat.

If she were any other person, I'd lean over and give her a kiss. Hang out for a sec and then take off for home. Sated as hell after the absolute best sex of my life.

Hands down.

But with Kit, I can't. No kissing those lips. They're off-limits.

Funny how kissing her mouth is all I can think of while I stumble out of bed and into my clothes. I turn to see that she's wrapped herself up in her blanket, burrito style.

"Need anything?"

She shakes her head, still dreamy, probably not fully come down yet from the absolutely bonkers sex. I'd give her aftercare if this were a thing. I'd stay for her.

"All right." I nod, jaw clenched. "See you tomorrow." I'm out the door and down the hall by the time she says goodbye because the last thing I want is one more oh-so-grateful thank you.

What I do want right now is those off-limits lips. More than I've wanted anything in my life.

And it's starting to feel like a problem.

26

KIT

The phone rings a few minutes after I get into work. "Parlor, this is Kitty," I say, mind not entirely on what I'm doing.

Immediately, there's dial tone, which creeps me out. I'm old enough to have seen those hang-up horror movies and, though it may be full on daytime outside, I'm alone here.

I don't like it. I lock the door. I'll have to open it when the staff arrives, but that's not an issue. I'd rather do that than be freaked out like this.

About twenty minutes later, there's a knock. I'm about ten feet from the door when I recognize my ex and let my footsteps fizzle to a stop. Fuck.

He cups his hands to the glass and peers inside. I move to the door and unlock it.

"Hey. Kitty."

"What?"

"Geez. Okay."

"You don't get to be the injured party."

"No? No?"

Carefully, I lodge my foot behind the door.

"You think you're all victim here, but let me tell you, Kitty, you aren't that easy to be with, okay? I mean...the number of times I came home after a long day of classes and you were unavailable or too tired to—"

He stops, mouth open, eyes, too, like he's just been bopped on the head—and remembered that fighting's not what he came here for. God, he's so transparent.

"Look, Kitty, I don't want to fight."

I give him a slow blink. Opening my mouth at this point will serve absolutely no purpose.

"I just need you to understand. Life's...expensive. Kids, pregnancy, I mean, Lily's going crazy, Kitty. She's exhausted and hungry and she just yells and then there's all the shit we've got to buy. You've got no idea how it feels to—"

"I'mma stop you there right now. Back up and go away, Clark. Go."

A car pulls into the lot. A pickup.

"No. No, this restaurant is half mine. The house! The house is half mine. It belongs to my baby. I put in years at the—"

"Everything okay, Kit?" Jake strolls up, somehow nonchalant and one hundred percent present at the same time. He knows exactly how I feel in this moment. He sees the door cracked, sees the man leaning over me, pointing with that index finger like it's one of his reproduction medieval swords. God, what a prick. What a stupid fucking prick.

"It's fine. Clark's leaving."

"Leaving? No. No, this is a public place. This is my business, too. This is—"

"Why don't you sell the Tesla, Clark? Huh? Sell that."

"No. No! We need the Tesla. Lily likes to—"

"Excuse me." Jake's voice is so low, the timbre, usually rich and warm, somehow hollow right now, metallic. "This your ex?"

I nod.

Jake looks at him, nodding himself, slowly, like he gets exactly what's going on.

Not that he can, really. I mean, Clark, the medievalist, whose trips to Europe I financed for years, is just trying to steal another penny from me, but what nobody realizes is that I'd give it to him if it meant I'd never have to see him again. Never have to run into pretty, young Lily at the coffee shop.

I've stopped going to the coffee shop now. She's hugely pregnant, living with the man I thought was my life, my future. I hope never to see her again.

"Let me through," Jake says.

Clark has to obey. Once he's in, Jake locks the door. We're walking to the bar when Clark screams that I'll be hearing from his lawyer.

"He harassing you?"

I shake my head and then change my mind, because the way I feel, scared out of my wits, is really close to how I'd feel if that were the case.

"He wants half the restaurant."

"Seriously?" Jake turns to stare out at where Clark's taking off in his ridiculously expensive car. "What a prick."

"He is. He is a prick. He wants half the house, too. After everything I financed. He has nothing to do with this place. Nothing."

Jake stares outside again, looking thoughtful.

I sink onto a bar stool, fold my arms onto the bar, and wonder when this part of my life can be over. "Can we, like, skip forward six months?" I ask. "Or, I don't know, a year? Can I be officially divorced and, just forget about Clark and his little Lily and his fucking out of wedlock child?"

He doesn't reply, though I can feel him still standing there.

Slowly, I raise my head.

"Out of wedlock?"

I grimace. "He's a medievalist."

"A medievalist?"

"You know. Studies and teaches and writes all about knights and kings and stuff."

"So, like chivalry and shit?"

I laugh. "Yeah. Yeah, just like that."

"He might want to practice what he preaches." He walks around the bar toward the kitchen, slinging an apron around his waist as he goes.

"You'd be surprised."

"Yeah? How so?"

"Men were real assholes to women back then."

Jake watches me, jaw tight and hard, before disappearing into the kitchen.

A couple hours later, he comes back out, plate in hand, sliding one arm into his coat.

"What's this?" I ask, looking up halfway through the week's liquor order.

"Black Forest."

"Seriously?

"Seriously." He looks at me, no smile at all on his face. There's a pause during which I wonder if he'll say screw the rules and lean over to kiss me. He might think it, but in the end, all he does is boop me on the nose. "Be back before service. Tell Frida there's a note to get her ready."

"All right. Everything okay?"

"All good," he says with that easy grin. And then he's gone.

Jake

Pretty fucking easy to find a medievalist when you want one.

This one happens to be the only professor in the university history department named Clark. And his schedule's listed on the school's website, which is pretty handy.

The department secretary lets me know that his office hours are over for the day, but he'll be headed out immediately after his seminar. He's got birthing classes, apparently.

I'm leaning against the building's brick wall when a slew of students come out, followed, eventually, by the man himself.

"Clark."

He pauses, turns. It takes a second, when he sees me, for his eyes to pop wide with recognition and by then, the place is deserted.

"What are you doing here?"

"Came to talk to you."

"Got nothing to say, man."

"No? Fine. I didn't come to listen."

His mouth opens and shuts again and, while he's

trying to puzzle out exactly how this is gonna go, I take a step—one step—into his space and he's cornered. A rookie move. But this guy hasn't done a day of time in his life.

"Give me your phone," I tell him.

"Are you kidding me? No. You've got to be."

One more step and he knows just how big I am, just how little I care.

"Your fucking phone."

He hands it over. I shove it in front of his face and the phone opens, like magic. Quickly, I find Kit's number and delete it. With his unwilling help, I install an app that lets me track him, then hand it back.

"What'd you do?"

"Made sure you don't go near her again."

"Go near her? She's still my wife you know, you fucking—"

My mind goes narrow, my focus as sharp as it's ever been. I move, put my hand at his throat, the other hovers just over his balls.

"I will fucking kill you."

"What? You've got to be—"

"I will *kill* you." I look down into his eyes and let him see the violence in mine. Then, in case he doesn't quite get it, I translate into words he'll understand. "That is not hyperbole."

"Hyperb..." He swallows. It's loud out here, despite the traffic at the edge of campus, but I hear that dry sound. I see his pupils go wide. I know the signs of fear and this man is in the thick of it. "Where the hell did Kitty find you? Thugs R Us?"

"I don't get that reference."

"Geez, how old are you, dude? Like twenty?"

The fucking gall. I back slightly away, more annoyed by him now than angry. "How old's Lily?"

Touché.

His blinking speeds up. "I can't believe she sent you here."

"She's got no idea I came after you." And by the time he works up the courage to reach out to Kit and complain, I'll be long gone.

That knowledge drills a hole in my gut.

"She wouldn't like you doing this. Threatening me like this."

I let a smile pull at my lips. I can be creepy as fuck when the occasion requires it. "You think you know what she likes?"

He opens his mouth to reply and then drops it, belatedly struck by understanding. Mottled color seeps up his face. He knows now, as surely as I know, that I satisfy the woman in ways he can't begin to imagine.

I hand him back his phone. "Leave Kit alone and you won't hear from me again."

I've turned to go by the time he works up the courage to say, "I know who you are, you know."

My only response is a raised-eyebrow look.

"You're internet famous."

"What?"

"Your video. My girlfriend—" He clears his throat, looks away, runs one trembling hand through floppy hair. "The students. They're all talking about it."

"About what?"

"You beating the shit out of that guy."

My pulse picks up. "Guy?"

"In a parking lot? Against a car? That's you. Crap, I thought that looked like Kitty pulling you off him.

You're the hashtag 'Parking Lot Hero.' Like, you literally pick some guy up by the neck, like he weighs nothing. The... Fuck. You know what? I believe you, okay? I believe that you're capable of hurting me. I can't..." He looks away, sort of theatrically flummoxed, and then back. "I can't believe she'd consort with someone like you, but then again, she does have that shitty, felonious brother, doesn't she? Fuck." The phone in his hand starts ringing. He looks at it, drops his hand to his side, and mutters another "*Fuck!* Just... I've got to go."

He takes off, not quite running, phone pressed to his ear.

I pull out my phone and do a search, wondering if I've gone and fucked everything up, now that there's video evidence.

It takes a while, but I finally find it on one of the big social media sites.

It's me all right. #ParkingLotHero. Whoever posted it was dining at Parlor that night and she, clearly, along with more than 2 million other people, thought the other guy deserved what he got. I watch the whole thing, closely, and the distance, the lack of any real iden-tifying characteristics, like a license plate, a restaurant name, or my face, allow me to finally breathe enough to get in my truck and head to the restaurant.

But I'm buzzing, hard, with adrenaline when I get there.

Kit

"My place tonight."

"What?" I blink up to see a very stern-faced Jake, just back from who knows where.

"Let's do my place."

"Oh. I think we're not on the schedule until—"

"Fuck the schedule. Fuck the contract. I want new rules, Katarina."

"What's going on?"

"I'm over the rules. They're obsolete."

"They're important."

"Bullshit. They're hypocritical nonsense. I'm tired of being the bad guy, bending rules. Tired of breaking them, too."

"We don't need to—"

"*You sucked my cock*, Katarina." He leans close enough so no one can hear, looks me straight in the eye and in a low, gruff growl, says, "You licked it like a fucking lollipop." Mortification turns my skin to pure fire. I cast a quick look over my shoulder at where Cora and Toni are rolling silver. "We're well past your rules and you know it."

I can't catch my breath.

"You pregnant yet?"

"I...I don't know."

"All right. Well, let's get you that baby."

I can't think of a single reply. Or anything else I'd rather be doing.

27

———

Kɪᴛ

The shift goes by painfully slowly. Everything I do feels too slow, too syrupy, nervous, and also caught in someone else's headlights.

The waitstaff takes forever to leave. Finally, *finally*, I lock the door behind Cora, then Toni, then Frida.

When Jake turns the kitchen light off and comes out, I set the credit card receipts down so he can't see how hard my hand's trembling.

"You ready?" He asks, like there was no six-hour break in our conversation. No offering of red velvet cake with cream cheese frosting brought out to me on a plate, wordlessly. Just the cake and a look. Just him watching while I take my first bite and then work very hard not to moan through my second. That's two cakes in one day. I can't help but feel like things are ramping up.

Through it all, the way we seem to communicate without words feels...meaningful. Real.

It scares the crap out of me.

"What, um, what changes did you want to make?"

"One." He leans over the bar, eyes glittering with a light that's somehow both burning hot and ice cold and cuts straight through to my marrow. "We've already established that I touch. I lick. I suck. I bite."

Oh, god. My knees go weak. Bite? He wants to bite me?

Crap, he already has, hasn't he?

It takes everything I've got not to reach up and run my fingers over where he did it the other night.

"You afraid of this?" With the flick of one thick finger between us, he somehow encompasses whatever *this* is.

"No. *No.*" I back up a step and bump into a chair, feeling hemmed in. "This wasn't the deal, okay? We agreed."

"We did. You're right."

Somehow, though perfectly adequate, his words only make me feel worse. Guilty and dishonest. Like I'm the one doing something wrong here.

Which I'm not. He's pushing things.

But you let him get away with it. Every time.

Okay, that voice needs to shut the hell up.

There are *still* rules. This isn't about affection or communication. And it's definitely not about the attraction simmering—*boiling*—between us.

An attraction I was sure I'd imagined until he offered to knock me up, as he put it. Since then... Oh, god, since then everything's gone to absolute hell.

"Come over to mine for a drink, okay? No rules against that." He's got that opaque thing going in his eyes again—they're hard and dark, the blue nothing but eerie rings around his bottomless pupils. For some reason I can't begin to explain that hardness both irritates and excites me. "Pretty sure we've got a session on the schedule for tomorrow night."

My thighs tighten in response to that sentence. My entire body's on a string and he's just leading it around, entirely separate from my brain.

"Um, yes. Yes, we do."

"We're moving it. I want the session tonight." When I don't respond, he smiles. "Grab your keys. Let's go."

I should insist that I'm in charge here. At work and, yes, for the other thing we're doing, too. Nobody bosses me around like this.

But I guess we're both pretty aware now that none of this is what it's supposed to be.

Entirely complicit, I slide the cash into the bag uncounted, take it back to my office with the receipts, and lock it in the safe, then walk back up front with my keys and purse and coat.

Throughout all of this, I've got plenty of opportunities to back out. To change my mind, to argue that he's wrong and take off, angry. I do none of that. Instead, I go out like a zombie, get in my car, and follow him back to his place.

We pull up to what looks like a garage, but sort of old school. A vintage brick warehouse that's been redone in the last twenty years. It's got huge roll-up doors, which would make amazing front windows for a restaurant. I'd call the place The Garage or something equally unimaginative.

He leads me around to the side through a door and into a space that looks exactly like one of those old-fashioned New York gyms from '80s movies about boxers. Smells like it, too.

"What is this place?"

"Place I bought years ago."

I blink. "You own this?"

"A friend was being evicted a while back. He needed cash and I figured it was a good place to put some cash." He leads me up a narrow iron staircase to a sort of catwalk overlooking the whole space, which from this vantage is truly massive. "Got the building at a seized property auction."

"Wow." I lean over the railing and look down at all the punching bags and weights and the big ring in the middle of it. "It's kinda nice."

"Yeah?" He leans beside me and stares down. "Ricky'd appreciate the compliment, although…"

I wait.

"Ah, nothing. He's retiring. I'm selling the building." He shrugs and, despite his easy smile, there's something behind the words that feels strained. "Meeting with a real estate agent tomorrow. End of an era, I guess."

"You have to sell?"

"Don't need the money, but with nobody to run the place…"

"Nobody wants the business?"

His head shake is quick "Not much money in it. More of a community service than anything."

I look up at him, curious at how level, almost monotone, his voice has gotten. "How so?"

His stance is relaxed, but there's a muscle ticking in his jaw, a strain to his neck. "Ricky's the guy who saved me. Before prison and after."

I watch him, waiting for him to go on, hungry for any morsel of insight he's willing to share.

"Think I told you I was a brawler as a kid." I nod. "Well, Ricky's gym's where I learned to fight. To take that energy and focus it." He lets out a bitter, humorless sound. "When I got out, Mom had…" He sniffs, looks away. I fight the urge to reach out and put an arm around him. "Ricky gave me a place to stay. Helped me figure out a job."

"He sounds like a good guy."

"The best." His smile's more of a grimace. "He's still saving kids down at the gym."

"Yeah? Kids like you?"

"Some things don't change."

"Except he's retiring?"

"Got himself a lady friend." Now he's grinning. "She wants to go on cruises, not hang out in a smelly gym filled with people beating the crap out of each other for fun."

"You don't know anyone who could take over?"

He swallows, seems to consider, and then says an abrupt, "No," and turns to a door behind us. "Come on in." He unlocks it, letting us into an industrial-looking lobby area, complete with one of those open freight elevators and everything.

"You're kidding me."

He grins, shuts the door behind me, and turns to a last set of double doors. "I kid you not." Another lock opened, doors thrown wide and…

"Oh. This is *nice.*"

"Whole building belonged to an outlaw biker gang. This was the president's digs before the feds got him— all of 'em, actually—on racketeering charges." He turns on a light and puts out a hand for my jacket, which he hangs on a set of antler coat hooks by the door.

"You hunt?"

"Nah. That was here when I bought it." His head

shake is dismissive. "I'm only recently allowed to own a firearm."

"Oh. Oh, I hadn't thought about that."

"Not much interested in shooting guns. I could use a bow and arrow, I guess. If I got a sudden hankering for fresh meat."

I ignore the innuendo—intentional or not. "So, a motorcycle club. That's pretty wild."

"Yep." He leads the way to a wide-open kitchen and the massive, rough-brick-walled space beyond. "Had it deep cleaned before staying here the first time. Twice." From a big, professional grade fridge, he pulls out a wine bottle and a beer. "Get you a drink?"

I pause, look at him, and then down at the selection. "I..." A puff of air escapes me. "Is this a date?" My light laugh is so clearly forced, he's got to hear it.

"You want it to be?

"I don't date."

"Fair enough." He grins, completely unfazed. "I'm gonna have a beer to unwind after a long, busy shift. Want one?"

I nod, although I'm not sure I do. What I really want is a moment to think.

He knocks the cap off on the counter's edge and hands it to me, indicating the massive leather sofa in his living room. "Sit."

I comply, itchy at how easy I'm being. But also... maybe part of the itch is that I like this bossy side he pulls out occasionally. A lot.

"You always like this?"

"No." He opens his own beer and walks over to tap it against mine. "Just with you."

"I'm not sure I like it."

"Noted." I watch him take a long swig, head back, Adam's apple bobbing. "You're *not sure* you like it." He sits in a huge leather armchair that somehow looks small once he inhabits it. Relieved by his choice to sit across from me, I settle deeper into the sofa, as far from his wide-spread knees as I can get. "See, *not sure* that you like it kind of insinuates that you're not sure either way. Not sure you like it. Not sure you don't."

I open my mouth to object and realize he might be right. There's something to his bossiness. Something almost...relaxing maybe?

Maybe it's all the decision fatigue from living with a man who never took charge for so long. Or maybe being the owner of a successful business and a house that's falling apart. Maybe it's that I've been alone, making the decisions, doing the things, and when he tells me what to do, it's a vacation.

No way will I admit to any of that, though. And right now, we probably need to focus on getting this whole thing back on track.

"I...we..." I take a swig from my bottle, start to set it down and then drain half of it. "I think you're right. Things have changed and we need to re-establish boundaries."

"Ah. So, you're into a little negotiation?" He takes a sip of beer and smirks. The expression is maddening and cocky and it looks so good on him, I have to turn away. "Should I call my lawyer?"

"You know, Jake, maybe that's not such a bad idea." Maybe if I'm prissy, it'll destabilize him the way he's done me.

"Oh, yeah?"

"I don't know if I'm pregnant yet, but the moment it happens—"

"You taken a test yet?"

Oh, I'm so busted. No. No, I haven't. And I can't go into the whys right now, because if I do, I might have to face the truth of my denial. What I come up with is, "Hasn't been long enough," which has the benefit of being the truth, although it doesn't begin to explain why I don't want to know if what we've done has worked. Knowing, after all, would mean stopping. "The point is, I..." I finish off my drink and set down the empty bottle and straighten up as best I can in this slouchy, too comfortable sofa. Then, because I'm a mess inside and can't focus when he sits there like that, staring at me like I'm lunch, I spit out, "I only need you for one thing, okay? Once you do your... Once you finish, we're done."

"Are we?" He leans forward and he's got that look again—the one that tells me he's not the kind of lion who toys with his food. He's the one who goes straight in for the kill. The kind that devours its prey and leaves nothing behind but a pile of shining white bones, picked clean.

Well, and maybe an essential organ or two. Like my heart.

Shit. Why did I go and think of that? What is wrong with me? This is sex. I've done sex before. I'm an expert at the no-strings part. No heart involvement whatsoever.

"You know what?" I stand, all business. "Let's do this. Let's do our session."

"Sit down, Kitty. We're not done."

28

———

Kɪ**ᴛ**

Why do I hate it when he calls me that?

Because Kitty's not my name? Or is it that it's what everyone at work calls me? Maybe the problem is actually that he says my full name—Katarina—when he's buried inside me and now it's how I think of myself on his tongue. On his lips. On that sandblasted voice.

Whatever the case, I drop back onto my seat like he's pushed a button, and let my head fall into my hands.

"Tell me what's wrong, Kit."

"I— I don't know. We can't... *Oh, God!* Why is this so hard?" I meet his steel-bright eyes for a half-second and look away. "Look, we can't make this a...a..."

"Spit it out. Whatever it is. Say it."

"A real thing. *Real.* That's what I'm trying to say. I'm trying to explain that this is practical, not emotional. It's not fucking *real.*"

My voice is too loud, the buildup so strong that it makes the ensuing silence seem all the deeper.

He says nothing. I stare at my hands. Two of my nails are chipped. They're always chipped. Working behind a bar is why I don't usually put on polish.

I did this week, though.

Because I knew I'd see him.

Crap. Crappity. Crap.

After a few more moments, he stands. I don't move, but my mind's racing as he stalks back to the kitchen. When he returns, it's with two more beers. Good. Maybe we'll just have another beer and I can go and we'll pretend none of this happened.

With the kind of single-minded focus he exhibits while plating a daily special or lining up to fuck me behind my bar, he opens my beer, then takes his seat again. I still can't look him in the eye. Not when he's watching me like that. Not when I'm the only thing with a pulse in his vicinity and I know—I just know— how it feels to be in his sights.

"Let's negotiate, all right, Kit? It's all I'm asking."

On an inhale, my gaze lifts to meet his with the kind of shock I've only felt when hit by something hard and solid at very high speeds. Like that softball one time in middle school. Or the time my friend's car was T-boned by a minivan, turning our afternoon of Christmas shopping into a backache that still comes back to haunt me on rainy afternoons.

"We've already established that I want the lights on. Every single time I fuck you. I want to look."

His words fizzle through me, leaving me weak and out of breath.

"We know that touching's on the table. And I say whatever dirty shit I want while it's happening." He squints, watching me like he can see through the layers of skin and bone to the organs going haywire down deep. "The way your cunt clenches around me every time tells me you fucking love it. Am I wrong?" His big body hunches toward me and my brain's got no control over the way mine cants to meet him. I'm a flower tilting toward the sun. "You got any objections to that, now's the time."

I want to say... I should tell him... We really shouldn't...

My mouth is so dry I have to swallow twice before I can get my voice working again. Not that I know how to respond. I'd need brain cells for that and he's just about fried them.

"Nothing?"

"I..." My vision's gone a little dark at the edges—that is this man's power over my libido. I swear he's hypnotized my body into obeying his brain instead of mine. It's a miracle that I finally dredge up the word, "Kissing." I clear my throat. "No kissing."

"Fine," he spits out, somehow pissed that I'm working to maintain at least some healthy boundaries. "But I get to make you come whenever and however I please."

Wait. *What?*

"Right now. Here. On the sofa. I make you come, hard, before I take you to bed and fuck you. Those are *my* rules."

I'm nodding. I didn't tell my muscles to move, but like his good little puppet, they're obeying the man pulling the strings. What I want has no bearing in the face of such certainty.

"Good. Finish that." Those eerie blue eyes flick to my beer, like he's making me take my medicine.

Shaking, I obey. What choice do I have? My being's slipped from its moorings and he's the only thing keeping my skin and flesh attached to my bones. I take the bottle and sip slowly until it's gone, then set the empty down.

"All right." He stands and shoves the big driftwood and iron coffee table aside, then settles onto his knees on the glossy hardwood floor right in front of me. "Stand up."

The second I do it, he reaches under my skirt for my underwear, which he drags down.

"Good girl," he whispers as I flop back to the sofa, aware of how ridiculous I look sitting here bare-assed on leather with my panties hanging off one foot. He grasps my knees and spreads my legs wide and for a handful of seconds his face goes utterly blank.

"Katarina," he whispers and, just that tortured sound is enough to send a frantic whimper spiraling up from my chest. "Fuck, baby, you're beautiful."

He looks up, into my face when he says this, swallows, and then drags that gaze back down again, inexorably drawn to that place.

In my contrary way, because this wasn't supposed to be a thing, dammit, I still haven't shaved properly since we started this thing. I regret that now for a handful of seconds and then decide that it's not my problem what he thinks. I don't care if he likes hair or doesn't or if the patchwork situation down there is unattractive as hell. I don't care because none of this was supposed to be...*anything*.

"Do it." What was supposed to be an order to make him hurry up and get it over with sounds like a plea.

"I'll do it when I'm ready," he replies with a quelling look. "You'll sit there and you'll wait." A grim smirk. "My rules now."

And here's the thing: the rules *are* his, suddenly. Entirely his. He's taken the stupid contract and twisted it around and now we're not here for me at all.

I didn't sign up for this.

"Stop."

He glances up at me, searches my face, then slides his gaze down my body again. "You don't want me to."

"Jake..." My voice trails off into nothing.

"*My* rules." Rough hands on my knees stroke up to my inner thighs. "You want me to stop, you say..." While he tilts his head consideringly, eyes glued to that hot, needy place between my legs, his hands turn and his knuckles make their lazy way back to my knees and then up again. "What do you like?"

"Um... Chandeliers."

"You gonna remember that? *Chandelier*."

"What?"

"While we're fucking? If you want to stop? Will you remember to say chandelier?"

"Are we...getting kinky or something?"

"I don't know. You want to?"

"I don't..." My mouth and eyes are wide open and my legs are open and I'm sitting here with him on the floor before me and the whole thing is as surreal as anything I've experienced. It seems wise, in this weird, out of body moment, to be entirely sure of what I'm saying. "I don't want you to hurt me."

"I wouldn't."

"I...I think maybe what we've been doing is a little kinky already, right?"

He nods. "Probably."

"And you want to do...more? Other stuff?"

He considers. "You make me feel...wild, Katarina. Like a fuckin' beast. You make me want to..." He shakes his head, like he can't actually believe what he's saying. "I want to take you down. Hunt you. I want to bite you, claim you. I don't know. It's not a thing I've done or felt before, but it's like..." He starts to laugh and it fizzles out when I try to close my legs and he gently, slowly, pries them back open, his gaze on mine the whole time. "Like that. Just like that."

And though there's no way I could describe exactly what that look, that moment, just communicated, I get it, deep in my bones. Somehow, the way we went about this opened me up to a whole new sexual...world and, like a language learned as a kid, I just know—I know— that this is how it would be between us.

How it should be.

God, admit it, Kit. This is how it is.

"I... I want an easier word. Something I won't forget when...it's happening." I cast around for something. "Red. I want to use red."

"Got it. Anything else?"

I shake my head.

"Say it."

"Uh..." I shut my eyes through another lazy exploration of my sensitive skin. "Red."

"You need me to stop, I'll stop if you use that word." His smile is diamond hard. "But you better mean it."

I don't protest. Don't utter a word.

"No...no kissing," I finally whisper in a final, pathetic attempt to control some part of this.

But like a lion let loose from its cage, Jake Brand is tearing through everything in his way. "I heard you the first five hundred times," he growls, too closely focused on his objective to bother with eye contact. "Now lie back and let me feast on this beautiful pussy."

29

———————

JAKE

Not fucking real, she said. *Not fucking real?*

I don't know why the hell those words pissed me off like they did. But, goddamnit, the woman's got no idea. None.

For some inexplicable reason, those words were a red flag, waved in front of me.

She thinks what we're doing, what we've got is *not real?*

I don't even know what it means. What is real when it comes to sex? Doesn't matter. The fact is, Katarina Esteban sealed her own goddamn fate when she tried telling me that this connection's all in my head.

I know better. Hell, I knew the second I saw her.

When I walked in and saw those big eyes, sad and lost and still somehow determined.

The thing is, she knew it, too. She felt this attraction. That's why we're here today. Why my knees are grinding into the refinished hardwood plank of a place that never once felt like a home until she walked into it.

Call me opportunistic or single-minded or whatever the hell you want, but ever since I got to town, there's been one thing and one thing only on my mind and if she prefers denial, well, I'm happy enough to take responsibility for both of us. For every goddamn thing.

Kit's carrying enough on her shoulders with the restaurant and her house and whatever painful past she's lugging around.

I've got the rest. I've got this. Which isn't a relationship, fine. But it is fucking *real*.

Practical. Not emotional. Those were her words and, in a weird way, I'm all right with that. I don't need her to cry on my shoulder. I need her to give it up to me. That's practical, right?

Yep. Practical Jake Brand. That's me. Doing things because they make sense, not because I'll die if I don't.

Like this pussy, right here. Fuck...look at it. Pink and soft, with a little hair on the outer lips. I like that hair. Like how silky it looks.

And I fucking love how she smells up close. Musky and warm. Sex and woman and something else. Something precious and real and just out of my grasp.

None of this is within my grasp, is it? And yet, that fucked-up inner part of me is somehow convinced that it should be mine. It feels like mine.

It's why I gave her the safe word. I've never felt like this before—like someone else *belongs* to me—and there's danger there.

I'd laugh if I had any sense of humor left. It flew the goddamn coop, though, when she told me this thing... Wasn't. *Real.*

Practical? You know what? Fuck that, too.

I turn and run my lips along the soft, dimpled skin

of her plump inner thigh. Then, because kissing is still off the table, which pisses me off, along with a million other things, I draw them back and scrape her with my teeth instead. At her full body shudder, I turn and do the same to the other side.

Make it last. That's the plan. Make her so fucking hungry she'll beg and beg and beg and then...

Fuck. I don't know. Then what? What is the end game here?

Happy families with her in her cute little yellow house?

Nah. That ain't happening. I'm leaving. Besides, I'm not a family man.

She doesn't want a baby daddy anyway.

This is sex. Pure, filthy sex.

On that thought, I angle my head and let my teeth sink the slightest bit into her flesh, smiling at the way she tenses up and tries to close her legs.

"You want me to stop?" Eyeing her, I edge closer to her warm cunt, shiny wet and ready. "Hm? Or you want me to put my mouth on this puffy little pussy and let you ride my face 'til you come?"

When she doesn't reply, I force myself to lean back and look at her. "Tell me."

"What?"

"Tell me you want to come on my tongue." Instead of tightening my grip the way I want, I loosen it, show her she can stop anytime. "Tell me you want it."

"I...I..."

"Your safe word's right there if you need it, Kit. Red. All you've got to do is open your mouth and say it. Or..." I lean in, shut my eyes, and breathe her in, mouth watering with need. "You can tell me you want it."

It takes her a minute of internal hemming and hawing, but eventually, she gets there. "I want it."

"Yeah." I nod, letting my nose skim that crease separating her thigh from my objective. "Fuck yeah you do."

She gasps when I go in and nip at the tendon leading right to where I want to be, then slide my tongue home.

The second my nose finally touches all that sweetness, her eyes screw shut and I lose it.

Did I say slow? Hell, no. There's nothing slow about this chemistry. This shit is volatile. Dangerous. Lightning fast with flashing lights and blaring alarms and warning signs and still, I want to burn right up along with it.

Before I can stop myself, I've pried her legs wider, thrown one thick thigh over my shoulder and sunk my entire face into her.

That's it. The moment I lose track of everything but her.

I've thought about this. A million times. Every night at work. Picture myself on the floor every time she sits on one of those bar stools at the end of the shift, lifting her skirt and just diving in. Like it's mine. Like she's mine.

Reality is so much better, dammit. And not just the taste or the smell of her while I lick and suck and flick my tongue over her little clit, but the sounds. The way she grips my hair so tight it hurts and that pain focuses me. The way her hips rise to meet my tongue when I fuck her with it. The way that, now that they've got permission, my hands are all the fuck over the place, touching, stroking, twisting.

There's no in-between here. It's all or nothing and we've moved well past the nothing stage.

All. Mine. Everything.

Her hips buck, knocking me back and I growl and slide both hands under this ass—this ass I've been dreaming of—lift her up and drag her right to my mouth. She's a meal, a platter made just for me. "You fight, baby girl," I mutter against the softest pink flesh I've ever tasted. "Fight for it."

She makes a sound that's like a complaint, needy and annoyed, and even that lights me up just right.

The woman's irritated that I'm making her come. Annoyed that I'm forcing her to take it. And fuck if that's not just another one of my fucked-up buttons.

Giving her a hungry sound of my own, I swipe my tongue up her middle, going deep and shallow and then playing her clit like an instrument.

She squirms and I tighten my hold and pull her in closer and then there's no real movement. Just pressure.

I'm half up, her wrapped around me like a vine and we're as close as we can get and suddenly, there's only one way this'll be better.

Arms around her torso, I heave myself up. She squeals and clings to me, giggling as I twist and flop onto my back, the sofa—which I'm thankful was made for a man my size. Once I'm settled at one end, I drag her up to straddle my chest and, when she looks like she'll protest, higher. "Fuck my face, Kit. Come on. Do it, please," I beg her when she starts to protest. "Sit on me."

She pauses and looks down and the view's like every wet dream I've ever had rolled into one perfect woman.

"I'm heavy." She plants her hands on my shoulders and tries to scoot back.

"That's good. I want your weight. Give it to me." The second I say the words, I realize just how much I mean them. I want to take the weight off her. Make it my own. "All of it. Come on. Up. Let me soak in you. Let me make you feel good."

I don't let her think about it before tugging her over me, onto me, and then—fuck...*fuck*, my cock's gonna explode.

There's nothing in the world aside from this pussy.

Right here, in this moment, I could die a happy man.

30

———

KIT

Oh god. Oh, god.

I can't... What...

I can't describe how it feels to be consumed by Jake Brand.

I can hardly believe it's even happening.

It's so different from the other times. He's not slinking toward me like a lion bent on seduction. Oh, hell no. No, this is a full-on frontal assault.

I moan and my hips swivel. My hands settle on the sofa arm. I lean forward, taking weight off him.

Jake snarls, wraps his arms tighter, and pulls down. He'll suffocate. I'll kill him.

The man is in no way toying with his food. He's absorbing it like it's his last meal and the bell's about to ring and he's seconds from getting thrown out on his ass.

"Holy shit. Holy shit," I whisper, over and over again. It's glorious. He is. We are, like this.

Being taken. Consumed with such fierce intensity that if our cells could join, he'd do it.

I'd do it. Mesh with him. Let him tie me in a knot and tighten it, tighten it, the way my insides are coiling up hard.

I'd do anything to keep riding his face like this. Anything to reach the climax he's forcing on me like I'm not the one on top. Like my hands are tied and these limbs are useless and all I'm made for is taking, receiving, feeding him, feeding pleasure.

"Oh, god. God, god. Jake, it's..."

Too much. Way too much.

I'm sitting on him, but the man's calling the shots. The hands forcing my hips to grind down, the shoulders spreading my legs too wide, the tongue taking and taking and taking until giving's not such a chore at all.

Letting go, for the first time, isn't even a choice, is it? Not when it's forced on you.

Not when I'm in the driver's seat, but my body's not my own and my mind's left the building and—

"Oh. Oh!" That's my voice. Hijacked by his teeth right now, his nose, which is splitting me open while his tongue fucks into me. The rough, callused fist scraping up my sweater, tugging at my bra, dragging the cup down and then—

I scream. And it's not a pretty little sound or one of those breathy porn noises. It's a full-on thing, hurtling out of me at the exact speed of the orgasm that just claimed my lungs and seized my abs and my heart and shut down every other muscle in my body. Everything— every part of me—is spinning off in pursuit of that one goal.

Coming. Coming. Which isn't anywhere near an adequate word for this *seizure* that's taken hold, coiling me up and up, knotting me tighter in search of that last drop of pleasure.

Just...one...

"Oh, god."

"Say it." He's somehow gotten his mouth free.

"Oh god."

"Say my name. Say it."

I blink down at his shiny, beautiful face, slick from me. This isn't real. This man between my thighs. It can't be.

"Fucking say it while you come, Katarina. *Say it.*"

"Jake," I whine as his finger sinks inside me and everything coalesces and the bit of me that was left to take has been *taken*.

After a painful split second of tension, so intense it actually hurts, I go boneless. Spine liquid. Flesh a hot, sweet syrup.

My eyes shut and I go somewhere. Warm and soft. Easy. Nothing hurts.

If I could, I'd stay like this forever. Goddamn, let me stay here forever.

31

─────

JAKE

Kit slumps over me and I help her slide down my body so she's covering me, heavy and boneless and warm as a big kitten. My arms automatically wrap around her and I bend and put my lips to the top of her head, start to kiss her soft, dark hair, and freeze.

No kissing.

Something inside me tightens up and it's a fucking shiv to my gut because it's two things, twisting two different ways.

Part of me wants to obey her wishes. Do what she says, be the good man. The just man. The man my dad expected me to be. That man knows that none of this is about me, it's about Kit and the family she's trying to make. I'm a handy tool being offered at just the right place, right time.

The other part, the fucked-up part, is a gnawing ache she set off deep inside me, urging me to take more than she's wanting to give. Every time we do this, I figure the ache will fade.

Every time, it gets so much fucking worse.

When I think about what she's really asking for—that family. Her and any kid she has—and how badly that roof of hers needs fixing, how the front walkway's gonna be a menace when she's hauling a kid and it's icy out and she's wearing those goddamn shoes with the tiny heels that make her look like pure sex. If nobody fixes the walkway, she'll get a heel stuck one night coming home and twist her ankle and—

I'm up and out from under her, swiping an arm across my face, so goddamn resentful and at the same time, what the hell is wrong with me?

I'm not the guy you end up with. I'm not forever.

Jesus, who even fucking wants forever?

I'm halfway across the room by the time she makes a little noise. It's a kitten waking up noise and it's the sweetest sound and she's so beautifully messy there on the sofa, panties hanging off one foot and her entire ass out.

"Jake?" She squints up at me, clearly sees something in my expression that tells her things are off, and awkwardly gets up. That leads to her stepping on her panties and falling back onto the couch and struggling to get both legs on.

I force my insides to harden against all this awkward cuteness from a woman who's usually so put together, so dignified. I should send her home. Tell her the whole fucking thing's cancelled.

But the ache in my balls tells me that isn't happening.

Instead, I say, "Let's do this," in the same way I look at the water and take a big breath before an underwater welding dive.

"Oh. Right, how do you want to—"

"You ready to fuck?" I interrupt, voice hard as steel, while my chest cavity feels filled with razor wire.

I know I sound like a dick. I *am* a goddamn dick. Even in prison, I was known as someone not to mess with. A young brawler with a death wish. Only got worse after Mom died. Couldn't see the fucking point anymore.

Frank was there. Thank fuck for Frank.

Ah, hell. *Frank.*

He'd never be okay with this—fucking her bare, giving her a kid. None of this would fly.

Fuck, he'd kill me.

"Oh, you're ready to—"

"Yeah. Let's go. Open your legs."

The shift in her expression from soft and hazy to surprised and then wary hits me way below the belt. Or above it, I guess. Hell, it's vibrating through every part of me, like a gong.

I know I shouldn't do this. Any of it. I should shove her out that door and send her home and leave her alone forever. It's what she wants. A family of her own. No attachments.

We've got that in common. I've perfected the art of the free, no-strings existence and she's looking for a no-strings family. I get it. Viscerally.

I'm a complication this woman didn't ask for. The best thing I can do now is fill her up and send her home.

I look her up and down, slow and dirty, and choke out, "Take off your shirt and open those legs," in a voice that feels like it's gone through a wood chipper. Then, to dig a deeper trench between reality and that fantasy world I accidentally fell into, I palm my dick and add, "Let's get this over with."

Kit

"*Over* with?"

Something just happened. I have no idea what, but it's obvious in Jake's rigid stance, the glare bordering on belligerence, following every one of my moves like a hawk.

"What are you doing, Jake?" I ask, voice quiet as I attempt to get my underwear back in place. "What's wrong?"

"Nothing's wrong. Just ready to move this to the bedroom."

There are unseen levels to Jake, I realize, as we stand here glaring at each other, post orgasm. Depths I'd never guessed at the first couple times we met.

He's not just the easygoing guy or the rough guy or the efficient guy in the kitchen. He's all of these things and more and the Jake across from me right now is intimidation itself.

My movements slow and cautious, I get the skirt over my thighs and stand to let it cover my knees. "You okay?"

"Great."

He doesn't look great. He looks pissed, which makes zero sense given that I just did exactly what he begged me to do and literally sat on his face.

My cheeks flush red at the thought. "I think I should go."

"I think you should take that shirt off."

My pulse kicks up at the low, dark thing lurking in his tone. "Do you?"

His nod is measured, even, his eyes at half-mast. My heart's thumping wildly in my chest, which could be a by-product of the most mind-blowing orgasm of my life. It could also be my body's instinctual response to whatever it is he's doing.

Carefully, my eyes glued to his, I edge one foot right, all the while struggling to get my clothes together.

"What are you doing, Kit?"

"Nothing," I whisper. It's a complete lie. I am definitely doing something, although I can't formulate into words exactly what that something is.

This feels like a game, suddenly. A very dangerous game that I very badly want to play, despite how scary it is.

"You are. You're disobeying my direct order." He watches me through narrowed eyes.

I snort, hoping the sound covers the subtle shift of my body weight. "I don't follow orders."

His nostrils flare. "You remember that safe word?"

Everything inside me lurches. Oh, god. Oh, god, what is this? What are we doing? Shaky now, I nod, every move slow and careful.

"Say it."

"Red," I whisper as I inch farther over. One foot, then another.

"You want to use it?"

"Do I need to?" Another step to the side, slightly farther from him. Also slightly closer to the door.

"Up to you."

"Would you stop if I said it?"

"Always." He blinks back the beast and looks at me, gaze clear and sharp. "In a heartbeat."

I nod, trusting him in a way I'd never have guessed I could trust anyone. "Then I'm good."

His chest expands. "I...fuck. If you run right now, I'm gonna chase you down. You want that?"

Out of breath, buzzing so hard I can barely focus, I look him right in the eye and say, "You can try."

I jump into action, fast. My foot lands wrong. I stumble. Look up. He's coming.

All I can do is sprint.

Toward the door. My keys are on the counter, but that doesn't register until it's too late. The door's through there. Right *there*. Shit, he's behind me. I hear him, not rushing like I am, which is creepy and also my body's on fire with wanting it. I'm so wet—from before, from this—I know I've soaked through my underwear. Quick as I can, I feint and race around the big kitchen island, only he's heading around the other side and every single time I've thought of him as a predator comes racing in.

I was right. I was *right*.

Hell of a thing, isn't it, when confirmation comes too late?

Too late, my ass. I've wanted this from the start. In a flash I remember the moment he walked into the dark bar and lowered those mirrored glasses. The way his eyes hit mine, like something physical.

A fucking sledgehammer.

I'm halfway around the island when he changes tactics, plants a hand in the middle and vaults right over the damn thing. One giant arm circles my middle, ripping a squeal from my lungs—half scream, half laugh. My feet leave the floor.

Instinct makes me kick, hard.

He grunts, shifts my weight to get a better hold and we're moving. I flail again which serves only to kick my stupid panties halfway down my legs. Rather than gathering me tighter to him the way I expect, he lets me go, smack in the middle of a long corridor, and pushes me to the floor beneath him. I'm face-down on a long skinny rug. A runner. It's soft and thick enough to cushion my naked knees as I push up in an attempt to crawl forward.

"Don't fucking move."

I ignore him, struggling hard to get away.

Suddenly, he's yanked the cotton from one of my legs and he's over me, on top of me, huge and heavy, so hard there's nothing I could do to get out if I wanted.

Do I want to? It's hard to tell through this blazing inferno of adrenaline.

My back arches hard, pushing my ass against his erection and everything—every cell inside me—goes molten. It's not blood flowing through my veins now, it's lava, thick and hot, searing everything in its path.

"When I tell you to take off your shirt, Katarina," he mutters, his voice a razor wrapped in velvet. "I want it off." His weight shifts to one straight arm, hemming me in while his hips dip, staking my bottom half to the floor.

My brain is so confused at the sound of a zipper coming down, but then his hot cock slaps my bottom and I know exactly what's coming.

I don't know why I keep fighting him.

Maybe it's because he's about to fuck me on his

hallway floor with his pants pushed down around his hips and fighting seems right.

Maybe my inner animal doesn't realize that it's all game and can't let go of its mission.

Maybe the fight makes it better.

Oh, it does. I'm ten times more worked up because of the struggle. I want this with a desperation I'm not sure I've ever felt.

Whatever the case, I'm shocked into stunned, still silence when he shoves my legs open, lines himself up and slams in.

For a handful of seconds, he's deep, deep inside me, behind me, above me, around me, and I can't think a single thought that makes sense.

I can only feel. Full, slick, swollen, excited, angry, lost, and then...

Found.

Some part of my brain comes back online as he pulls halfway out and, rather than follow his retreat the way I want, I try to escape again and the way he comes after me then... Like something feral and wild and fully out of control.

It's the culmination of every hungry eye-fuck, every unsaid word.

This penetration, is harder, tighter. He grunts, the sound right beside my ear and it feels like a thick, angry sort of vengeance. With an irritated snarl, he slides one arm under my top half and another under my belly and he holds me, fucking me hard and close, like something he's hunted down and caught and can't risk letting go of lest it slither away.

My arms are pinned to my body and the only thing between my face and severe rug burn is the way he's gathered me up against his frame, holding me where he wants me while he mounts me from on top.

My tender insides clench around him and he growls into my ear.

I squirm and he tightens his hold, fucking me harder, faster than he ever has and then, because it wouldn't be sex without a little smutty talk from this man, he pushes his hot face against my neck and says, "I love these fucking tits."

One hand edges up and palms one, through my shirt and my bra.

I can't help but whine in response.

"I love this sweet pussy. This whole fucking body. It's..." A rough, sloppy series of thrusts makes me gasp for air and then, unbidden, from out of nowhere, I'm close to coming again. Not a wide-open orgasm like the last one, but a tight, painful little thing, slippery and secret.

"There it is. There's my girl. Oh, fuck. Oh, fuck, do it, come on this cock my sweet, sweet girl. Fuck, I love it when you come. I love it when—"

We climax together. I hear a low, animal moan and know it's mine because it scrapes on its way out. He's pressed deep inside me, I'm curled in on myself, my head turned to the side right where his lips are. His mouth.

I want to taste him, want to feel him kissing me. I want that connection, to look in his eyes while I soar and he fills me up, but at the last minute, he cants his head to the side and down and his mouth lands innocuously in the crook of my neck and my orgasm ekes out one last shudder when his teeth take their place and sink in.

He's the one who turned away from that kiss.

In the thick of the moment, full of his cock and his seed and an emotion I can't look at head-on, I would have gladly broken every rule I've ever had.

I'd have done it for him.

I don't know what to make of that.

I don't know what to do at all anymore.

32

———

I breathe her in, close my eyes, give myself the gift of this moment. Just her body and mine, together. It's elemental and right in a way that scares the shit out of me.

Forever. That's what I want and that's what pushes me back to reality. To the time and place where she's using me and I'm using her and we're on a floor after fucking like animals.

There's nothing more to this. Nothing at all.

"You'd better not thank me." Tearing myself away from the most beautiful woman I've ever laid eyes on, I roll away from her onto a hallway floor that is way too hard for my knees.

"Huh?"

"I mean it. Don't thank me. I don't like it."

"Oh. Okay then." She sounds lost.

My heart feels wrong in my chest.

"This isn't a service I'm providing. It's...an itch I'm scratching." What a lie. It's not an itch anymore, it's something much, much bigger. It's a hole I'm trying to fill. Or something.

"It still itching?" There's a smile in her voice.

I force a smirk to my face and admit the truth. "Much, much worse than before."

"Clark called me a bitch, guess now I'm down to itch. Maybe someday I'll just be a tch."

"You're *not* a bitch." Just thinking about that little prick raises my ire again. I wish I'd ground his face into the university's brick walkway.

"Oh, I know." She turns over with a groan, puts her chin on my chest and looks at me. "I'm an itch."

"You're a fuckin'..." My brain supplies nothing except, "*Treasure*," which surprises a laugh from her. She's laughing, but I can't breathe. I can't breathe and that's not good when your job involves diving underwater.

"What? Oh my god. Where did that come from?"

"You are a treasure. Okay, one..." Warming to any subject that doesn't involve my heart, I sit up with my back to the wall, and she shifts so she's lying face-up, head in my lap. The breath I've been trying to catch quickens. "You're all sparkly."

"Sparkly?"

"Shh, let me finish."

"Oh, sorry."

"So, you're sparkly. You know, like you glow from the inside out. Two, you're...deep." Her shout of laughter is the best sound. The best. "Hard to get to, and..."

I put my hand over her mouth to smother her snorting. "And you're worth the fucking dive."

"Dive," she repeats, muffled by my palm.

"Like a treasure. At the bottom of the sea."

"I guess you'd know."

I pause, my chest doing this weird thing where it goes tight and sort of expands at the same time. Christ, is it a heart attack?

"You okay? Jake?"

I nod, picturing myself out on the platform. Whenever I have to dive to weld underwater—literally the most dangerous gig in the world—I go in knowing that it doesn't matter if I come back up or not. The hazard pay's worth it when you don't give a shit.

And I don't give a shit.

Right?

"I'm good. I'm good."

She shifts until she's sitting across from me, legs drawn up, clearly uncomfortable in nothing but her top. Her makeup's kind of smeared and her cheeks are bright red, her lips, the most bitable, kissable curve nature could have made. "What's going on?" she asks laying a hand on my leg in a way that feels natural, easy.

"Just thinking."

"Okay."

"Got a couple weeks before I take off."

She watches me, wary.

"We should...we should make sure we give you that baby."

Her smile is hesitant. "I thought we were doing that."

"Yeah, but... It's not an itch for me now."

"What is it?"

"It's a mission."

Her features tilt up in shock, surprise, a bit of a smile, too. "O-kaaay. What's going on? What changed?"

"I want to give you a baby. I want you to have that. And also..." That thing in my ribcage clenches, twists. I lift a hand and rub it. "I want to give...*you* to some baby." I drop my head in my hands. "Christ."

"You want to give me to a baby?"

"I...I'm not good at this. I only talk to guys, usually."

"Oh. I'm your first woman? Is this a weird conversational virginity thing 'cause I am not a proponent of virginity nonsense talk."

I elbow her playfully and she elbows me back. "No. I'm good with women. I *know* women. I *like* women. I just don't usually...care."

There's a pause. Quiet. Her thinking things I wish she wouldn't and me fighting this tightening vise around my middle. If it gets any worse, I'm calling 911.

"You care," she whispers, looking me dead in the eye.

I sigh.

My head flops back and thunks against the wall.

Dammit. I do. I really fucking do.

33

———

KIT

He cares. Oh, god. Oh, god, I do, too. That's why this is so hard, isn't it?

If I care and he cares, then... "This isn't a relationship," I spit out, like I'm fifteen years old and Sven Larsson just told me he loves me. But just saying the words hurts.

Especially when what I really want to say is, *Stay. Please stay. Stay and see where this goes.*

His face goes hard and blank. "No?"

I shake my head, unable to face that look. He doesn't want to stay here, working in a kitchen. He's a world traveler, an adventurer. I'm a distraction for him, that's all. An itch that needs scratching. "Relationships are..."

"Too much work?"

"They don't end well," I offer. It's a tiny piece of me, though there's no way he'll know that. It also happens to be nothing but the truth.

He nods, eyes focused somewhere in the middle distance. "Like I said, I've never really had one."

"Not one? *Ever?*"

"Geez. Make me feel weird about it. I mean, I've..." When he looks my way and flicks his eyes down toward my bottom half, I know exactly what he means. "I've fucked around. I guess I'm not exactly relationship material."

For some incomprehensible reason, this gets my back up. "Why not?"

Are you kidding me? his expression says. "Look at me, Kit. Does this face really give you the wild urge to put a ring on it?"

I pause, the question flickering through me like surprise, shock.

There's no way to let the truth out. It'll just wind up hurting. Me, him.

On the surface, he's got a face that says almost nothing, and a body that says a whole lot. The ink alone is a chronicle—a lifetime's worth of stories. Most of them probably pretty grim.

None of it feels like the truth.

There's stuff in his eyes that doesn't fit the rebel without a cause skin he's holding up for display. There's a challenge in his gaze, right on the surface. A glimmer that calls out, *Go ahead, scratch a little deeper, try to find something worth saving. Worth caring about.* Behind all that, there's a hint of vulnerability I wouldn't have guessed at upon first meeting him. I also suspect it's not something he's aware of himself.

There's pain there and experience and a shit-ton of the bits of his history that have made him who he is, and there's something else. That vulnerable thing, that unguarded little question? It calls to some naive little piece of my soul that should have been snuffed out ages ago.

"Rings are overrated," I whisper.

"But you still want a kid."

"I want a family," I insist. "I want to take care of someone. To be a part of something."

He nods, slowly, his eyes scanning my face like he's taking in all the bits and pieces of me and trying to get them to make sense.

"Your house is like that. It's a family place."

"Yeah, I...I hope so."

"Needs a new roof." He grins. "And a dog."

I snort. "Seriously? When would I have time to take care of a dog?"

His brows lift. "Uh. You know a kid is a lot more work than a dog, right?"

"Of course I know that," I say, far more irritated at his question than I should be.

"I didn't mean—"

"I'm fully aware of what I'm getting myself into." I pause, full, so full of emotion that I can feel it threatening to leak out already. "I should go." I stand awkwardly. The last thing I need is to break down in front of him again, like I did at my place. God, what is wrong with me? Back and forth and up and down. I'm a mess.

"Katarina." He tilts his head back to look up at me and he's so earnest, so beautiful, it pulls at something deep in my heart. "I know I'm not relationship material, okay? I get that." I open my mouth, but he cuts through my protestations. "You don't have to tell me that I'm not dad material either. You and I both know that's not what this is about. Hasn't been from the start."

He stands until he's towering over me in the hall.

"But you are so fucking hot to me and what we've been doing... Shit, I've never been this turned on." He swallows, hard. We're still talking about sex, right? "Don't try to deny you're hot as hell for me, for this. Don't lie to me."

"I won't," I say, sounding young and belligerent, as if I'm not several years older than the guy. "I'm not."

"You want me."

Ugh, what an asshole, forcing me to say it. Never mind that it's the truth.

I just barely hold back from rolling my eyes like some annoyed teenager. "You know I do, Jake, but—"

"But what? But you don't like to feel good? You don't like coming so hard you can't talk after? Come on. Just... For once in your life, why don't you let someone else deal with things, huh? Just spend the night, spread your legs, lie back and enjoy it? How about that? How about for these next couple of weeks, you let me do the work?"

"I...I..." I'm blank. Completely devoid of words. What the hell am I supposed to say to this guy? Finally, a quiet, "Okay," just slips from my lips. Easy as that.

In the next moment, it's like a weight has come off me. I'm light, floating. Everything seems so unbelievably simple that I can't believe it ever struck me as being complex.

"Good. Now hold on." He bends and grabs me and I squeal, half fighting him as he throws me over his back and stalks down the hall to his room, slapping my ass with a resounding smack that I feel way, deep down in my core. "'Cause we've got a whole lot of fuckin' to do in not nearly enough time."

Jake

There is a whole lot to be said for sleepovers.

Especially when there's no rubber involved. Nothing at all between me and this woman.

No reason to get out of bed, except when she's hungry at one in the morning and we both need water following the third time I take her.

After that, she turns on her side and I wrap my arm around her and bury my face in the crook of her neck and fall asleep to the sound of her sighs.

When I wake up, it's still dark and I'm still spooning her. One soft arm reaches back to wind around my neck, I lean in...stroke my lips to her cheek. She arches her ass toward me and, like we've done it this way a million times, I'm inside her. Eyes shut, arms full, cock exactly where it needs to be. After a couple slow, easy thrusts, we barely move. Just her doing something inside that I've never felt before. It's a clenching and unclenching, her hips subtly grinding. Not even sure I'll come like this, but for some reason, the orgasm doesn't seem to matter.

I don't reach around for her clit. I don't pump my hips. I stay buried inside her, warm and safe as a hug, lips pressed right where she smells so entirely of her it's pure heaven. It's home. It's exactly where I'm meant to be.

Half dreaming, I yawn into her shoulder and she stretches with a noise like a happy, sated cat and settles deeper into me and the next thing, I'm asleep.

When I wake up before dawn, she's gone.

34

———

KIT

We get into a rhythm, Jake and I. Every day and evening, we work at the restaurant and every night, we go back to his place and we do it. In his bed.

It's almost—almost—like a relationship.

Except for the kissing part.

And the part where this thing has a deadline.

I haven't gotten my period yet.

Nor have I bought a pregnancy test.

Why bother until I'm sure, right?

That's the practical part of me talking, because false negatives on those things are common, so it seems wasteful, really, to buy one and then have to get another in a week or two.

But really, if I let myself be brutally honest for a second, I have to admit that I don't want to know. If I knew for sure that I was pregnant, then I'd have to put a stop to what we're doing.

And I don't want to.

Every night, Jake is harder to leave and every day, it gets harder to imagine life without him.

Which is why, when the first truly viable candidate to replace him comes in after sending me her resumé, I almost turn her away. *The job's not available*, I want to tell her. *It's taken.*

But I'm too much of a survivor to do that. Instead, I lie and tell her I was going to reply to her email. I tell her to come on back and meet Jake, our current chef, who's on his way out in less than a week.

Less than a week.

The pain that slices through me when I think that would be debilitating if I didn't clench my jaw and stiffen my spine and pretend that my rib cage wasn't collapsing in on itself.

I even invite her to the staff cookout we're having at my place in a couple days. Cora and Riley are getting married and we're closing for a full day to celebrate.

I bought a bunch of drinks and stuff to grill and we're doing it at my place.

Jake, being Jake, shows up an hour early, with a huge, three-tiered cake in hand.

"It's beautiful."

"It's lavender," he tells me, like the cake's for me, not for our guests of honor. "And lemon." He sniffs, turning to one side maybe a little embarrassed to admit it, then back to face me with a look so intense it pummels me, straight in the heart. "Reminds me of you."

The balm I gave him. The way sex smelled that day, the two of us, wrapped in beeswax and flowers and aloe in my bed.

I don't want you to go, I think, letting the words vibrate inside me, painful and real.

He heads out to light the grills and I put together a few last things, throw on a sweatshirt against the early spring chill, and join him.

Just the look he gives me when I walk outside—just that—makes me feel more in my body, my bones, than I ever felt with Clark.

That, that's why this is a bad idea. All of it.

When this is over, it won't just hurt, like with Clark, it will break me apart, inside and out.

That's how much he means. How much he matters.

Frida and Annette show up, followed by Toni and Raf. Then the new future chef, Yemi, who's brought something called Mandazi, which is a fried Nigerian dessert that tastes like coconut and heaven in your mouth.

There's a handful of buskids who work for me mostly during the summer when the patio opens and business triples. They're all high school and young college students. Cora and Riley finally arrive and the party gets going in earnest.

There's food and drinks, music. Annette, Raf, Yemi, and the buskids dig a football out of Lord knows where, Frida pulls out her guitar and starts singing exactly like Joni Mitchell, and Cora and I grab fleeces and blankets and watch as Jake lights the improvised fire pit he literally just built in my backyard with a handful of bricks from my basement and a shovel.

"What are you thinking?" I ask Cora as we sip on hot toddies and look out at the crew, happily enjoying the event.

As always, my eyes go back to Jake—always to Jake—as he heads out to join the others at football.

"I think I totally misread things a while a back,"

Cora says.

"Huh?" Jake catches the ball with a theatrical *oouufff* sound, searches for someone to pass it to, and picks Raf, the smallest, shyest person out there. When he throws it, it's with the easy, unconscious grace of a guy who knows his way around a football. And a restaurant. And a woman's body.

There's that feeling again. The emptiness. The loss.

I hate it, but nothing will make it go away.

"The Jake thing," she replies.

I turn to look at her and she cackles, joint and mug in one hand, while the other slaps her knee. "Yeah." She points at me. "Yeah, we got your number, right Frida?"

"Hm?" Frida asks in the middle of singing about holy wine tasting bitter and sweet. "What?"

"Jake will be missed."

"By all of us," I say, my cheeks the kind of red that comes from a blustery spring and a too-close fire and women I respect trying to pry their way into my soul.

"By you," they say simultaneously and, without warning, the tears come.

"Oh, oh, honey." Cora's up and scoots over to my side of the fire, while Frida keeps strumming, her dark eyes warm and knowing on me. "Oh, come on, no. No! Frida!"

"What? Can't stop Joni midway through." She tilts her head over to where the others are still playing. I glance over and catch Jake watching me and go redder still. "They'll hear us," she stage whispers and, I guess she's right.

"He's leaving," I say, as if they know everything already anyway. Which they probably do. I'm the one who's been fooling myself that a restaurant's not just exactly like a family. "Five days," I whisper, voice clogged.

"He'll be back."

I shake my head. "No, he won't."

"Wouldn't be so sure," Frida half-sings in a low, bluesy voice.

Cora's arm tightens around my shoulders. She blows her smoke away from me. "You guys have kept the whole thing awfully secret."

"It's not a relationship."

The women share a look. "Sure looks like one."

"How? How does it look like one? We don't even kiss."

The guitar strums to a dissonant stop and both of them look at me, hard, before going back to what they were doing. Smoking and playing.

"What, exactly, does that mean?"

"I... Shit." I slug back my drink and set the mug down, wrap the blanket tighter around me, and drop my forehead to my knees, and I let myself imagine, really hard for the first time, what it would be like if he stayed. If we had a baby together—or not—if this could be real. Like, just the two of us.

"Holy shit," Cora whispers, sounding scandalized and excited in a way that does not bode well for the notion that she might ask no more questions. "What are you two up to?"

I sigh and then, after catching another look from him and going even redder, I'm sure, I admit, "We're trying to, um, get me pregnant."

Saying it deflates me so fast, I'm almost floating. Relief, oddly, is what I feel most of all. Saying it, admitting. Sharing.

"Holy, motherfucking shit." Cora shakes her head in obvious shock. "That is baller, babe. Baller."

"Don't know what baller means." Frida bends to snag her joint back from Cora. "But I'd be willing to bet this isn't the last we see of that man." She takes a long, deep toke and looks over at me, her dark eyes narrowed against the smoke. "Mark my words."

I don't even dare let myself hope. The disappointment, at this point, might kill me.

Jake

What if? I keep thinking while leaving her house the next morning. What if?

What if I come back? What if I make Kit my home base?

No. No, she needs someone around, if she's gonna be a mom. The dream for her doesn't involve an absentee dad.

Does it involve a dad at all? Nope.

But the thought's there. Constantly. Every second. So present it takes my breath away, makes me worry about the state of my lungs. Maybe I should get checked out before heading out to the next platform.

"Where's the real estate agent?" asks Ricky, the second I get into the gym. "And where you been all night?"

"Okay, first of all..." I stop, given that he's blocking my path, and turn to look at a couple guys sparring in the ring. "I still haven't called. And second, none of your business."

"Oh, really? That so?"

"Yep. I'll call her today."

"Wish you wouldn't."

"Then why'd you ask?"

"You're leaving in a couple days, boy-o. And Dolores wants her cruise."

"Well, tell Dolores..."

"What?"

"I'll pay for the cruise. You deserve a break."

Ricky's face—all soft wrinkles and bones that lost their structural integrity in fights that happened before I was even born—goes hard as his battle-scarred fists. "You've got a woman here."

"I don't—"

"You've got a woman and you're still leaving, when what you really want is to keep the gym running, because you know it's a good place—a necessary place—but you're an idiot who thinks you don't deserve happiness. That's what's happening. That's why you won't call, why you're still acting like you're leaving."

There it is again, all the air's left my body—I'm out of breath, empty, only this time it hits me like a bowling ball to the gut. Or one of Ricky's fists.

"You could stand to stick around for a while, you know, kid."

"I'm not a kid."

"No. No, you're a man. A good man. You're a man who deserves a break. A man who could use a good woman. Or, hell, maybe you're seeing guys? Dude, I'm not gonna judge. Whatever floats your—"

"She doesn't *want* that. Me. A... Fuck, Ricky. This isn't about that, okay? Just...leave it alone." Up in the ring, Travis, a kid who's here literally every day, and quite a few nights, delivers a punch that sends his opponent to the mat.

"Hey, hey, hold up, hold up. That's it. *Ding ding ding!*" Ricky yells as he runs over to check on the fighters.

I take advantage of the opportunity to head up to my place, where I lock the door and put on music. I sit at my computer and check the weather to see if that North Sea storm's going to affect things, and then, because I know I'll need to eventually, I start packing my shit up.

Hours later, toward the end of the shift, Kit and Cora and I stare out at the rainy parking lot and watch the last customers drive off through a sea of puddles.

I've got four days left and Yemi's starting tomorrow. There's probably just enough time for me to get in a truckload of gravel and fill those potholes so they don't ruin Kit's car.

"It's a mess," Kitty says.

"It's not letting up." Cora's clearly glum at the idea of staying any later than she has to.

"Go home, Cora. I'll finish up."

"I'm not leaving you to do all the closing stuff. It's mop night."

"Go. Seriously."

"Frida left an hour ago," I remind her.

"You know I'll pay you your hours."

Cora makes an ugly sound and rolls her eyes at me. "She'd tip me, too, if I let her." She looks at Kit. "No. No, you can't pay me extra out of pocket because it's been a slow night. That's not how restaurant work goes."

"Okay, but you shouldn't have to—"

"Uh-uh." Cora shakes her head at me. "You're already the only place in town that does health insurance and a retirement plan. I'm not letting you tip me for existing."

Kit sighs as Cora walks off, still staring out at the sheets of rain.

"Want to close now?" I ask her.

She shrugs. "Doesn't seem worth staying open."

"My place?" I ask, low enough that only she hears.

I watch her chest lift and fall at a decidedly quicker rate. Watch her mouth drop slightly open. She barely nods and that tiny movement pushes my own breath right out of me, sending me into what feels almost exactly like anoxia. Like I'm stuck at depth without oxygen and I'll never make it back to the surface in time.

We close up quickly, though neither of us ever cuts corners. I follow her to my place, slow as hell through a rain like I haven't seen in ages.

At least not on land.

We race through it and get inside the gym, lock up and run upstairs, the metal steps squealing under our rubber soles.

I throw open the door and grab her waist while she walks in, give her a tickle and smile when she giggles and squirms.

Then, before she's gone five paces, she stops short.

I close the door with a clang, follow her gaze, and see the bags I packed earlier.

Slowly, like slogging through water, I watch her look over at me, watch her eyes get big and sad. It's terrible knowing I put that look there, although I'm not sure I get how it happened. Or why.

"You're ready to go." Her voice is light as air.

I nod.

It takes a while for the pressure to ease out of the

moment and when it does, I see right away that every-thing's changed.

"Kit," I say as she finishes toeing off her shoes and heads straight down the hall to my room. "Wait up."

Her pace doesn't change. She continues on, all busi-ness. My favorite sultry, hip shaking walk a thing of the past.

By the time I get my boots off and grab a towel, I find her sitting up in my bed, under the sheets, naked.

I open my mouth to comment and then hold it in because, fuck, this shit is complicated.

Wasn't supposed to be, but it is.

I hand her the towel and soak up every second of her body doing practical, everyday things.

Instead of the easy banter we've worked up to these past couple of weeks, it's with a kind of thick quiet that I undress and get into bed.

She watches me every second, though, and I wonder if it's the same for her. Will she miss this like water? Like air? Are her insides shoring themselves up, too, against what's about to happen?

Once I'm naked and, contrary to every other time we've been together, only half hard, even with her eyes on me, she slides over and I get into the warm place in my bed and fuck if that isn't the strangest, most beau-tiful thing I've ever felt. A warm spot, waiting for me.

I clear my throat, thinking I'll say something to improve the mood, but not a solitary word comes to mind. So, instead, I do what works for us. I move under the blankets, down her body, one slick slide of my tongue at a time, to that uncomplicated, hot, fragrant place between her legs. And I make love to her. Maybe for the last time.

35

———

Kɪᴛ

"What happens if there's a storm?" I ask, staring straight up into the quiet, dark night.

"Hm?" He flops over onto his back.

"While you're, you know, underwater." I gulp. "Welding?"

"We'd avoid that."

"Okay. Good. Okay." The stuff I've been reading online these past few days keeps swirling, and the more it swirls, the bigger it seems and, to be perfectly honest, it's really not okay at all. "Do they need you to go underwater?"

"It's what I'm hired for."

"Every time?"

"This platform's got a few issues. It's an older one."

Oh, god. I can't get these images out of my head. A rusty, creaking metal eyesore in the middle of a wild, stormy sea. Cold, cold rain battering down. "Why Norway?"

"Hm? Well, the company I work for sends me out to different locations, based on need and—"

"Why you?"

He takes a while to answer. When he finally does, his words take the panic I've been shoving back and turn it into something rabid, too huge to hide. "I'm good at it. I'm a good diver, a good welder, steady under pressure. I don't mind danger and I get the technical aspects."

"I mind danger." I work hard to keep the fear from my voice. "I mean, for you. I mind that you put yourself out there, that you could get hurt. I read it's the most dangerous job in the world."

He doesn't immediately answer, which is answer enough. He turns onto his side and, in the dark, with the sound of rain pounding on the metal roof above us, he puts his rough, callused hand to my cheek. It smells oh-so-slightly of the balm I gave him.

"You worried about me, baby?"

I clench my jaw, emotion filling my throat and sinuses, and nod.

"I'll be fine."

I nod again, hating that a single tear's managed to escape my eye. "How...how will I know?"

"What?"

"How will I know you're okay? How will... What if..."

Another tear slips out. This one he swipes gently with his thumb.

"I... Fuck."

I almost eke out a laugh at that, but can't quite force it that last inch from my mouth.

"I'll keep in touch."

A shaky breath escapes me as I imagine the check-ins. "I'm alive!" they'll say. Texts or emails or whatever he can manage from out in the middle of the ocean.

"I, um, I... I haven't sold this place yet."

I sniffle. "Okay."

"So, I might have to come back. I know you said you didn't want me to—"

"It's fine." I say, relief pouring through me, warm as whiskey. "It's fine."

"Yeah?"

I nod and lean toward him, wanting a kiss more than my next breath, but so scared of the pain. Instead of pressing my lips to his, I veer to the side and kiss his cheek, then his shoulder, and give him my back, the way I've done these many nights. He'll wrap me up in his body and hold me tight and we can both pretend this isn't ending in a few days.

We can pretend it's something it's not.

Except, as I fall asleep, with his face tucked into the crook of my neck, I'm not sure what exactly it is anymore and what part of it is pretend.

I wake up in the dark, hours later, crying, which hasn't happened in ages. And it's not a few tears, it's the deep, wracking, internal pain kind of crying that will absolutely turn to ugly sobs.

The dream wasn't about Clark. Or the baby I miscarried in my twenties. It's not about a car wreck, which is what I dreamed about on bad nights for most of my life after my parents died. It was Jake. Just Jake. And me. And *our baby*.

And we were happy.

Just stay, I've wanted to tell him a million times over the past few days. At the restaurant, when he brought me my third-to-last piece of Jake cake and I almost lost it right there in front of Cora's knowing gaze. That night I knocked on his door and he opened it and I fell into his hug like I belonged there. Last night, when he spooned me and whispered how beautiful I was, right against my ear, and all I wanted—the only thing in the world—was to turn and kiss him, but I know, *I know*, the pain isn't something I'll get over.

I'm here now, crying from that dream and I realize my error.

It's too late.

I'll never get over this. Him. Never.

I love him not just with my body and my head, but with the deepest, realest part of me. A part I've tried hard to protect since losing my parents as a confused kid.

What happened with Clark—the way I thought I loved him? That was surface only. It was an easy love. Forgettable.

But those packed bags by Jake's front door last night, ready and waiting? The second I saw them, something shifted.

Oh, god. I've got to get out of this bed. I've got to go.

Now.

Quietly, quickly, I pry his heavy arm off me, roll out of bed and root around for my shirt. The bra's a lost cause. In the hallway, I find my skirt, struggle to get my underwear up, and snag my shoes and keys, walking barefoot to the door.

Out, down the cold metal steps, breathing hard and fast through my nose, but somehow keeping the tears in check. They hurt, trying to force their way out, but I know better than to let them.

It's okay. It's good, even. The hurt's focusing me, keeping my steps quiet, careful.

I get to the big metal outer door and unlock it, then swing it open and jump with a startled scream when something separates from the shadows.

"Shit. Shit, lady. Stop. Stop. Sorry." I'm about to slam the door shut, but I pause. "Sorry, is Ricky here?"

"Ricky?"

"Or Jake. He here?"

"What?" I peer at the kid in front of me. He's tall, but can't be more than twelve or thirteen years old. He's got the nasal voice of a boy in full-blown puberty and the hunched shoulders of a young man not yet used to his long, lanky body.

"Jake lets me crash here sometimes. On the mats over there, see? In the corner."

I turn and blink through the dark at a pile of those thick, soft-looking mats. There's what might be a towel or a blanket folded up beside it.

"Jake does that? He lets you stay here?"

The kid shrugs. "Just on days I'm not allowed home."

"Not allowed?" I lower my volume at the last minute. The last thing I need is Jake coming down and dragging me back up to his room. I could handle sleeping together every night as long as I woke up on my own. But waking up groggy beside sweet, sleepy, bed-Jake? I don't think my shields would stay up. I don't have that kind of stamina.

"Dad's an asshole," the kid says, his voice thick.

"Oh, I'm...I'm sorry." I squint back at him in the dark. "Look, I don't know what to do here. It's not my gym and I don't feel like it's my place to—"

From upstairs, a door slams. Crap. Jake.

He's coming down here, fast, no doubt, trying to catch me. I can't face him right now, not with the way I'm feeling. Like I've just ripped myself open and now I'm bare and if he takes one more piece of what's inside me, I'll break again.

"Listen, that's him, okay? Ask him..."

The door at the top of the stairs flies open and I don't want to see him. I can't. How can I when I've made the biggest, worst mistake of all?

Like an absolute fool, I've gone and fallen in love with the man. And nothing, *nothing* I've lived through could have prepared me for how much I know this is going to hurt.

I take off.

Jake

By the time I make it down the stairs, I expect her crappy old Rav 4 engine to turn over. I figure she'll be gone, pulled out of the lot with a squeal of tires and one last goodbye that tells me I pushed things way too far last night. I get to the door and tense up when Travis waves at me like some black and white scarecrow from a Tim Burton movie.

"D'you see her?" I'm out of breath and out of control. Like I had her one minute, in my arms, warm and soft and everything and now she's gone and that was it. My one fucking chance to—

What? Fuck, I don't know.

He nods, sniffing back what sounds like a cold's worth of snot. "Yeah. She's out there."

"Where'd she go?" I'm all business. "She tell you?"

He shakes his head. "Nah, man. Just...took off."

"How'd she seem?"

"I don't know."

"Like, upset, or..."

"Yeah. Yeah, like that."

"Fuck." I'm about to walk out when my eyes land on the kid and I look at him, like *really* look at the way he's standing, and everything inside me goes still. "What's going on?"

"Nothin' bruh. Just needed a place to crash."

"Why're you holding your arm like that, Travis? What's wrong?" Half of me's dying to run after Kit, but the other half can't move.

"I'm good. Just tired. Just—"

I hit a switch, the overheads come on with a metallic thump, and everything inside me goes tense. "What happened?" I hear how deadly I sound. Quiet, low. So far past pissed, I can't feel a thing.

"Nothing, man, I—"

"Who did this?"

Outside, a car door slams. A moment later, Kit's jogging back toward the rectangle of light that's spilled out into the lot. She stops in the doorway, eyes massive, wild. After the briefest of connections between us, our gazes both land at Travis.

"What happened?"

His head's down, but that doesn't hide the soaking wet hair, the blood-smeared cheek, the black eye, the fucking split lip or the weird angle of his arm. The kid's skin and bones. I can see where his shoulder's dislocated.

I'll kill whoever's responsible. He's a kid. "Who did this?"

He shakes his head, sniffling again.

"Who did this to you, Travis? Who beat the crap out of a—"

"My dad. My *fuckin' asshole dad, okay?*" he screams. The words echo through the empty space, interrupted by another sniffle.

Shit, the kid doesn't have a cold, he's been crying.

He's hurt, more than physically. So hurt he's crying tears of betrayal, of pain rooted deep in his genes and I'm yelling at him and... "Here." I pull off the sweatshirt I threw on and Kit moves in and helps me set it gently over Travis's wide, bony shoulders.

"Hang on a sec." I look at Kit, quietly asking *you got this?* At her small nod, I say, "Stay here with Kit, okay. I'll be right back."

The fact that he just nods and stands there tells me he's in a lot of pain. I've seen this kid spar in the ring. He's one hell of a tough guy.

I hate that this, right here, is probably why.

I'm weirdly calm as I get shoes on and grab a shirt and jacket, wallet and keys, then take three bottles of water from the fridge and a handful of the dried beef jerky I snack on when I'm working out a lot.

Like recently. Every time I couldn't sleep, from thinking about Kit.

My feet clang as I come back downstairs, relieved at the calm I see in her eyes. I hand Travis a water.

"I'll drive," Kit says, leading us to her car. When I try to sit in back, Travis insists on taking the back, leaving the two of us up front. It's quiet as the car heads out of the lot, tires swooshing over wet pavement.

Hadn't even noticed it was raining. I look down, run a hand over my jacket, collect the water droplets there.

In the backseat, Travis refuses the jerky.

I'm betting he's starving, but he says his jaw hurts too much to eat.

Kit glances at me. Even in the dark, I feel the weight of that look. I want another. I crave the connection.

"How old are you?" she asks in a voice that's calm and reasonable. Just a regular day in the neighborhood.

"Thirteen," he mumbles.

"Your mom, is she..."

He shrugs. "She's at home."

"She know this happened?" I ask.

He stops sniffling long enough to let out a long, shuddery exhale and I know, without hearing the answer, what he's going to say.

"I tried, you know? I tried. He's always hitting her and I tried to make him stop, but I'm just too...fucking... weak." Every word's punctuated by a sob and that piece of me, deep inside, that's been hiding for all these years wakes up and *feels*.

It's unbearable, I remember, to let yourself feel. To know that you aren't loved the way you're meant to be and you're not good enough, not nearly strong enough to save the people who matter.

It takes a few seconds of silence for me to realize that Kit's attention's on me again, intense, despite her eyes' focus on the road.

Fabric rustles and something touches me. Her hand. On mine.

I stare at it for a few seconds before returning her squeeze.

Then she holds me. Just like that. Not too tight or

loose. I hold her back. The same way. No pressure. No expectations.

Just accepting comfort when I hardly remember what that feels like.

It's the easiest thing I've ever done.

Kit

"My dad died when I was a little older than Travis," Jake tells me like he's reciting the day's specials.

The too-bright fluorescents of the ER waiting room bathe us both in a sickly light that would be unflattering at the best of times. After an almost sleepless night, Jake's face looks gaunt, his ink stark. I'm pretty sure I look like refried ghoul.

I watch him, still, silent.

"Couple years later, my mom got remarried to an *upstanding citizen*. Rich guy. Family money. Political connections." He's facing forward, staring straight ahead, at nothing but an empty row of molded plastic chairs. "Still lives around here. Last I heard he had a mansion in Remington with his...third wife? Fourth? Mom loved Dad. But, you know, the diner, always work-ing...it was tough. Real tough. When he got sick and passed, she sold it. For a while, we were good. Mom had these friends and used to go out and do things she never got to do when the diner owned her life. But then she met *him*." A slow, measured inhalation lifts his chest. He doesn't otherwise move from that straight-backed position. "Thomas A. Bentley. Tommy to his friends." He smirks. "The third."

I give him a low scoffing sound, just so he knows I'm

listening. To our right, the ER doors swoosh open and a young couple comes in with a crying baby. My belly clenches.

When my attention returns to Jake, he continues. "I never liked Tommy. Didn't trust him. He took us out to eat this one time, before they were married. Steak house up on the highway."

I know the one he means. It's still there. Still full of stodgy old, red-nosed white men leering at waitresses in short skirts. There's a piano and a guy who sings jazz standards every weekend. Their steaks are huge and expensive and come alone on the plate. Sides of potatoes and mushrooms and green beans are extra. Clark's parents took us there when he got his PhD. In a way, I guess I wanted Parlor to be a kind of antidote to restaurants like that. A place that feels rich and lush, but where the food's simple, and full of flavor, the service friendly and above all, human. Everyone is welcome. Not just straight, rich white men.

"Mom went to the bathroom and I watched him watch the waitresses like they were as available for consumption as the steak on his plate. A woman walked by and he called her over and held out a folded bill. Maybe ten bucks. When she reached for it, he pulled it back, teased her a couple times like that. She was...not happy. After she took off, having well earned that cash, he turned to me with a wink and said 'Tips for tits.'"

"Oh my God."

"Yeah." He looks at me and then faces forward again. Behind us, the baby's still crying, the family talking in hushed tones while they wait for the check-in person to call them. "Dad always said you could see right into a person's soul by the way they treat waitstaff, cashiers, cleaners, folks in the service industry."

I nod. It's true. It's absolutely true. You know what kind of person you're dealing with from that very first interaction.

He sighs. "They got married." He pauses. "I...I think she needed or wanted the security. I think she felt like she...deserved the money, the privilege, after doing the diner thing for so long? Supporting my dad, not having something of her own? I don't know. She was still young. Maybe she had stars in her eyes. I, on the other hand, did not. So...when he started...hitting her..." I hold in a gasp. "Can't say I was all that surprised."

"I'm so sorry, Jake."

He shakes his head. Doesn't want my apologies or commiseration. Doesn't want a damn thing. This is why he's like he is. Self-sufficient, contained, and alone. "After the fact, I figured out that he'd probably been doing it for a while. We were living in this fucked-up house, just huge, with a woman who came in to cook and a cleaner and these guys who mowed *constantly*. I avoided that asshole, kind of did my own thing. Barely saw Mom at that point."

The way he's telling this story, in something close to a monotone, his back ramrod straight, his face utterly expressionless, tells me it's coming. The thing, the big, big thing that made this man into who he is today. He was a kid, I keep thinking. He was just like Travis, who's back there, getting checked out by doctors and interviewed by social workers.

He was a kid.

"Thing is, I was already big at that point. And I was...pissed. I'd started going to Ricky's gym, every day after school. Learned boxing and kick-boxing and jiu jitsu and I was kicking ass in the ring. Real quick. Tommy, now he'd played college football. He was big, too. And the bastard had a gun."

A chill slides up my spine. "The night it happened, I'd just turned seventeen. I was fuckin' feral at that point. Barely at their house, spending nights in the gym, like Travis. Went home for clothes or to get Mom to sign things for school, and she was in bed. Bleeding. Face just..." His exhalation is controlled, quiet. "He'd beaten her to a pulp. I should have gotten her out of there—I wanted to—but she wouldn't come. And he wouldn't let me. Pulled that fucking pistol out. I was so beyond everything, so enraged that I went after him anyway. We fought. I got a few hits in. Got him on the floor. Broke his nose, his teeth. Messed him up. Went to get Mom and she...she wouldn't come. Wouldn't leave him. She was mad. At *me*. I had no right, she told me. No...no *right*."

I look down at where his hands are gripping his jeans-clad knees. I want to hold one. I want to hold *him*.

"Tommy Bentley wasn't just a big, privileged fish in our little pond. He was a lawyer. Lots of lawyer friends. Judges, too. I was sent off real quick. Tried as an adult. Treated like absolute shit."

"What about your mom?" I ask, though I'm pretty certain I don't want to hear the answer to this question.

"Mom? Oh, Mom sided with him. With the cops. With...the judge. Every step of the way, she upheld that asshole's testimony. Only person who showed up for me was Ricky." He gives a quick, spare nod. "Ricky."

I reach out and put my hand over his. He looks

down and stares, then after a second or two, turns his hand over and returns my squeeze.

"I was sentenced to five years for what should have been a misdemeanor. He, uh, claimed self-defense. Said I had the gun. Mom..." He turns and looks right at me and there's something so shellshocked in his eyes, so vulnerable, that all I want in this moment is to comfort him.

"Come here." I lean toward him, put my hands on his cheeks, pull him down to my level. Not for any reason but to be here. To show him that I'm here.

His forehead thunks lightly against mine and we're close, close, sharing air and warmth and this tiny space between us.

"She died, Kit. Mom died while I was inside. She got cancer. She was...*riddled* with it. That's the word I remember. Riddled."

"Oh, Jake. I'm so sorry."

"I can't forgive her," he whispers, barely shaking his head, barely speaking. "Even after all the therapy, all the fucking work, I still can't."

"You don't have to," I reply.

"She came to see me once. I wouldn't. I wouldn't do it."

I'd thought Clark broke my heart. I'd thought he'd cracked it right down the middle, but that was nothing to how this man's just pulverized it. In my chest, there's nothing left but powder.

"See now? See why I can't do the whole family thing?"

"Yeah." I laugh-sniffle, only barely conscious that tears track down my face. "I totally get it. I do, but...you cared, Jake. You were the only one. *You* were the family.

You, on your own, trying to hold her up, hold the whole thing together. You were there for her and she...her fears or whatever kept her from doing the right thing."

"Fuck, you're just like Frank."

"What? No way. Frank's annoying."

"Frank said the same shit. Told me I was the only right one in that whole mess." He glances up for a split second. I think this is the closest I've ever really looked at him, in bright light, and his irises are as delicate as cracked ice. "Frank also taught me to stay alive inside. I owe him my life."

"You don't owe him."

"It was bad, Kit."

"Frank wouldn't expect anything in return."

"Pretty sure he'd expect me *not* to knock his sister up."

Almost smiling, I look at him, close up, those long lashes, the very faint fan of laugh lines around his eyes, and I have such a depth of emotion that, for a handful of seconds, the world around me corkscrews. It's the worst kind of vertigo. The kind that doesn't settle after you blink. The kind that isn't just a momentary lapse, but a permanent shift. A pressure change that reaches all the way to my marrow.

He hasn't broken my heart, I realize, drinking up every detail of his face. He's dug it out of the rubble it's been hiding in all this time. Forced it out into the light, where it's tiny and weak and shivering from cold, but also weirdly whole.

"What happened with Frank," I share, a paltry offering in return for the confidences he's just given me. "When he was sentenced and went to prison, I was a mess, you know. I lost my brother to a system that isn't remotely kind or fair. My parents were gone. They'd died."

"Frank told me. Car crash."

I keep going, because I want him to understand. I want him to see how I got here.

"Yeah. Yeah. And Frank was my rock, before that. My grandmother and Frank. Then what he did…well, I couldn't hate him for it, no matter how bad it seemed. Our Grandma Esteban couldn't pay for his defense. And I…tried." I huff out a sound that's not even close to a laugh, remembering how I quit every one of my many extracurricular activities in order to wait tables. "Frank wouldn't let me. He was so pissed when he found out I quit theatre and soccer. That fall, he made me go to college, as if nothing had happened. Like our whole world hadn't been flipped upside down. Told me he wouldn't take a cent from me."

"He was proud of you, Kit. He still is."

I shake my head ruefully. "Frank always hated Clark. Only met him once, when we went to visit, and still, he *knew*. But, Clark was a shoulder to cry on. *Stability*. I thought. The years went by and I pushed on and on, held him up, supported him while he went to school. We were going to make a family. I was going to go back and finish my degree. And that fucking asshole didn't keep a *single one* of his promises. I was the stable one, the supporter, the heart of everything. I tried. I mean, I worked and worked and I can't even talk about how things were in the bedroom and… I'm forty years old and all I wanted, all I want, the only thing that matters…is love."

When he lifts his eyes and meets mine, the shock of

that connection reverberates right at the center of my being.

Love. That's it. Love.

"Kiss me," I whisper against his lips.

"*Now* you say it. Now? *Here?*" His eyes flick to the side and, for the first time in ages I hear the sounds that exist outside our little bubble. Crying baby, silent weeping, in the distance, a siren. From the back, a voice is screaming that someone's stolen their eyebrow.

"No way. Not here. Nope. Come here." He grabs my hand and stands. Together, we walk out the front door into the chilly night.

36

Jake

I drag her outside, take a quick look around and head left to where there's a little green area with benches and bushes. It's relatively quiet here in the predawn light. Early morning traffic sounds in the distance, the highway not too far off.

I push through a stand of bushes to a dark, private hollow between the shrubs and the hospital's wall.

There's nothing left. No barriers. Nothing but the yawning truths we've shared.

I press her to the rough red brick and lean in and our mouths come together like swords clashing. No, not swords, shields. Walls.

Her lips move under mine. They're hesitant, almost, stiff. I press harder and then her fists are in my hair and mine in hers and we grind together, striving, forcing.

I release a frustrated growl, she whimpers, and then her hold moves to pull my shirt from my pants and I stop her. "No."

She blinks up at me. I see shock on her face, embarrassment. She tries to turn away, but I lean down and put my forehead to hers like when we were inside and say, "Kit. Katarina, sweetheart." Her name's a caress against her face. I don't know how to say the things pouring out of my soul, but I sure don't want to do it by kissing her fast and rushed. By taking her quick and hard against the hospital wall like her body's all I care about.

I force myself to go slow, to not rush, to take my time with this thing that means so much.

A kiss on her cheek, so soft against the skin of my lips. On her ear, precious and delicate and beautifully complicated. The side of her neck, which smells like her —like us—down to her shoulder. Goosebumps scatter out and I realize she's not wearing enough clothes for this.

She tries to hold on to my arms as I lean back and take off the jacket I barely remember throwing on in my place while racing to get back to Travis, knowing she was down there with him. Knowing she'd come back.

After a brief protest, she lets me put the jacket over her shoulders, lets me wrap my arms around her, and hums low when I kiss her head, her ear again, place pecks along the other side of her throat.

I bend to skate more kisses over her collar bone, one and the other. Each is a gift. Her hands drop from my arms when I tilt her head back and nibble that sweet, velvet place below her jaw, using lips and tongue to travel up to her chin. I'm out of breath by the time I stare at the tip of her nose and put a kiss there, another at the corner of my eye. Each tender touch is an offering. Her forehead, where I linger, is a solemn benediction.

Until finally, I bend to press my forehead to hers again, look her straight in the eye, and give Katarina Esteban my whole heart.

Along with the mouth to mouth contact we've denied ourselves for too long.

At first, it's just a press, a delicate slide, slow, tender, so tender.

My lips move, stroking, brushing and pressing, my tongue urging, and then the wet tip of hers to mine. Questions and gliding responses.

The taste of her. The smell. The way my insides have broken loose from their moorings and there's nothing holding me to earth but this connection. It's fucking crazy how good she feels.

I didn't know. How could I have fucking known it could be like this?

Another slide of our tongues and we're playing now, dancing, enjoying this moment with a purity I've never experienced once in my life.

Maybe as a child. Maybe this sweet, innocent exploration is like learning to use your hands or to draw a circle or as natural as, fuck, giving your mom her first baby smile.

"Fuck, Katarina, you're...you're so strong. So goddamn righteous, so *good*." Each sound's a dry rattle forced straight from my insides. "I've wanted you—loved you—since that first moment I walked in and saw those sad eyes. I know you can't give yourself to a guy like me. I get that. I know I'm not the father you'd want for your kids, but let me hold you. Let me help you. Let me be the guy you don't have to be strong with. Give me some of this weight from your shoulders so you don't have to hold it up by yourself all the time." Another kiss, quick, hungry, sipping from her, gathering up her taste in case this is the one and only chance. "Give me your pain, Katarina. Give me all the bad shit because you only deserve the good."

Kit

"Stop," I whisper against him. And then, when he keeps muttering that I'm too strong and a pillar and all kinds of other nonsense about how he'll hold me up as long as I let him, I mutter, "Shut up," and shove him far enough back so I can reach for his zipper. He's hard, thick.

We both watch as I slowly pull him out, the sounds of the world waking up beyond this place too far to matter.

His face right now is lost, his eyes glazed at half-mast.

I stroke him once, twice. His head drops back, those bright eyes disappear behind heavy lids.

I want him lost like this forever, his body—his pleasure—in my hands.

His heart.

Shit. His *heart*.

A tear slides from my eye down my cheek. I don't bother wiping it. It's been nothing but emotion today and I can't imagine that's about to change.

Instead, I let it fill me. The pain and the tenderness. The affection and all the other stuff I'm feeling for this man who's already taken on my burdens, who's shown me with his body and his actions how much he cares.

I reach down and drag my skirt up, catching his light

eyes on me. His big, rough hands go straight to my waist, my hips, his mouth returns to take mine like he's been waiting for just this opportunity.

The kiss builds and builds again and his hand's on my ass, the other stretching my poor panties to one side, and he effortlessly heaves me up against the rough wall and he's there, filling me one slow inch at a time. As soon as he's fully seated, our mouths return to exploring and teasing and tasting, learning to make love under fresh terms.

"I'm scared," I tell him, my sighs mingling with his on the surface of our sensitive skin. "I'm so scared."

He hums into my mouth, tightens his hold on me as he thrusts and I tighten my legs as we move together. We both gasp at the tight fit, the swollen pleasure, the quiet intensity of this new position, sharing things that are more than skin deep.

"I'm here," he whispers as our hips circle tighter, harder, our bodies barely moving under the shelter of my skirt.

"What if..."

"I'm here."

It's not the words that eventually get to me, not the way he easily handles my body or his cock fills me to bursting. More than want and relief and the hunger I'd excised from my wishlist a hundred years ago, it's his gaze on mine that does it, steady and serious and sure of this one thing. Of me. Us.

When he reaches down and rubs me between my legs and I clamp tighter to him, the thing that finally pushes me over is his mouth hot on mine and the words, "I love you," on his tongue.

By the time the whole thing's over, only a handful of

minutes have passed. We were quick, by necessity, and once we get ourselves straightened up and sneak out from the shelter behind the shrubbery, past the park benches and out to where the hospital's fully awake, I feel every inch as exhausted and battered as I must look.

I head to the restroom as soon as we get in and clean up as best I can. Jake's waiting for me when I come out.

"Talked to the social worker." He holds up a card. "Said she'd update me, if she can."

We're in my car, driving us home when, out of the blue, he says, "You done a test yet? Recently?"

"What?" My body jumps so hard it takes an effort not to jerk the wheel.

"Pregnancy test. You done one?"

Eyes glued to the road, I shake my head.

"You, uh... You want to stop off? Get one?"

"Now?"

He hums, a frustrated sound. I don't know exactly what's going through his mind, but I understand the sentiment.

"I want to know if I'm gonna be a dad."

I turn and look at him, straight on for so long, he mutters, "Watch it."

I turn back to the road, barely seeing it.

"What is this? Are you...are you offering? Do you want that?"

My breathing's going haywire. My mind's a mess.

"*Look*. You heard my story. I'd be a terrible dad." I make a pissed off sound in my throat, which he ignores. "I'd be the worst person for the job. I mean, who the hell wants an ex-felon in their life? I've spent more nights in prison cells and fuckin' oil rigs than in a real home, a real bed." I'm blinking hard, but say nothing. "Now, since I met you, I know this one thing. One."

To the right is a strip mall. The drugstore's lights are on. While he's talking, I swing into the lot and park.

"If you were mine, Kit. And, who knows, maybe had a little human growing inside you? I'd take such fucking good care of you."

I turn and look at him, my entire being soft and vulnerable as a fresh bruise.

"I'm a walking red flag, Kit." He looks at me and I can see how he's convincing himself, too, while he talks. "But with you, for you and..." His eyes go down, then back up. "For my family, if I had one, every one of my red flags would become a weapon, a shield between you and the rest of the world. I'd be an asset, never a problem."

"You're not a problem, Jake."

"I'm single-minded. I can be an asshole. When I left prison, Ricky helped me get back on my feet, but mostly it was this hard head of mine that pushed me forward. I had a goal: to make money. To get rich. 'Cause money's the only fucking thing in this world that seemed to matter. If I worked hard enough, if I did nothing but that, one day Tommy fucking Bentley and his old cash, old power wouldn't scare me."

"Then I met you." He searches my face, looking blindsided for a handful of seconds, and leans in. "And suddenly, I got it. The thing I've been missing all these years. That safety that money buys? It's got nothing on the way I feel when I'm in your presence. Beside you." His hands take mine and press them together. "Inside you."

"Jake, I—"

"A red fucking flag, baby. That's me. A whole fucking string of 'em. But I'm *your* red flag, Kit." He bends, puts his lips to my knuckles and gives me a kiss that'll be seared into my soul forever. When he meets my eyes again, I see a fire burning inside them. For me. For us. "I'm yours. With or without a baby. If you want me. I'll be your fuckin' red flag. Forever."

I can't get to him fast enough. By the time I get my seatbelt off and lean over to kiss him, I'm already wrapped in his arms, surrounded.

When our lips meet, it's explosive—like everything with us. Probably a good thing some asshole honks, laughing as they pull into the spot next to us. Otherwise, I'm not entirely convinced I wouldn't have done the man right here in the CVS parking lot.

We don't go into the store for a test. The man's ripped his chest open and shown me his insides and now all I want is to be alone with him again. In his arms.

I drive to my place because at this point, there's no way I'm spending another second in this pair of panties.

We trip on the walkway and Jake catches me. "I'm buying supplies and I'm fixing this fuckin' thing."

I laugh, although already, some part of me wonders how this'll work. He's leaving in three days. Three. Days.

Oh, no, it's down to two.

We make it up onto the porch and, after a long-drawn-out kiss while I attempt, unsuccessfully, to open the door, we're finally in the living room and he's backed me up against the door. His hand's already dragging up my skirt and the kissing's getting messier and I look up and there's a man standing there, in the hall leading to my bedroom.

I freeze, a shocked, "What the hell?" tumbling from my lips as I blink for a few seconds, blindsided by the unexpected sight of my brother, much bigger than I remember him, tattooed, tough as nails, and clearly pissed all the way off.

"What the fuck is going on here?"

37

JAKE

I turn, slow, careful.

Frank, who I saw almost six weeks ago when I went to pay him a visit, looks about ready to explode.

With good reason.

"Frank. Oh my god, you're home? You're home. You're home!" Kit races over to him and throws her arms around him. They hug long enough to give him time to lower his head and put his cheek against her hair and then lift it up to give me a death glare.

I'm a dead man. There's no question about it. Frank's close to my height and much wider. Clearly he's been lifting inside. He looks harder, too, around the neck, the jaw. He's got so much ink now I'm shocked his face isn't covered.

Then again, Frank was always one of the smart ones. He knew perception was everything. Knew he'd get out one day and need to get a job. He took classes in prison, studied his ass off, got a fucking law degree. Not that you'd guess it to look at him.

After a moment, he loosens his sister's hold and sets her away from him, eyes on mine like missiles to their target. Steady and sure. He doesn't even have to threaten. Hell, I know I'm in the wrong. I shouldn't have done this. Any of it.

He doesn't want me with his sister. He'd want someone better.

"Brother," he says in that way that makes me wonder where he's hidden the shiv and what part of my body he'll strike.

"Good to see you, Frank."

"Yeah? Then what the hell are you doing over there?" For a handful of seconds, I watch him, not understanding what he means in the slightest. Then he moves and I tense up for the blow I know is coming.

He grabs me in a bearhug that's so fucking tight I figure he's opted for the less popular option of crushing me to a powder. But then he's slapping my back and telling me he's so fucking glad to see me and he sounds choked up.

It takes me a sec to give in and hug him back. It's probably the lack of sleep and all the shit that's gone down in the last day, but when he pulls away, emotion clogs my sinuses in a way I don't usually let it. I look down.

Silence.

When I glance back up, his eyes are swinging from me to Kit and back again. "So what's the deal here? This a thing?"

Kit looks over at me and back to him without speaking.

"I'd like that," I finally say. "I'd like this to be...something."

"Whoa. You two just figuring it out?"

She gazes at me, nodding. "Yeah. Yeah, it's new."

"This mean you're moving here?"

My brows go up. "Got a contract in a couple days."

"You're leaving?"

"No." As soon as I say it, it's the truth. "I'm staying."

"Nice." He gives an evil grin. "Fucking worked."

"What worked?" Kit asks.

"My plan. Been waiting for you and that prick to break up." He slaps me on the back, hard. "Told you Jake was the best guy I know."

"Jesus Frank," Kit mutters, shaking her head at me with big eyes, which suddenly, go wider. "Wait. How are you here? You didn't like, bust out or anything did you?"

Frank laughs. "Fuck, no. I'm on parole. It's official." His face goes slack and I feel his shock in my bones. "I'm a free man."

EPILOGUE

Jake

The roof's fixed. As of now, the front walk's officially finished. That took longer than anticipated, because Kit wanted cute little cottage garden flagstones and I wanted something we could roll a stroller down. Not that a stroller was necessarily in the cards, but we wanted different things.

Actually, the same, but different.

Kit wants ambiance, atmosphere. She wants it to feel good. I get that. It's the whole premise behind her restaurant, after all, and the place is magic.

I, on the other hand, want my woman safe. I want the best for her.

So, I talked to a mason and figured out what stones to use and it's now a cemented flagstone walkway.

"Looks good, man."

I smile at Travis, who's now got a whole lot of skin in the game. "Sure does." I nod. "Thanks for helping out."

"Wasn't nothing."

It was, but I don't mention that.

I look up at where Ricky and Frank are putting up the porch swing—reinforced for my weight, plus pregnant Kit's.

Because she is carrying my child.

Our baby.

Fuck me. My heart. My *lungs*.

Every time I think about it, they go haywire. I can't breathe. Can't even see right when the edges of my vision get dark.

"Come on, guys. Let's go grill."

We walk around back, Ricky and Frank trailing after us. The whole Parlor crew's here, plus Yemi's sister and whoever the hell else people wanted to bring. Riley brought a literal pig from his farm a couple days ago, so we've got that roasting in a pit. Annette—the vegan—isn't happy, but she never seems to be happy unless Frida's got her wrapped in her arms.

Which I fully understand.

Ricky's other half, Dolores, comes over and slots a lemonade into my hand, and Kit's right beside her, giving one to Travis.

You can't tell there's a baby in her belly yet, but already that little person's changed parts of me you can't see.

"You good?" I ask as she comes over to slide under my arm and let me pull her into my side and kiss her forehead, her cheek, her lemonade-chilled lips. Every kiss is a thing between us, never taken for granted.

"Yeah. Yeah, you?"

"I'm fucking amazing, baby."

She grins. "Should we tell 'em yet?"

"What, that the random pig roast isn't just a pig roast?"

"Yeah. Yeah, yeah, come on. Let's do it. You guys! Hey!"

"Hold on. Hold on, baby." I lift my head. "Trav, get over here, man. We need you with us."

The kid walks over, head down, shoulders curved forward. He's taller than anyone else here and he's only fourteen at this point. Doctor's got no idea how big he'll end up being, but I keep saying to Kit it's a damn good thing she's got a restaurant, or else our foster kid would eat us out of house and home. As it stands, he's making a decent dent in the restaurant.

"We got an announcement," Travis says to the folks who've come over today. Frank and Ricky and Dolores and Frida and everybody from the restaurant.

This is my family. My people. This is the life I'm lucky enough to have found.

Travis looks at us with a grin, his face bright red. "They're having a baby," he tells the group.

Ricky whoops and takes off his baseball cap, throwing it high.

Dolores giggles as she runs over to hug first Kit and then me. The woman's a giggler. Five feet nothing, with bright dyed red hair and lots and lots of makeup, high heels and leopard print everything. And she giggles. Constantly. It's cute, though honestly, I don't know how Ricky stands it.

Slowly, Frank makes his way down the porch stairs to me. He sticks out his hand and I shake it.

"Congratulations," he says, low, just for me.

"Thanks."

"Hey, uncle Frank," Kit sings as she comes over to

accept a hug from him, too. "You better get ready. You are officially our number one babysitter."

"Not sure I'm babysitter material."

"You'll do just fine."

"I'll babysit," says Travis. The kid offers to do everything. All the time.

I share a glance with Kit.

We've got to find a way to make him understand he's not a paying guest here. He's part of the family.

"Boy or girl?" Ricky asks.

Kit and I share another look, this one lingering. "We don't want to know."

"What?" Dolores's voice goes high, screechy. "How'm I gonna know what color clothes to buy?"

Annette shakes her head.

"Babies care about stuff like that?" Travis, as he so often does, chimes in with just the right answer at the awkward moments.

"No," says Frida. "No, they *really* don't give a crap," with the same inflection she'd use to tell me her fried oysters were up. She cocks an eyebrow at Dolores, as if to dare her to talk about pink and blue and that other nonsense. "I'd say you're pretty safe with leopard print."

Frank snickers and Ricky smacks him on the arm and a smiling Kit turns to look up at me, her eyes all soft and warm and full of love for me and everyone else here.

Family. That's what this is. The rightness I remember from when I was a kid, the safety in being with those who care.

"How's it going over at the gym?" asks Ricky, who's finally rid himself of that responsibility.

"Membership's up," says Frank. He's taken over the apartment and helps me manage the business.

We've been working with a local non-profit to make the community service aspect of the place official and suddenly, there's an influx of interest where for years there wasn't much.

Yemi's at the restaurant full time and I help out when I can. I always make sure Kit takes days off.

Then there's Travis. Our foster kid. I want to adopt him, but this shit takes time. The system, as several of us know, isn't always easy to navigate.

And his mom's trying to do right by him. We'll see what happens. I want the kid happy. It's all that matters. Maybe he'll wind up with her. Maybe that's a good thing.

"We've got more news," I call out, swallowing hard as I turn to look at my woman. "So, the papers came in and...Kit's divorce is final."

"We're getting married!" she squeals, unable to hold out long enough to keep them all in suspense.

Again, Dolores's reaction's the biggest and again, the rest of us are laughing at how excited the woman gets. Kit pulls the ring out of her pocket, slips it on, and shows it around. Dolores is too obsessed to let anyone near.

My eyes slide over to catch a look from Frank, a slight nod. He knows exactly what happened that day at the university between me and her ex. I told him the whole goddamn thing. If anything ever happens to me, I know that Frank, beyond a doubt, has my back.

It's a damn good feeling.

Ricky sidles over. "You asshole."

"What?"

He punches my arm and pulls a box from his pocket, slaps it into my palm. "Stole my goddamn thunder."

When I see the diamond in the little blue velvet box, I laugh so hard I'm bent double by the time the others notice.

Everybody stops talking. "What's his deal?" Annette asks, her voice always good at cutting through all the bullshit.

Frida mutters something about how it's nonstop with me these days. I'm always giggling (her word) about something.

I open my mouth to call her out, but... The laughing. The happiness?

Man, she's right.

"Jesus, give me back that thing." Ricky pulls the box from my hand. "Come here, Dolores."

As the others follow the action, Kit comes over to wrap her arms around me and give me a kiss.

"I fucking love you," I mutter against the most precious lips in the world.

"I know you do," she says, grinning hard.

"That's not what you're supposed to say to your fiancé."

"Oh, what am I supposed to say to my fiancé?"

"You say, I love you too, Jake."

"I love you too, Jake."

Even though she's just parroted the sentence, I still feel it, vibrating through me like a wrench to ice cold metal. "So, I made a decision, baby."

"Okay."

"I'm not going back out," I tell her, low and secret and for her ears only. "No more contracts on the rig."

She goes still. "You sure? It's a lot of money."

"I'm selling the houses."

Her brows go up. She knows those places were my nest egg. My safety net.

"Let's put an addition on the house."

"What'll you do for work?"

"What, cooking for you isn't enough? And the gym?"

"You'll be here all the time."

I nod, put my forehead to hers, and watch her eyes cloud over with emotion.

"That's the best news. Of all."

"Better than a *baby*? Marriage?"

"Jake Brand, I want *you*. The rest is just icing."

"I'm the cake," I say, with a shit eating grin. "You fuckin' *love* cake."

"Yes, Jake." Slowly, she nods, leans in and gives me a kiss that is in no way appropriate for this setting. We might have to sneak off somewhere. Soon. "I *love* cake."

"And, baby, cake loves you."

THE END

Read Kit and Jake's Bonus Epilogue here: https://BookHip.com/VXNKZLT

Read on for a taste of Frank's book, WELL PAID...

Thank you so much for reading this book. If you enjoyed it, please consider reviewing or recommending it to others so they can find it, too!

WELL PAID SNEAK PEEK

Villains are often actually heroes. And vice-versa.

This is a fact that I know intimately, to the very depths of my soul.

And yet, that first glimpse of Frank Collado—murderer, felon, and my own personal savior—still scares the living daylights out of me. The man looks like someone who'd corner you and hurt you. Take things you have no intention of giving.

It is possibly the size of him, although I've gotten used to big men. It might be his expression—closed off and hard. Or the scars. Three of them, crisscrossing his face like someone's used him as a tic-tac-toe board and his eye is the center O.

There's a beat, as I step around the end of the cereal aisle, when my body reacts to him as if he's a predator.

Run. Run. Run! it screams.

But I've never been on the flight end of the spectrum, or fight for that matter. Sadly, I'm a freezer, all the way. I stand here, stuck in place, one foot literally raised like I'm some granola-toting Bambi, and stare.

He's out. He's out and I had no idea. Did he bust out of prison and come straight here to find me?

Right. After fifteen years, he finally decided to ruin his good record and come for the woman he refused to see the whole time he was inside.

Not once did he let me visit.

"Frank?" I whisper, once my lungs inflate again.

He turns. Looks at me.

And nothing. No recognition. No friendliness at all.

My ego shouldn't be hurt by this. I mean, the man killed for me, after all, so it's not like he hasn't given enough, but somehow... I suppose somehow I'd thought he'd be happy to see me when our paths did eventually cross.

That is clearly not the case.

Thick, black brows lift, dark eyes squint and rake over me and, no, I'm certainly not looking my best—my god, I'm fifteen years older than the girl he knew back then. I'm in my thirties. Not young and fresh and pretty.

"Hey," he finally says, the sound of him so much more resonant than I remember. Like the rest of him, his voice has changed, gotten deeper, harder, rougher. His body is the most intimidating thing I've ever seen. Rather than the tall, muscular perfection I've gotten used to over the past decade, there's something coarse about the way he holds himself, like his body is a coiled spring or a razor poised to slice, his energy so closely leashed there's no masking it with jeans and a tight T.

Apparently Frank went off to prison as an angry young man and came out a hardened one. I don't think I've ever seen anyone so patently brutal.

"How...how are you?" My own voice is a fluttery, weak-sounding thing and I hate it. I want to show him how strong I am, how resilient. "I didn't know you were out."

"Out on parole." A muscle flexes in his too-hard jaw, like he's annoyed that I've stopped him mid-shop.

I glance down at the basket in his hand and see a half-gallon of milk, a steak, a bag of frozen peas and a loaf of white bread.

"You been alright?" he asks.

Suddenly, more than anything, I'm hurt by his nonchalance. *Why didn't you call me?* I want to ask. *Why didn't you let me visit? Why did you send my letters back? Why are you just standing there instead of bending down and wrapping me up in those—*

Every thought leaves my head when my gaze lands on his hand, the knuckles white from the chokehold he's got on his basket. Then I scan back up his body and see the rigidity in his shoulders, the tension in his wide neck. Oh my goodness, he's as nervous as I am. Maybe more so.

My insides shift again, no longer upset that he's avoided me, into compassion, perhaps even affection. I take a step forward, hand out, and blink when he sways slightly back.

Oh. Oh, god.

"I'm sorry, are you..." Scared of *me?* An ugly noise of disbelief escapes me before I dredge a calm, bland expression from somewhere deep inside and look up at him, as if this meeting isn't affecting me at all. "I'm good," I say, nodding slightly. "You?"

He nods, too. "Yep. All right."

"You been out for a while?"

"Close to a year."

A *year?* Hurt hits me right in the chest. I swallow it back with a nod. "Okay. Okay. You, uh, you busy?"

He casts a look over his shoulder like he's looking for a way out and the pain squeezes into my throat and up, up. In the next moment, it occurs to me that, because of how I've worded it, he thinks I mean right now.

Almost relieved, I go on. "I mean to say, are you working? Staying busy?"

"Yeah." A quick flick of his night-dark eyes to mine sends a shocking curl of warmth into my abdomen. "Took over my brother-in-law's gym."

"Huh." I nod. "That's wonderful! Excellent!" Oh, god, me with the superlatives. *Shut up, Evie!*

"You?"

"Oh, yes." The first real smile I've been able to muster slides onto my face. "I make furniture now."

"Cool." He's too busy looking furtively around to give me any more eye contact and it occurs to me that this could be one of those prison survival things. Hypervigilance, maybe?

Or, more likely, he'd rather avoid me and is currently searching for the closest exit.

Probably the latter. I can't imagine this man getting attacked in prison. The other inmates probably stayed as far away from Frank Collado as possible.

Then again, he got that scar somehow, so he wasn't completely safe and I'm an idiot to think he could have been.

"You, uh... Would you like to go grab a quick coffee, or—"

"No, thanks."

His quick denial's the final straw in this wholly embarrassing exchange. Clearly the man is not interested.

And that hurts like hell.

"Alright, then. Take care now." I give him a huge, fake smile and a wave and set off straight for the exit, dropping my basket off along the way.

Iain will understand. He knows how I feel about Frank and what he did for me back when life got so bad I didn't see a way out.

He knows and he cares and he *always* makes everything better.

As I race, flushed and near tears, from the scene of a reunion I'd never imagined going quite so badly, I can't help but wonder: does Frank have someone who makes everything better?

More than anything, I hope he does.

Pre-order Frank, Evie, and Iain's story here: www.adrianaanders.com/wellpaid

Get a one-time email every time I've got a book out: https://www.subscribepage.com/Releases

Keep in touch through one of the links below.

Newsletter:
www.adrianaanders.com/newsletter
Bookbub:
www.bookbub.com/profile/adriana-anders
Facebook:
facebook.com/adrianaandersauthor
Join my reader group:

facebook.com/groups/booksmarttarts
Follow me on Instagram:
instagram.com/adriana.anders
Tweet with me:
twitter.com/adrianasboudoir

ACKNOWLEDGMENTS

Thank you for being here. Truly. I could not do this without your support. While you're here, if you have the time and inclination to give this book a rating or a review, that would mean the world to me and, if on top of that, you'd like to stay in touch? My goodness... are we becoming a thing?

Okay, maybe not. I'm a little eager, like my heroes, to take things to the next level. Forgive me.

In the meantime, I've got people to thank for making this book come to life. As with every book I've written, WELL BRED didn't write itself and it didn't happen in a vacuum. First off, I need to thank Michelle, who is truly the very best. She's not just a PA, she's an amazing friend, a cheerleader, a first reader, and so so so much more. I couldn't be happier to have her on my team. I also need to thank Molly O'Keefe for reading these words and giving such brilliant (as always) feedback. Thank you to Annika Martin (and friends) for the sticker club (yay!) that made this book actually get finished and to my Cville crew: Daphne Green, Joanna Bourne, Elizabeth Safleur, and Sofie Couch for your brilliant ideas and your constancy throughout this some-times never-ending process. You are my rocks.

Esther, thank you for being a beta reader extraordi-naire, and Kim Cannon, your editing was, as always spot on.

Andie J. Christopher, Rusty Keller, and Amanda Bouchet, I am just so fortunate to have you as my people.

Finally, I should probably mention my kids who didn't distract me nearly as much as they did when they were tiny (sob!) and Le Husband, who is always there when I need him.

Love you all!

ALSO BY ADRIANA ANDERS

The Whatever it Takes Series

Well Paid - coming soon

The Camp Haven Series

Kink Camp: Hunted

Possession

The Rough & Rugby Series

We'll Never Have Paris

The French Kiss-Off - coming soon!

The Dom-Com Coming soon! Subscribe to release day emails here.

Daddy Crush More available on the Radish Reading App!

The Survival Instincts Series

Deep Blue

Whiteout

Uncharted

More to come...

Love at Last Series

Loving the Secret Billionaire

Loving the Wounded Warrior

Loving the Mountain Man

The Blank Canvas Series

Under Her Skin

By Her Touch

In His Hands

ABOUT ADRIANA ANDERS

Adriana Anders is the award-winning author of Romantic Suspense, Rom-Coms, Contemporary, and Erotic Romance. Her books have received critical acclaim from the New York Times, OprahMag, Entertainment Weekly, Booklist, Bustle, USA Today Happy Ever After, Book Riot, Romantic Times, Publishers' Weekly, and Kirkus, amongst other publications. Today, she resides with her husband and two children on the coast of France, writing the love stories of her heart. Visit Adriana's Website for her current booklist: adrianaanders.com

Sign up for Adriana's newsletter
Like Adriana Anders on Facebook
Join Adriana's reader group

BB bookbub.com/profile/adriana-anders
X x.com/AdrianasBoudoir
O instagram.com/adriana.anders
P pinterest.com/adrianasboudoir
f facebook.com/adrianaandersauthor

9 798989 019830